When was the last time someone had cared enough to listen to her fears, offer support?

"I just want the best for Ciara and Aiden," Maddie said. "They deserve more than I had—a roof that doesn't leak when it rains. A family that isn't falling apart from work and weariness. Am I selfish for hoping I won't have to go into debt for all that?"

"No," Michael answered. "There's nothing selfish about you, Maddie. You work harder than anyone I've ever met, and you're being clever about it, if you ask me. You're building a business to support you and Ciara and Aiden. That's something to be proud of." As if to prove it, he bent and kissed her on her forehead.

A warning rose inside her, insistent, demanding. She had a future all planned, and it didn't include falling in love. That way led to sorrow. She knew that.

Why then had she offered Michael a chance to stake a claim on her heart?

Regina Scott has always wanted to be a writer. Since her first book was published in 1998, her stories have traveled the globe, with translations in many languages. Fascinated by history, she learned to fence and sail a tall ship. She and her husband reside in Washington State with their overactive Irish terrier. You can find her online blogging at nineteenteen.com. Learn more about her at reginascott.com or connect with her on Facebook at facebook.com/authorreginascott.

Books by Regina Scott

Love Inspired Historical

Frontier Bachelors

The Bride Ship
Would-Be Wilderness Wife
Frontier Engagement
Instant Frontier Family

The Master Matchmakers

The Courting Campaign
The Wife Campaign
The Husband Campaign

The Everard Legacy

The Rogue's Reform
The Captain's Courtship
The Rake's Redemption
The Heiress's Homecoming

Visit the Author Profile page at Harlequin.com.

REGINA SCOTT

Instant Frontier Family

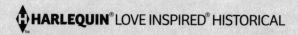
HARLEQUIN® LOVE INSPIRED® HISTORICAL

Recycling programs
for this product may
not exist in your area.

™ LOVE INSPIRED BOOKS

ISBN-13: 978-0-373-28342-2

Instant Frontier Family

www.Harlequin.com

Printed in U.S.A.

Dear friends, let us love one another, for love comes from God. Everyone who loves has been born of God and knows God.
—*1 John* 4:7

To Kris, who knew where Maddie needed to live
and that she needed a cat; and to the Lord,
who gives me friends and family,
both two-footed and four-footed, to love.

Chapter One

Seattle, Washington Territory
October 1866

Maddie O'Rourke stood on the pier beside Mr. Yesler's mill, waiting for the ship to come in. Every inch of her tingled, from her carefully braided red hair under her green velvet hat to her toes inside the leather boots. After nearly a year of working and striving, she was about to reunite with her little brother and sister.

She shifted on the scarred wooden planks, the bell of her wide russet skirts swinging in the cool fall sunlight. She could hear the whine of saws from the mill, the hammering that told of new buildings going up behind her. Gentlemen crowded around her, ready to receive the passengers and cargo from the sailing ship that had swept into Elliott Bay an hour ago. Among those about to disembark would be Ciara and Aiden. Maddie could only pray, as she had for months, that her brother and sister had forgiven her for abandoning them in New York.

But what else could she have done? Her income then as a laundress had barely been enough to pay her room and board, let alone support two others. She and her half siblings had struggled along for months after Da and her stepmother had been killed in that horrible tenement fire. It had been a dark time for them all, one she'd prefer to forget.

Only the advertisement in the paper, announcing the need for teachers, seamstresses and laundresses in far-off Washington Territory, at exorbitant salaries, had given her hope. She'd managed to scrape together enough money to join the Mercer expedition to Seattle and find a safe place for Ciara and Aiden to stay until she could send for them. But though she had plenty of work here, the costs were high, and she hadn't been able to bring her family to her or pay for a lady to accompany them on the ship.

Until now.

The brine-scented breeze off the blue waters brushed her cheek, setting her net veil to fluttering and tugging a strand of hair free of her coronet braid. So much had changed in the past few months since her friend Rina Fosgrave had suggested a different future to Maddie. No more was Maddie a nameless laundress lugging pounds of dirty linens up three flights of stairs to labor over a steaming tub as she had in New York. Now she was Miss Madeleine O'Rourke, owner of Seattle's finest bakery, upstanding, respected, admired...

"You're a little late on my shirts, Miss Maddie."

Maddie kept her smile polite as she turned to the older logger who stood beside her, his bushy brows furrowed in frustration. If she'd learned anything since starting work at the age of nine, sixteen years ago now, it was to never disappoint a customer. There was always another girl ready to scrub her fingers raw for a penny a shirt. And Maddie was well aware there was another bakery in Seattle.

"My deepest apologies, Mr. Porter," she said, batting her lashes for good measure. "I'll deliver them to the boardinghouse me own self tomorrow at the latest. I can't be keeping my best customer waiting, now, can I?"

At her praise, Mr. Porter turned as red as the flannel sticking out of the neck of his plaid cotton shirt. Stammering his thanks, he ducked his grizzled head and turned away.

Maddie smiled after him. Gentlemen had reacted with endearing embarrassment to her teasing since she was sixteen and her scrawny body had blossomed with curves. She'd heard enough compliments over the years to know the fellows liked the rich color of her fiery hair, the twinkle they claimed resided in her dark brown eyes. Her flirting made all the gentlemen, young and old and in between, smile for a time. There was nothing wrong with that.

But this laundry delivery would be her last. The woman who was coming with Ciara and Aiden could take over the remaining laundry chores, to Maddie's everlasting relief. Whether that lady flirted with her customers was her own choice. Maddie would be focused on making the bakery a success so she could repay entrepreneur Clay Howard every penny he'd invested in her, with interest.

Her nerves tingled again as she turned her gaze once more to the ship. The vessel was a two-masted steamer much like the one that had brought her most of the way here. That ship had been filled with women like her, seeking a better life. This one was bringing her own heart's desire.

A longboat had been lowered over the side, filled

with passengers. Were Ciara and Aiden among them? How much longer would she have to wait?

"Nice day for a stroll, eh, Miss Maddie?"

Maddie nodded to the gentleman who had been so bold as to step up to her this time. He was one of the clerks in the Kellogg brothers' mercantile, where she'd bought her supplies for the bakery. "A fine day to be sure, Mr. Weinclef."

He squeezed the rim of the hat in his hands so hard she thought he might strangle the blocked wool. "I'd be happy to stroll with you."

"To the moon and back!" one of his friends called from the edge of the pier, and others laughed.

Mr. Weinclef turned a sickly white.

"Sure-n but you're a sweet gentleman to be offering," Maddie said with a smile designed to turn his friends green with envy. "Perhaps you'd be so kind as to sit with me in services this Sunday."

"I…I'd be delighted, ma'am," he said. He seized her hand and pumped it up and down so hard her hat tipped to one side on her braid. "Thank you, thank you so much!"

Maddie managed to retrieve her hand before he scurried off. Righting her hat, she turned once more to the waiting ship. She'd never lacked for gentlemanly company in New York, though she'd been careful to keep from making a commitment. Here in Seattle it was far worse, with needy bachelors falling over themselves to make her acquaintance, seek a moment of her time.

She knew some of the ladies who had come west with her were already betrothed. She'd attended several weddings, been a bridesmaid at two. But that wasn't how she planned to lead her life. She'd seen how hard work and privation could make any marriage a struggle.

Look at Da and his second wife. Look at her life with her father and her late mother in Ireland, for that matter. It seemed love between a husband and wife could not last in adversity. Why pretend otherwise? Why set herself up for more heartache?

She put up her hand to shade her eyes from the sun, already low over the Olympic Mountains across Puget Sound. Every yard the longboat bobbed closer, every wave it crested, her body tensed the more.

Oh, please, Lord. I know You have better things to be doing than to deal with the likes of me, but perhaps You could spare a few moments. I tend to speak my mind, and I'm not long on patience. Would You help me make us a family again? Ciara and Aiden deserve that.

The burly-armed sailors were putting their backs into their work as they rowed the boat toward the pier. Now she could make out a girl and a boy nestled among the other passengers, and she thought her heart might push its way out of her fitted bodice, it swelled so much. Oh, how they'd grown! Ciara's hair, a proper brown, was past her shoulders in a thick braid, and wee Aiden's dark head was nearly to the shoulder of his sister's blue coat. The seven-year-old was glancing about with wide eyes as if he'd never seen such a place.

Of course, he hadn't. How strange Seattle must look to him after being raised in Five Points, the Irish neighborhood in New York. When she'd first walked past the whitewashed houses dwarfed by towering firs all around, she'd thought she'd arrived in another world entirely.

She felt a little foreign now. Would her brother and sister talk to her as they used to, sharing their fears, their triumphs? Would they still say their prayers together at night? She couldn't take her gaze off them as the boat bumped the pier and men surged forward to catch the lines, make the boat fast and help the passengers ashore.

Calm now. Show them what a fine lady you've become. Show them that allowing you to go ahead was worth them staying behind.

Her smile felt shaky as she stepped forward.

A man leaped from the boat to land on the pier. She had only a moment to register height and broad shoulders before he turned to lift first Ciara and then Aiden to the planks as if neither weighed more than a feather. His heavy dark blue coat and rough brown trousers made him look like a sailor, but instead of helping the rest of the passengers to alight as the other sailors were doing, he took Ciara's hand in one of his and Aiden's in the other and turned toward Maddie. The look in his eyes was more challenge than welcome. It was almost as if he was Ciara and Aiden's father, determined to lead them into a new life and protect them from any harm.

"Maddie!" Aiden broke from the man and ran toward her. All her resolve to be a grand lady evaporated like fog burning off in the sun. She bent and caught him as he hurtled into her, hugging him close.

"Oh, me darling boy! I've missed you so!"

"Me too." He pulled back and scrunched up his round face. "It took forever to get here."

"It was two months, twenty-six days and four hours," Ciara corrected him as she approached at a more ladylike pace. "But that was a very long time." She glanced up at Maddie with the deep brown eyes they'd inherited from their father. "How nice to see you again, sister."

Though Maddie had longed to hear that word from Ciara, she couldn't help thinking that the girl was even more determined to play the lady than Maddie was. She wasn't sure whether to tease Ciara or respond in kind. Ciara didn't allow her time to choose. She tugged on the sailor's hand, forcing him forward until he nearly bumped into Maddie.

"This is Mr. Michael Haggerty," Ciara announced, gazing up at him with so much pride, Maddie might have thought her sister had sewn him together from whole cloth. "He's come to marry you."

Maddie's head jerked up, and she stepped back to eye the fellow. With hair black as a crow's wing swept back from his square-jawed face and eyes bluer than the Sound on a sunny day, he wasn't a bad-looking sort. There was character in those solid cheekbones, determination in the firm lips. He even nodded respectfully as his gaze met hers. But no amount of good manners and handsome looks was going to win him a place in her affections.

"Mr. Haggerty came all this way for nothing, then," she told them all, raising her chin. "I've no reason to marry, him or any other man, and that's the last that needs to be said on that score."

Michael Haggerty could not imagine a worse way to be introduced to his benefactor. Most ladies he knew would have cried out, demanded an apology at Ciara's announcement that he had come intending marriage. Miss Maddie O'Rourke had given him a proper set-down instead, her declaration softened only by the lilt of an Irish accent that reminded him of his aunt and all he'd left behind.

Now her glare flashed around the pier, daring anyone to disagree with her. Several men ducked away as if afraid she would discover they secretly harbored hopes of winning her.

Best to calm the waters if he wanted a chance at sailing through them.

"I think Miss Ciara is overstating the case," Michael said with a glance at the little girl. Ciara's proud look dripped away like water off a roof. In the time Michael had known her, first at the children's home his aunt kept in New York and later aboard ship, he'd seen the pattern many times. Ciara had been one of the older children at the home, a position that had earned her the respect and awe of most of the others. Her queenly demeanor lasted only until someone disagreed with her, and then she quickly reverted to the unsure eleven-year-old who dwelled inside.

"But he came all this way," she protested to her sister. "He took care of us."

"We like him," Aiden added, slipping his hand back into Michael's. That was Aiden, loyal as the day was long, to each of his sisters, to Michael, to anyone who befriended him. His trembling lower lip was enough to make anyone rethink whatever they'd been doing to cause his distress.

For a moment, Michael thought Aiden's look had touched Maddie as well, for her tension eased. "Glad I am that Mr. Haggerty was so kind to you both," she told her brother. "But that doesn't mean I owe him my hand in marriage."

Ciara stiffened as if she quite disagreed.

"No, ma'am," Michael said before the girl could build up a head of steam again. "I'm the one who owes you a debt. Your money paid for my passage."

Maddie frowned. She had delicate russet-colored brows over a pert nose and the creamiest skin Michael had ever seen. And that hair, thick as coals after a fire and twice as fiery. But a pretty exterior could hide a far less pleasing heart, he'd learned to his sorrow.

"I don't understand," she said. "I asked for a lady to escort my brother and sister, someone who could be helping me at my work."

That's what Aunt Sylvie had been intending to send her, until the threats to Michael's life had convinced her to beg him to go instead. But he didn't want to explain that now, not with people crowding around them on the pier, gazes already curious.

So Michael released his hold on Aiden and saluted as the men on the naval ships in New York harbor had been wont to do. "Able Seaman Michael Haggerty at your service, ma'am."

Her lips tightened until they were a pretty pink bow on her oval face. "I'm not a captain of a ship, Mr. Haggerty. I have no use for sailors."

Michael lowered his arm, determined not to give up so easily. "You must have some fixing and carrying that needs to be done, ma'am. All I ask is a chance to repay my debt to you."

She shook her head, threatening the placement of the tiny green hat that perched on her braid. He'd seen a few of those in New York, usually on women who couldn't be bothered to count the cost of the whimsical things.

The thought brought his aunt's voice to mind. *Don't you be going and judging all women like your Katie O'Doul. Not every lady sets her heart on breaking others'.*

"I've never held with indentured servants, sir," Maddie informed him. "Too many of our people labored under that system."

Our people. The Irish. Was she one of those who valued the home country more than the country they now called home? He'd been fighting the battle of misplaced allegiances for most of his life. The only reason he was here now was because he'd lost that battle in New York and lost the woman he'd thought he'd loved at the same time.

He wasn't about to lose more.

"Nevertheless, Miss O'Rourke," he said, "I'm a man who pays my debts. And I've grown quite fond of Miss Ciara and Master Aiden. Until I know they're safely settled, I'm afraid you'll have to suffer my presence."

It was a bold statement, so he wasn't surprised when her dark eyes flashed fire even as her hands tightened into fists at her sides. Oh, but he was in for a tongue-lashing now. As if Ciara thought so as well, she latched on to Michael's arm again.

"Oh, please, Maddie!" she cried. "Don't send Michael away!"

Aiden pressed himself against Michael's leg, face tightening with worry. "He's our friend."

Maddie O'Rourke drew in a deep breath. Michael knew the position in which he and the children had placed her. She was an unmarried woman, by all accounts, a laundress, Aunt Sylvie said, though no laundress Michael had ever met dressed half so well or carried herself with so much pride. But he truly didn't want to marry her. He wanted to make sure Ciara and Aiden were safe, and he needed a job so he could pay back what he owed and find his footing on the frontier.

"Have you no other friends or family in the area, Mr. Haggerty?" she asked as if trying to determine some other solution to the problem he presented. She raised her gaze to his, and he thought the movement was at least in part a way to ignore the pitiful looks on her siblings' faces.

"A fellow came with me on the boat," Michael said. "But he has only enough to pay room and board until he finds employment."

She sighed, fingers relaxing against the material of her skirts. "'Tis a difficult choice you're giving me, Mr. Haggerty. To begin with, I've no idea what to do with you. A woman working off her debt might have slept upstairs with the family. I've no bed available for a bachelor."

"I don't need much," Michael assured her. "I can make do with a blanket on the floor."

She frowned as if she wasn't acquainted with such humble behavior. In truth, he wasn't used to it either. He'd been proud enough, ambitious even: working on the docks in Brooklyn, rising among the ranks to a position of authority, engaged to the prettiest lass Irishtown had ever produced.

But his pride had lasted only as long as it had taken for the Dead Rabbits gang to try to force him into becoming a liar and a thief.

"And then there's the work," Maddie continued. "Have you any experience with the doing of laundry?"

"In truth, I've never tried it," Michael admitted. "But I've a strong back and a ready mind. I should be able to learn the way of it."

She shook her head. Perhaps she thought he denigrated her work by making it seem too easy. From what he'd seen, laundresses worked harder than most for less pay.

Ciara and Aiden were glancing back and forth between the two of them, as if willing their sister to give in. Maddie looked as if she couldn't or wouldn't budge, even for them.

You offered me light when all was darkness, Father. Show me the way now.

Michael reached out and took Maddie's ungloved hand in his. "Give me the opportunity to help, Miss O'Rourke."

Maddie gazed up at him, eyes narrowed as if she thought to see inside him and determine his worth. Michael held her gaze, wishing he could see inside her instead. Ciara and Aiden had talked often about their sister Maddie, and his Aunt Sylvie had sung her praises, but he couldn't understand her. Why would anyone leave a little brother and sister behind? Why travel halfway around the world? Had she been escaping trouble, like him? Or was she the cause of it, like Katie?

"Very well, Mr. Haggerty," she said, pulling back her hand. "You can stay with us, but only," she cautioned, finger in the air as Ciara cried out in delight and Aiden began jumping up and down, "until you secure a proper job. I suppose I can find some use for you."

"I'll do anything that needs doing, Miss O'Rourke," he vowed, "without complaint or compromise. You'll have no cause to regret your decision to help me."

"So you say," she answered, but Michael got the impression that she was regretting it already.

Chapter Two

Maddie could see that Michael Haggerty was going to be trouble. For one thing, Aiden and Ciara looked to him rather than her for guidance. She supposed that was a natural consequence of him serving as their escort aboard ship, but she could not allow it to continue. She had enough doubts about her abilities to raise her brother and sister.

And as for Ciara's insistence that Michael and Maddie must marry, that was nonsense. If Maddie wanted a brawny man in her life, she could have married one of the Wallin lads who were brothers to the man her good friend Catherine had married. Failing that, all Maddie had to do was whistle, and a dozen loggers and mill workers would have run to her side and dropped on bended knee to propose. Seattle was so desperate for marriageable females that she hardly needed to import a suitor all the way from New York!

Besides, why had Sylvie sent a man when Maddie had specified a woman? With her money going to pay Mr. Haggerty's way, Maddie had nothing with which to hire the lady she'd needed. And by the size of him, he'd more than eat his weight in wages!

He was watching her now with those blue, blue eyes, as if waiting for her orders. She straightened her spine. "Set to work, then, Mr. Haggerty. Find Ciara's and Aiden's things. They'll need to be carried home."

He saluted her again. "On my way, Captain O'Rourke."

Aiden giggled as Michael strode back toward the longboat.

Maddie drew in a breath. She could manage this. She must. In the next month, she had an opportunity to establish herself as the premier bakery in town by making all the cakes and rolls to be served at the biggest, most extravagant wedding Seattle had ever seen. Every man, woman and child would be singing her praises and lining up to purchase her products. Her future, and Ciara's and Aiden's futures, would be secure. She wasn't about to jeopardize that for the likes of Michael Haggerty.

She pressed her hands into her skirts and bent closer to Ciara and Aiden. "Who's ready to see their new home?"

"Me!" Aiden declared.

Ciara nodded eagerly.

With a smile, Maddie turned to allow them past her up the pier. "This way."

Aiden ran ahead, darting between the waiting people and the sailors on the narrow pier. Ciara walked beside Maddie as if trying to be a lady, but Maddie could see her sister's head turning this way and that as she took everything in.

"Seattle's different from Five Points," Maddie told her. "You'll find everything smaller, except the geography."

"Where are the tenements?" Ciara asked.

Maddie put an arm around her shoulders, realizing with a pang that she didn't have to bend all that much to do so. Her sister's eyes were nearly on a level with hers and pinched a bit around the corners with worry.

"Sure-n but there are no tenements here," Maddie confided.

Ciara stopped, eyes widening. "Then where does everyone live?"

Maddie pulled back with a smile. "That depends, so it does. Some live in rooms above their shops as we will. Some share a house with many bedrooms in it. Others have grand houses high on the hill. And some live out among the trees in cabins built of logs."

"Built of logs?" Now Ciara frowned. "Didn't the coppers stop them from cutting down the trees in the park?"

Maddie shook her head, trying not to let her sister see her amusement. "If you can believe it, the trees aren't in any park. They live out all on their own, everywhere."

Ciara put her hands on the hips of her blue coat. "You're teasing me."

Maddie gave her a hug. "No indeed, me darling girl. It's a whole new world here, and we have the privilege of helping to build it."

Ciara's brow cleared as Maddie released her. "We had the building of it back home too. That's what the Dead Rabbits did."

A shiver went through Maddie at the name of the dreaded Irish gang that had run Five Points. "The Dead Rabbits were violent, nasty creatures who used Irish pride to further their own gains," she told Ciara.

Her sister shook her head. "You don't understand. You were gone too long. The Dead Rabbits protect us, keep us safe. We need them."

Maddie stiffened. "Who's been filling your head with such nonsense?"

Ciara raised her chin. "I figured it out all by myself.

I'm grown now, you know. Oh, look! What's that?" She ran to the edge of the pier where Aiden had stopped to stare down at something in the water.

Maddie followed more slowly. She would never be able to see the vicious gang as heroes as Ciara did, but her sister was right about one thing. Life had definitely changed since Maddie had left New York. Sylvie Mc-Neilly, who ran the children's home where Maddie had left Ciara and Aiden, had little use for the gang violence that brought her another orphan every month. She would never have allowed Ciara or Aiden to admire the Dead Rabbits. So who had convinced Ciara otherwise?

If it was Michael Haggerty, he was about to find something considerably harder to deal with than sleeping on the floor.

Michael slung his cloth bag over his shoulder and picked up the children's carpetbag to start up the pier. He didn't want to lose sight of Maddie. He had a feeling she'd have liked nothing more than to leave him behind. His aunt had warned him as much.

"Maddie is a good person," Sylvie had assured him over the narrow table where she and all her children ate under the light of a single sputtering lamp. "You'll not be finding a kinder heart. But she's expecting the lass I promised her, not a big strapping lad the likes of you. See that you win her over straightaway. She can be a big help to you."

At the time, he'd agreed with his aunt that winning over Maddie O'Rourke would be key. He just didn't think the winning-over part was going particularly well. Try as he might, he couldn't understand her.

Help me, Father. I know she isn't Katie, but how can I be sure that she'll be any more faithful after leaving

*her brother and sister behind? These children need a
family, a secure future, not more heartache. I'm not
their father, but I feel like their brother. Show me how
to help them.*

"Hold up, me lad!"

The familiar voice stayed Michael's step. He had
known Patrick Flannery most of his life, though they'd
lost contact for the past few years as Michael worked
the Brooklyn docks and Patrick remained in Five Points.
Michael had been pleased to find his friend among those
heading to Washington Territory. With his warm blond
hair, green eyes and a spring in his step, Patrick was all
things good and bright about their heritage.

His friend craned his neck now to see up the pier,
battered top hat shading his eyes. "Is that her, then,
your warden?"

"She's not my jailer," Michael said, starting up the
pier.

Patrick kept pace, long legs flashing in his plaid trousers. "She holds the keys to your freedom, my lad. That
sounds like a jailer to me. What's she like, then? Is she
the fire-eater Ciara led us to believe?"

Ciara had bragged that her sister could do anything,
but Michael wasn't so sure. For all her confidence, Maddie O'Rourke had a fragility about her. Perhaps, like
her sister, a more tender woman dwelled inside the bold
shell.

But maybe that was just wishful thinking.

"Give me a day or two, Pat," Michael said as they
moved up the pier, shouldering their way through the
crowd. "And then I'll be able to tell you the truth about
Maddie O'Rourke."

"If anyone can, you can," Patrick said. "You're good
with understanding people. Me? I just like getting things

done. So, I'll explore the place and let you know me findings." He dropped back and allowed Michael to continue on alone.

Michael caught up to Maddie, Ciara and Aiden at the top of the pier, where they'd stopped. Aiden was down on his knees, bent over the water and grinning at a furry face that appeared to be grinning back.

"Ah, and here you've gone and made a new friend already," Michael teased him with a nod to the seal.

Aiden glanced up at him. "Can we bring him home?"

Maddie chuckled, a sound as warm as the color of her hair. "No, I'm afraid not. His family would miss him."

Aiden nodded as if he accepted that, then climbed to his feet. "The people here probably want him for the menagerie anyway."

"No menagerie," Maddie said. "All the wild animals here roam about free."

Aiden stared at her, and Michael couldn't tell whether the boy thought it a grand idea or a horrible one.

Ciara stomped one foot. "There you go again! You stop teasing us, Maddie!"

Maddie's smile disappeared. "It's the honest truth."

Ciara turned to Michael. "She said you don't need permission to cut down trees in the park either."

"What I said," Maddie clarified, "is that the trees aren't in a park. Here you can own your land, up to one hundred and sixty acres per lad or lass."

"Well, that's a whopper," Ciara said with a shake of her head.

"It's the truth," Michael told her. "It's from a law called the Homestead Act. I read about it. If you've an interest in farming and a stomach for hard work, you could go far."

He thought Maddie would thank him for supporting

her, but she frowned at him as if she wasn't sure what he was trying to achieve.

Ciara's frown eased. "Well, maybe you can farm, but that still doesn't mean you get to cut down trees anytime you please."

"You have to be cutting down the trees," Maddie told her. "Those one hundred and sixty acres you claimed most likely are covered in trees so thick you can barely squeeze through them. If you don't cut them down, you'd have no place to be planting your vegetables."

"Why would they plant vegetables?" Aiden asked. "Why don't they just buy them from the grocer?"

"I suspect you'll not find many green grocers just yet, my lad," Michael told him. "Or all that many farmers either. This is the wilderness. But that just means you can be anything you want to be."

Even saying the words made his heart lighten. No one to tell him what he must do, whom he must support in the name of protecting Irish interests. He could be his own man, follow whichever way the Lord pointed. He drew in a deep breath, savoring the crisp, salty air.

"I don't want to be a farmer," Aiden announced, heading toward the road beyond the pier with a skip. "I want to be a sailor, see the world."

"Now, where would you be getting that idea, I wonder?" Maddie said, following him with a sidelong look to Michael.

"Not from me," Michael assured her as Ciara came along as well. "I worked the docks in New York. I didn't sail the ships. And I'd think you'd have had enough of living on a ship by now, Aiden."

"You're right," Aiden said. "It was too small. I can't wait to run!"

Maddie grabbed his hand as if she feared he'd dash

off right then. "Not so fast, me lad. First you need to learn your way about."

With her free hand, she pointed up the steep hill in front of them. Michael had never seen anything like it. Though businesses were rising on each side, the rutted track running down the center was dark with mud. He could not imagine a wagon navigating it.

"That's the skid road," Maddie explained. "Lumbermen drag their chopped-down trees to the top and skid them right down to Mr. Yesler's mill over there, where workers cut them up for boards to make houses and ships. Some of the logs are so big across, a man looks like a wee child beside them."

"Now I know you're bamming me," Ciara said.

This time, Michael couldn't argue with her.

"Be that as it may," Maddie said, face turning stern, "it's a dangerous place for the likes of you. The men are rough, the logs heavy and fast. You're not to be going anywhere near it, understand?"

Aiden nodded solemnly. Ciara looked less sure, but she nodded too.

As if satisfied by their responses, Maddie set off walking, one hand still holding her brother's. Ciara walked on her other side. Michael could only fall in behind. Her heavy skirts twitched with her impatient stride, and he didn't think it was her siblings who concerned her. She didn't like him by half. He needed to work harder if he wanted to put himself in her good graces.

He tried to keep quiet as he followed her up the street. Humility had been a hard lesson, but nearly three months at sea had given him time to reflect. He had a chance for a future and he wasn't going to lose it by slipping back into old habits.

But Seattle, he saw, was even more sparsely populated than he'd supposed. He was used to tenement buildings crowding out the sunlight, masts of sailing ships so thick in the harbor he could have walked from one yardarm to another.

Here, single-story, whitewashed houses dotted the hillside, with dusky green trees taller than any he'd ever seen rising all around them. Two-story businesses were rare. The wide roads were heavy with black mud and crowded with wagons pulled by thick-necked oxen and wiry mules. And almost everyone he saw was male.

They were halfway up the hill, Maddie pointing out interesting shops to the children, when an older fellow in a fine suit, his whiskers thickest over his chin, stopped them. The tiny woman holding on to his arm must have been his wife.

"Good afternoon, Miss O'Rourke," he said as he tipped his hat. "Mrs. Horton was asking when we might purchase more of your exceptional ginger cookies."

"Now, dear," his wife chided him with an affectionate smile, blue eyes crinkling at the corners. "I'm sure Miss O'Rourke is much too busy preparing for the wedding to bake us cookies."

The wedding? Was Miss O'Rourke about to be married? A wealthy groom, eager to please his bride-to-be, would explain where the money had come from for passage as well as her fancy clothes and hat. What he couldn't understand was why the thought of a wedding disappointed him. Was he truly so hurt by Katie's desertion that he couldn't see others happy?

Maddie smiled at the couple. "Sure-n but I'll never be too busy for my best customers. I'll have a batch ready tomorrow afternoon, just for you."

Mr. Horton nodded, cheeks pink with obvious pleasure. "I'll come get them myself," he promised. "And good day to you and yours."

With a nod to the couple, Maddie led Ciara and Aiden on.

Ciara glanced back at them. "Who was that? And why did she ask about a wedding?"

Michael walked closer to hear the answer.

"That was Mr. and Mrs. Dexter Horton," Maddie replied, skirting around a rain barrel that sat at the corner of a building they were passing. "They've been loyal customers. They know I'm helping with a wedding for a friend who's marrying at the end of the month. It will be a grand affair."

Michael seized on the one word that made sense to him. "Customers. For your laundry?"

Maddie glanced back at him, and he thought a challenge lurked in those dark eyes. "First for my laundry, now for my bakery."

"A bakery?" Aiden hopped up and down beside her. "You mean with sweets and cakes?"

Maddie turned her smile on him, warmer and more tender, and something inside Michael reached for that smile like a plant seeking light. He thought he knew the source of the reaction. His parents had died when he was about Aiden's age; he hardly remembered them. Sylvie had been the one to look so kindly at him, to make him feel he was loved and appreciated. Was it any surprise he wanted the same for Aiden and Ciara?

But a bakery? How did a former laundress manage that, either from skill or with finances?

"Sweets indeed," Maddie promised Aiden, her voice glowing with excitement. "And breads and cakes. As much as you want."

That didn't sound like such a good idea. Michael

opened his mouth to tell her, then shut it again. She wouldn't thank him for the suggestion. Still, he couldn't help wondering whether she was trying to buy their affection.

She certainly didn't need to buy the affection of Seattle's citizens. That much was clear by the slow pace at which they progressed up the block of mercantiles. Every man acknowledged her as they passed, tipping his hat or otherwise greeting her as if she were the queen come to visit. By the looks in their eyes, more than one was smitten with her.

They tended to glare at Michael, who merely looked over their heads. He noticed, however, that Maddie didn't introduce any of them to the children. Was she unsure of the men or ashamed of her kin? The latter didn't seem likely, as she'd paid their passage and arranged for an escort.

"And here we are," she sang out, stopping before a narrow, two-story building at the end of the street. A wide window fronted a boardwalk, and a wooden sign over the door proclaimed the place the Pastry Emporium. Aiden's eyes lit.

"You own this?" he asked, voice heavy with awe.

"Not entirely," Maddie replied, taking out a ring of keys and inserting one in the door. "A gentleman here finds likely enterprises and funds them to grow. He was persuaded to support my endeavors. I'm paying him back a little at a time, with interest."

More than a little interest, most likely. Back home, there had always been shifty types ready to lend money, only to demand every penny for years while threatening their clients' health and the lives of their families. He could imagine Maddie wanting some way to support Ciara and Aiden, but at what cost?

As she opened the door, Ciara and Aiden scampered past her into the shop, and the scent of cinnamon floated out behind them. Maddie gazed at them, her face soft. She drew in a breath as if seeking assurance she could be all they needed. He could almost see the burdens pressing on her shoulders.

It wasn't right. First Sylvie and now Maddie—working themselves into an early grave to support family foisted upon them by fate.

Michael bent his head to hers. "Taken on more than you can handle?" he murmured, concerned and ready to offer his help.

She straightened her shoulders and narrowed her eyes at him. "Not at all, Mr. Haggerty. You'll learn I always know exactly what I'm about. If you intend to be of use, you'll have to keep up."

She marched into the shop, and he had to catch the door to keep it from slamming in front of him. He'd been raised to help those in distress, particularly a lady. What was he supposed to do when the lady wanted no help from him?

Chapter Three

The nerve of the man! How dare he question her decisions? She'd thought long and hard before taking out a loan to purchase the shop, and furnish it with the tools and supplies she'd need to establish herself as a baker. She was confident she could pay the money back in good time, so long as she proved herself at the wedding.

She forced herself to focus on Ciara and Aiden, who were glancing eagerly around the shop.

"This is where I'll be selling my goods," she told them, nodding to the long display counter where light glistened on specks of icing left over from the cinnamon rolls she'd sold that morning. "The high shelves behind it are for the confections and spices I hope to offer one day. And through that curtain is a fine kitchen with a brick oven big enough to cook all manner of sweets."

"Like in 'Hansel and Gretel,'" Aiden said, cocking his head to peer through a crack in the curtain. "Only that lady cooked children." He glanced back at the skeptical-looking Michael, frown forming.

Michael must have interpreted the look, for he came to put a hand to Aiden's back. "Your sister doesn't cook children," he assured the boy. He bent to put his mouth even with her brother's ear and lowered his voice. "But I'm not so sure about a longshoreman like me."

"No, silly," Aiden said. "You'd never fit in her oven."

"You haven't seen my oven," Maddie muttered to herself.

Just then the curtain gave a twitch, as if something waited on the other side. Maddie made herself smile. "Now, there's one other resident of my bakery you should be meeting. She's short and round-faced, with gray hair."

Ciara and Aiden looked at her, gazes quizzical.

"I thought you wanted Sylvie to send you a lady to help," Ciara said. "Why did you need Michael if you already had one?"

Why indeed? She couldn't help glancing his way, only to find him regarding her as if she were a piece to a puzzle that just didn't fit.

"You'll see in a moment," Maddie promised her brother and sister. She was merely glad Amelia Batterby hadn't made herself scarce when strangers arrived. Maddie ventured to the curtain and tugged it aside. A short-haired, gray cat peered up at her, amber eyes wide.

"You have a cat!" Aiden cried, lunging toward her.

Amelia Batterby disappeared like a puff of smoke.

"She's a bit skittish still," Maddie explained as Aiden's face fell. "She came to Seattle as a ship's cat, and a mighty explorer she was, escaping every time they made port and causing the captain all manner of concern. He was persuaded to leave her in my care, and she now earns her keep as a mouser. Just know that you mustn't let her outside, or she'll escape again."

Ciara angled her head to see through the curtain. "What's her name?"

"The captain called her Her Ladyship on account of

her proper ways, but I think she looked more like old Amelia Batterby."

Michael chuckled. "The lady who lived next to Sylvie. I remember her. She was always finding something to concern her."

Aiden shivered. "She scolded us whenever we even peeked out the door."

"But she always brought presents for Easter and Christmas," Michael reminded him.

"What presents does this Amelia Batterby bring?" Aiden asked Maddie.

"Mice and squirrels," Maddie told him. "And any other vermin that creep into the bakery."

Ciara winced.

"Maybe she'll catch you one night," Michael teased Aiden.

How easily he joked with her siblings, as if he were their brother and her the stranger come to live with them. She shouldn't be annoyed with him for such a gift, but she was.

"I'm too big for a cat to catch me," Aiden said. "But I like her. Can she sleep in the bed with us?"

"Very likely she does her best work at night," Michael told him. "But if she finds her way to the bed, I wouldn't be protesting."

And who was he to be deciding that? Although she agreed with him in this instance, she was the one who should have made the decision. And Michael should know that.

Drawing in a breath, she nodded to the far wall. "Did you notice that door to the side, Aiden? That leads to our home."

Aiden hurried to open the door, and he and Ciara

clambered up the wooden stairs. Maddie stepped in front of Michael, preventing him from following.

"We need to come to an understanding, Mr. Haggerty," she said. "You did your job bringing my brother and sister here. Now they're my responsibility. Leave any concerns about their upbringing to me." Satisfied she'd made her point, she turned for the stairs. A firm hand on her arm spun her back around.

All at once she wasn't looking at a penniless vagabond but a warrior prince ready to defend his country. There was steel in those blue eyes, determination written on every feature.

"I'll make you a deal, Miss O'Rourke," he said. "You prove to me you have what it takes to raise Ciara and Aiden, and I'll stop being concerned. But not one second sooner."

Heat licked up her. She'd had to fight with herself over the decision to raise her siblings. She had plenty of frustration left to fight him too. "I'll not be having you speak to me in such a tone, Michael Haggerty. I'm their bone and blood."

"And I'm the man who's listened to them cry themselves to sleep at night for the last three months," he countered. "I don't understand why you left them behind, and neither do they. I owe you a debt for paying my passage, but if you want my respect and theirs, you'll have to earn it."

There, he'd said it aloud. Aunt Sylvie had always claimed his tendency to stand up for the rights of others would get him into trouble. It had made him a pariah in New York. Likely it had just cost him room and board here. Maddie would be within her rights to toss him out on his ear for such a challenge. If she did, he'd have no recourse but to throw himself on the mercy of the church, if they even had a church yet in Seattle. He waited for her stinging rejoinder.

She took a step back from him and snapped a nod. "Done. And thank you for telling me about the crying. I'll be sure to watch for that. Bring up their things now, then we'll find someplace for you to sleep." She swept past him, lifting her skirts to climb the narrow staircase.

Bemused, Michael could only follow.

Upstairs, the space over the shop had been divided into four rooms—three smaller ones across the back and one larger one facing the street. The larger room held a fat-bellied stove and a tall sideboard along one wall, with a wooden table and chairs in the center. The red-and-white chintz curtains on the window and the red checkered cloth on the table brightened the space.

"Look, Michael," Aiden cried, gesturing toward the table. "Maddie got chairs enough for us all."

Maddie's cheeks turned a pleasing shade of pink. "Sure-n but I was expecting a lady to be coming with you. I thought she'd need somewhere to sit."

And she wasn't exactly sure she wanted him to take the lady's place at the table. Michael set the children's bag down on the floor. "And what might those rooms be, do you think?" he asked Aiden, nodding toward the three rooms across the back.

With two of the doors open, Michael could see that each of the smaller rooms held a bed on a wooden frame and pegs along the walls for hanging clothes. Ciara and Aiden threaded their way from one room to the next, exclaiming over the colorful quilts on the beds, the framed etching of a lady in a fancy dress that graced one wall.

Maddie stood watching, one arm hugging her waist. A moment ago, she'd been all fire; now she was as soft as smoke. She bit her lower lip as if waiting for Ciara and Aiden to find fault. He couldn't ignore the urge to assure her.

"You've done a fine job of making this a home," he murmured to her.

She drew in another breath as if she'd needed that affirmation, then reached up and removed the little hat to set it on the table. "So I was hoping," she told him. "I suppose it will depend on what they think."

Aiden darted out of the last room. "Who else boards here?" he asked.

"No one," Maddie said with a smile. "One of the rooms is for you, and the other is for Ciara. The last is mine."

Aiden stared at her a moment, then let out a whoop and dived into the nearest room. "This one's mine!"

"That one has a pink-and-white quilt," Ciara told him, following at a more stately pace. "It's clearly my room."

Aiden drew himself up. Michael readied himself to settle the squabble, but Maddie stepped between them. "Sure-n but they're all the same size. We can change the quilts and move the picture to another room, if you like."

Aiden made a face, backing away. "Nah. She can have her girlie room. I'll take the other." He dashed out the door.

Ciara perched on the bed and gave it a halfhearted bounce. She glanced up at Maddie. "Is this really to be mine?"

"All yours, me darling girl," Maddie assured her with a smile.

Ciara rose. "Good. Then you can leave."

Maddie blinked. "What?"

Ciara stood with her eyes narrowed. "You said it was mine. I can do with it as I please. I want to be alone. Now."

There went Her Highness, Queen Ciara again. For once, even her sister seemed at a loss for words. Michael knew he should allow Maddie to deal with the situation as she'd just demanded. But Ciara couldn't know how her attitude affected her sister, and he didn't like seeing either of them hurt.

So he dropped his bag outside the doors to the children's rooms and sketched a bow. "At once, Your Royal Highness. Just as soon as you remember your lowly servants here."

Though she raised her little chin, Ciara's cheeks were turning pink. "I never said you were servants."

Michael raised his brows. "Oh, didn't you? You seem to have forgotten that your sister paid for you to come here and gave you all this. There's such a thing as being grateful."

Ciara wrinkled her nose, which was nearly as pert as her sister's. "Why should I be grateful for having to come all this way, leaving all my friends behind? She ought to be grateful I'll even have anything to do with her."

Maddie sucked in a breath as if her sister's words had stung. Michael took a step back, waved at the door.

"Well, then, perhaps you should be the one to leave, you being such a put-upon lass. The captain said he was heading back to New York. Perhaps you can work your way home by clearing slops out of the kitchen and hosing out the head."

Ciara turned green. "You wouldn't do that."

Michael shrugged. "I don't see why not. I'm here to work off my passage. You don't seem to want to."

"You're not my father. You don't get to tell me what to do." She turned to Maddie. "You won't make me leave, will you, Maddie?"

Maddie glanced at Michael through the corners of her eyes. "I won't make you leave, me darling girl, but I can't be liking how you're treating me. This is to be your new home."

Ciara's mouth worked as if she was chewing on the idea. "All right," she said. "You can come in. But you have to knock first." She raised her voice. "And that goes for you too, Aiden O'Rourke."

From the other side of the wall came a rude noise. "Like I'd want to go in your stupid room."

Michael gestured to the bag outside their doors. "You'll each need to come and get your clothes and put them away. No dinner until it's done right."

"Fine." Ciara sashayed out of her room and bent over the bag. Aiden peered out his door, but wisely kept his distance until she had found her things.

"I best be getting food from the larder for dinner," Maddie murmured before hurrying down the stairs.

Michael sighed. He'd slipped back into his role as guardian even after telling Maddie he expected her to take up the task. But it wasn't easy handing her the role he'd played for as long as he could remember, first with Sylvie's other children, and then with Ciara and Aiden.

He hadn't been surprised to find two more faces at his aunt's table a few days after Christmas last year. Aunt Sylvie never could resist a call for help. In the crowded tenements that surrounded Five Points, someone was always dying of disease or disability, leaving children alone and frightened. Whenever possible, aunts and uncles and cousins distant and close stepped in, but sometimes no family or friends could be found.

So Sylvie took those children in, raised them as her own, scrubbed floors and sewed to make ends meet and accepted charity from all who offered. When Michael had first spotted the O'Rourke children, she'd had six others besides.

"What's their story?" he'd asked as he'd helped his aunt clear up after a meager dinner of cabbage soup and crackers.

Sylvie's ocean-blue eyes had turned down as she glanced at Ciara and Aiden huddled by the hearth. "Poor mites," she'd murmured with a shake of her head that had loosened her flyaway graying blond hair. "Lost their mum and da in that terrible fire a few months ago. Their older sister had the raising of them, but she struggled so. Now she has a chance to go with Mercer's Belles to Washington Territory. Sure-n but she'd be a fool not to take it."

He'd read the story in the papers that eventually ended up blowing down the streets of Five Points before someone used them to fill the holes in the walls or burned them for fuel. Some fellow from the wilderness claimed men in Seattle needed teachers and seamstresses. The editors seemed to think the women were more likely to be forced into marriage or worse.

"So she'll marry and go on with her life," he'd surmised. "She'll have what she needs, and she won't think of them again."

His aunt had set a sudsy hand on his arm. "Miss Katie O'Doul might have had her heart fixed on a crown, but Miss O'Rourke is another sort entirely."

That night, he'd been willing to give Maddie O'Rourke the benefit of the doubt. But a reporter had sailed with Mercer's Belles, and as his stories returned to be printed, Michael had struggled to find charity with Ciara and Aiden's sister.

Roger Conant, a good Irishman his aunt insisted, told of flirtations galore with the ship's officers, among the other passengers and at every port of call. How could Maddie O'Rourke be immune? He'd been the most surprised when the telegraph had arrived stating that passage had been paid for Ciara and Aiden and a lady to escort them.

"She must have found a rich husband," he'd told his aunt when she'd shared it with him after the excited children had gone to bed.

"She signs the cable Maddie O'Rourke," Sylvie had pointed out, showing him the closely worded note. "She's made her fortune, just as she'd hoped, and a great deal faster than anyone expected. And now the dear girl hopes to share it with her family."

She was trying to share it, all right. Michael didn't like thinking what such quarters must have cost her to build and furnish. She clearly wanted her brother and sister beside her, yet something told him she wasn't sure what to do with them now.

Leaving the children to put away their belongings, he followed her downstairs, locating her in the kitchen. The whitewashed walls enclosed a thick worktable with space below for bowls and rolling pins. Bright copper pots and dark iron pans hung from hooks over a squat wooden box with a lid. Its purpose defied him. One wall was built of red brick, with a small iron door at the bottom to cover the firebox and a wider door opening higher up for the oven.

Which just might have been big enough to fit a certain longshoreman.

Maddie was at a door in the wall to his right, digging through the supplies stored there. Casks and sacks crowded the floor; the shelves at the back were filled with tins of butter, cones of sugar in bright blue wrappers, jars of preserves, and bottles and vials of things he wasn't sure he could name.

She glanced at him as he came to a stop beside her, and he thought he saw something glistening on her cheek before she returned to her perusal of the supplies.

"It wasn't my place to settle that," he said. "Forgive me."

She reached out and pulled down a fat ham, molasses thick on its sides. "You had to settle it," she said, carrying the ham to the table. "I couldn't. They've changed. Once I was the world to them both, and when I told them what they should be doing, they did it."

As she pulled a knife from a drawer in the worktable, he ventured closer. She sliced through the meat with brisk efficiency, but her face remained tight.

"Ciara is growing up," he allowed. "Though don't tell her I said so. She'll take it as leave to make further demands."

Instead of smiling as he'd hoped, Maddie grimaced. "She's been like that since she was born. Da used to be teasing her like you did, calling her royalty." She rested the knife on the table. "She never was treating me that way. I'm thinking she blames me for leaving her behind."

She ducked her head, but Michael heard her sniff.

"It's hard to understand when someone you love leaves," he murmured, her pain like a wound inside him. "When my parents died, I remember feeling like I was the last person in the whole world."

She paused, slanting a glance up at him. "Who had the raising of you?"

He smiled. "Sylvie. She's sister to my mother. I don't know what I would have done without her."

Her hands started moving again. "But you didn't rail at her, tell her you had no use for her."

"I wasn't eleven," he pointed out with a shrug. "Or I might have. As it was, I was the first of her borrowed children, as she likes to call them. And she gave me many brothers and sisters over the years."

She took the remaining ham back to the larder. "Did you never mind having to share her?"

Had Maddie minded? Sylvie had said Ciara and Aiden's mother had been Maddie's stepmother. Maddie had to have been nearly grown when they came along.

"I never saw it as sharing," he told her. "Sylvie made you feel like the most important person in her world, like the two of you were partners. Her children were my family."

"Small wonder you're so good with Ciara and Aiden," she said, bending to gather some potatoes from a sack. "I just wanted to give them a home, a family again. I never thought they'd fight against me on that."

"Give them time," Michael advised as she carried the potatoes to the table. "You've had more than five months to accustom yourself to the place. For them, life changed when they boarded the ship, and it changed again when they left it."

She nodded. "I've just missed them so. All I wanted was for them to be happy." She glanced up at him. A drop of molasses darkened the tear on her cheek.

Unthinking, he reached out and wiped the smudge away with his thumb. Her skin was as silky and warm as it looked, and all at once he smelled cinnamon again, as if she were the sweet treat he was meant to savor.

Embarrassed by the thought, he stepped back as her face turned pink.

"You've given them every reason to be happy," he said. "A good home, a warm welcome. And what child wouldn't want to live over a bakery?"

She smiled then, brightening the room, lifting his heart. "Sure-n they say that the way to a man's heart is down his throat. That must be twice as true for children."

She gathered the food and a jar of preserves and headed for the door before Michael could stir himself to help. He thought she was right about Ciara and Aiden— good cooking and kind words would go a long way toward healing their hurts, helping them see the love their sister was trying to offer.

A shame it would take more than a bakery to make him ready to take a chance on love again.

Chapter Four

Maddie sat at the table, watching Michael, Ciara and Aiden tuck into the ham steaks, fricasseed potatoes and biscuits she'd prepared. She'd wanted to do more, but she'd barely finished her work in the bakery before changing to go meet them. Still, by the pace they lifted their forks, they were running a race and expected the loser to face a firing squad.

"Were they so stingy with the meals aboard ship?" she asked, fingers toying with a biscuit.

Aiden wiped his mouth with the back of his hand. "It was terrible! They only let us eat twice a day, and nothing but biscuits, biscuits, biscuits." He made a face and dived back into his potatoes.

Ciara wrinkled her nose. "Hard biscuits too. Nothing like these." She lifted the remaining half of her biscuit daintily, rubbed it in the blackberry preserves Catherine had helped Maddie put up and stuffed it into her mouth.

Maddie tried not to cringe. She'd have to work on their manners, if they'd allow her to teach them anything.

Michael had been silent much of the meal, though he'd eaten plenty, as Maddie had expected. Now he sighed almost longingly as he laid down his fork. "I've dined at a few restaurants in New York. None of them ever served biscuits as good as these."

Maddie's face warmed. "It does my heart good to hear my work appreciated." She winked at Aiden. "Now, let's just hope the fine citizens of Seattle agree with you."

"If they don't agree, they're stupid," Aiden said, shoving back his empty plate. He glanced up at Maddie. "When do we get sweets?"

Michael gazed at the wall, but he wasn't fooling her. She'd seen the light in those blue eyes when her brother mentioned sweets. Like the loggers and miners around Seattle, he must have a craving for sugary things. That also boded well for business.

She rose and went to the sideboard for the tin she'd filled earlier that day. "I'll have cinnamon rolls ready when you wake tomorrow," she promised Aiden. "For now, you'll have to make do with gingersnaps."

She brought a dozen to the table, and Aiden grabbed a handful before slipping from his chair.

"I'll just take these to my room for safekeeping," he said.

Ciara shook her head as he scurried from the table. "The rats will get them before you do, silly."

"There will be no rats in my establishment," Maddie called after him, "and I'll be thanking the Lord for that." She fought a shudder at the memory of the beady eyes and pointy snouts she'd seen on occasion in New York.

Ciara reached down and brushed her fingers against a gray tail that was peeking out from under the table. "Amelia Batterby would not stand for it," she said with great surety.

Maddie met Michael's gaze across the table and caught him smiling.

Ciara climbed from her seat. "I'm going to my room. You may call me when breakfast is ready tomorrow."

There went Her Highness again. Michael must not have liked the stance any better, for he spoke up, with a look at Maddie. "What about school? Don't Ciara and Aiden need to attend?"

Ciara turned to stare at him, and Aiden shot out of his room.

"They have a school here?" he asked, wide-eyed.

"Indeed we do," Maddie told them, feeling a tug of pride at her adopted city. "In the Territorial University no less."

She waited for Ciara to protest the unorthodox arrangement, but her sister seemed to fold in on herself. "I don't want to go to a university."

"I do," Aiden announced, bouncing on the balls of his feet. "I'll get to play with bigger boys."

"It's not like that," Maddie explained. "There aren't enough students of an age to be studying at the university, so the president opened a grammar school." She was only glad the president was no longer Asa Mercer, for she hadn't been impressed with him and his grasping ways when he'd brought her and her traveling companions out to Seattle earlier that year. She rose to gather up the dishes.

"Let me," Michael said, rising as well. He took the dishes and carried them to the sideboard. It was a gentlemanly gesture, but she thought he was merely trying to keep himself too busy to jump into the middle of the conversation.

"I still don't want to go," Ciara insisted. "They're probably mean. Isn't there an Irish school?"

So that was the problem. Back home, because of the

violence, many of the Irish children had learned at their parents' knees or in groups in a crowded flat.

"No Irish school," Maddie told her. "No German school either. Here everyone learns together."

Ciara's scowl said she didn't much like that idea.

"It's a new world we've come to," Michael said. He opened his mouth as if to say more, than clamped it shut again and resolutely turned his face toward the sideboard.

"Indeed it is," Maddie said. She moved to his side, pointing to the bucket of water waiting for the dishes and then the kettle steaming on the stove. With a nod, he set to work.

Now there was a rare man. Maddie couldn't help the thought as she returned to her seat and gestured her siblings toward the chairs on each side of her. Da had been good about helping with the children, but her stepmother had been the one to labor over the stove, the dishes and the laundry, even though she worked cleaning houses for the wealthy folks uptown during the day.

Now Ciara returned to the table reluctantly, Aiden with unabashed curiosity.

"Perhaps we should be deciding on some rules," Maddie said as they took their seats. "We already agreed there'd be no playing on the skid road."

"You said that," Ciara grumbled.

Maddie ignored her. Impossible to ignore was the way Michael looked to Maddie with a nod as if encouraging her to continue, or the sight of his muscles as he took off his coat and rolled up his sleeves for the washing.

"I expect you to attend school, do your best," she told Ciara and Aiden, trying not to think about the man standing behind her with his arms up to the elbows in water. "The quarter started in September, but I've made arrangements for you to join the class on Monday."

Both her siblings paled at that. Maddie pushed on.

"I expect you to be helping around here as well. Aiden, I'll show you how to pump the water and bring it in. I want a filled bucket in the kitchen and up here. I've friends who keep the woodpile stocked, but you'll need to bring the logs and kindling up here for the stove."

Aiden grinned. "I can do that."

Maddie only hoped her sister would be as accepting. "Ciara, your job will be to make the beds in the morning, sweep the floor, watch your brother and help me with the cooking."

Ciara humphed and crossed her arms over her chest. "That's servant work. Servants should be paid."

"You aren't servants," Maddie said, meeting their gazes in turn. "You're members of this household. We all work together and we all share the rewards."

Aiden perked up. "Like cakes."

Maddie nodded. "Like cakes and the other goods from the bakery. But we cannot be eating all our wares or we'll have nothing to sell and no money to buy what we need."

They both sobered at that, nodding their agreement. Like Maddie, they must remember the times when Da and their mum had been out of work, and food had been hard to come by.

"I expect you to be kind to each other and me," Maddie finished. "And under no circumstances will you allow Amelia Batterby out of doors. She'll run off or be eaten by one of the fearsome creatures in the woods, bears and cougars and wolves. Neither of you is to go into the forest alone. Take an adult who knows the area with you."

She couldn't help glancing at Michael. He had stopped washing at some point and was listening to her, his head cocked so that a lock of black hair fell over his forehead. Why did her fingers itch to tuck it back?

Now he nodded agreement but did not offer commentary. She'd asked him to stay out of her business, but his silence somehow felt worse than his interference.

She turned back to her siblings. Aiden was already fidgeting in his chair, gaze toward his bedroom door, where Amelia Batterby was giving herself a bath. Ciara was watching Maddie with a smug smile, as if she knew Maddie was having trouble keeping a dark-haired Irishman out of her thoughts.

"Off to bed with you, then," Maddie told them. "I'll come hear your prayers shortly."

They seemed to accept that, for they rose and left her for their rooms. She turned to Michael. "Well, Mr. Haggerty? Have you nothing to say about the matter?"

He shrugged, hands splashing in the water. "Not my place to say, as you pointed out. But if you want my opinion, I think you handled that well."

She wasn't sure why that warmed her so. She didn't need his approval. She didn't need his help. She certainly didn't need his distracting presence.

"Thank you," she said, determined to be no more than polite. She eyed him a moment. He'd rubbed soap on her dishrag, and the bubbles were dripping from his fingers. Long, strong fingers they were also meant for far more than washing her dishes or eating her biscuits.

Maddie drew in a breath, preparing herself to take up the next difficult subject. "And then, Mr. Haggerty," she said, "there's the matter of what I'm supposed to do with you."

* * *

So she'd come to a decision. Michael could tell by
the way she raised her chin. Though he stood taller in
response, he couldn't match her for seriousness.

"I'm a bit old to go to school like Ciara and Aiden,"
he offered, trying not to smile.

"You're never too old to learn," she countered. "And
I imagine the university president would be over the
moon to have a second student old enough to graduate.
But going to school won't be paying your debt, which
is what you said you wanted."

More than anything. But to pay his debt to her, he
needed work, either at her bakery or at some other business in Seattle.

"So what, then?" he asked.

She nodded toward the floor. "You can sleep near the
stove, and I'll provide you food until you can provide for
yourself. I haven't a blanket to spare right now with the
children arriving. Did you bring bedclothes with you?"

"Sylvie sent a blanket with me for the boat," he said.
"I can use that."

"Good. Sure-n it won't be a soft bed, but I've had
worse."

Had she? He knew she and the children had lived in
the tenements of Five Points, most of which were fur-
nished with beds. It was the number of people sharing
those beds, as entire families crowded into a single
room, that made life difficult.

"After I've finished the morning baking," she continued, "I'll show you the doing of the laundry."

That ought to be less than amusing. Him, Irishtown's
finest, doing laundry. But he was determined to pay her
back, so he merely nodded. "Yes, ma'am."

She made a face, nose scrunching and mouth tightening into a bow. "And you can stop calling me 'ma'am,'" she told him. "You make me feel as old as a granny."

He couldn't help his grin at that. No granny he'd ever known had looked half so fetching with her eyes snapping fire.

"Yes, Miss O'Rourke," he agreed.

She blew out a breath. "Would it be killing you to call me Maddie?"

"No trouble at all, Maddie," he assured her, liking the feel of the name on his tongue. "And you might try calling me Michael. It's a mite easier to say than Mr. Haggerty."

She gave him a nod, but didn't come out and say his first name. "Very well. Then there's the matter of the rules."

"I heard them," Michael said. "And I'll honor them. Since I don't know the area, I won't be taking the children on any outings among the trees."

"You'll not be taking the children on outings anywhere," she informed him. "I told you—you may sleep here and eat here, and it goes without saying that you'll be doing the laundry here until you find a job. I can see the effort you're making not to come between me and Ciara and Aiden, and I thank you for it. But the sooner you find work and a place of your own, the better it will be for all of us."

He knew she was right, yet still a part of him balked. He'd spent nearly three months watching over Ciara and Aiden, rejoicing with them when they excelled, encouraging them when they feared, admonishing them when they strayed. She couldn't ask him to simply turn off those feelings, leave the children behind like unwanted baggage.

But tonight might not be the best moment to argue

his case. The better approach would be to bide his time, show her how helpful he could be. Then maybe she'd let him remain a part of Ciara's and Aiden's lives. He'd had to leave everyone else he loved back in New York. They were his last ties to his old life.

"I'll start looking for work tomorrow," he promised. "As soon as I finish the little tasks you have for me."

Her smile curved up. "You might not be calling my laundry little once you've seen the piles awaiting you, Michael Haggerty. Finish the dishes if you've the will. I'll be back shortly." She turned and swept toward Aiden's room.

She was going to make him earn every penny of that ticket money. He found he didn't mind. His gaze followed her into the bedchamber, where Aiden knelt beside his bed with bowed head. Maddie gathered up her skirts and knelt beside him, listening as the boy murmured prayers for friends and family.

Michael rubbed at the plates in the cooling water, his own mind turning upward. *Prayer comes easily for him, Father. There have been times it didn't come so easily for me. Thank You for new opportunities. Help me to make the most of them.*

Aiden climbed into bed, and Maddie pulled the covers up around him. As if granting Aiden's earlier request, Amelia Batterby leaped up and curled onto the foot. Bending, Maddie pressed a kiss against her brother's forehead. Michael felt as if her lips touched his skin instead, gentle, sweet.

What was wrong with him? So what if she was as pretty as Katie? He wasn't going to let a woman, particularly one he wasn't so sure about, into his confidence again.

He still remembered the first time he'd seen Katie,

the way she'd smiled, the sunlight on her golden hair. He'd felt top of the world when she'd singled him out of all her suitors. He'd thought them both in love, but she'd had her eyes on a brighter future, one that involved fame won at the misfortune of others. He couldn't be that man.

He tried to focus on his work, rinsing off the dishes in a bowl of water one at a time, then drying them, but the simple task could not take his mind off what was happening in the other room. Now Ciara was saying her prayers with Maddie, hands clasped and face lifted up. Sylvie used to kneel at his side when he was Ciara's age, encouraging him, guiding him. Good for Maddie for wanting to take that role with her siblings.

"And bless the Dead Rabbits and all those who work to protect us," Ciara said.

Michael stiffened. He could see Maddie raise her head as well. The gang had cost more than one of Sylvie's children a parent, forced Michael out of his home and job. Why would Ciara want to bless them?

"Sure-n it's a fine thing to bless your enemies," he heard Maddie say. "Perhaps we should ask the Lord to change their hearts instead, help them use their influence to the good."

"They already do," Ciara protested, but Maddie must have given her a look, for she humphed and raised her eyes again. "And help the Dead Rabbits do more good things. And make Katie O'Doul sorry she ever hurt Michael."

Michael nearly dropped the plate. He shouldn't be surprised Ciara knew about Katie's defection. He and his aunt had talked about the matter often enough in the evenings when they thought the children were asleep. But Sylvie's flat was small and cramped; nothing remained a secret for long. And much as a part of him would once have considered asking the Lord for vengeance, he knew it was wrong. Katie had made her choice just as he had, and they each must live with the consequences.

"Are you sure that's how you want to be ending your prayers?" Maddie prompted her sister.

Ciara humphed again. "Fine." She cleared her throat. "And I suppose You should help Katie O'Doul do Your will as well. Amen." She dropped her hands. "Now will you leave me be?"

Maddie leaned over and kissed her forehead. "Only after I've wished you sweet dreams, me darling girl. I'll see you in the morning."

"Well, of course," Ciara said, but her cheeks were a pleased pink as Maddie took the lamp and left the room.

He thought she might turn in for the night as well, but she joined him at the sideboard and plucked the towel from his shoulder as if intending to help him finish his task. Her sigh told him she was none too sure about her siblings.

"They're settling in already," he told her. "It will only get easier from here."

"I hope you're right," Maddie said, taking the dishes he'd already dried and stacking them on the shelves above the sideboard. "It would be nice if something was easy."

"That was a long boat ride coming out here," he said, offering her a smile.

She chuckled. "Try it with sixty-odd females all determined to find a mate before they even reach shore."

He decided not to tell her about the stories in the newspaper. "You arrived unscathed."

"Unscathed and unwed and thankful for both," she

assured him. She accepted the last plate from him, and their fingers brushed. Her touch was warmer than the water.

He shook the suds off his hands, feeling as if he needed to shake off the feelings she raised in him as well. "I thought Asa Mercer brought all you ladies just to wed."

Her face was reddening. "Sure-n and he didn't tell us that he had the husbands all picked out until we were almost here! He even accepted bride prices for us. Well, I wanted no part of that. I came here for one reason—to make a home for Ciara and Aiden, and forget all about New York."

They had that in common, the need to start over. "Sylvie said you lost your father and stepmother in the tenement fire last year," Michael murmured. "I'm sorry for your loss."

"'Twas a sad, sad time," she answered, setting the plate on the shelf. "I just wanted to hold Ciara and Aiden close, never let go. Leaving them behind was the hardest thing I've ever done, for all I knew it was the only way. I had to go somewhere I could be more, so I could be enough for them." She glanced toward him. "I suppose that makes no sense to you."

"More than you might think," he said, remembering his reasons for leaving New York. "What should I do with this water?"

"Leave it by the door to the stairs. I'll take it down with me in the morning and use it to scrub the floors."

She stepped away from the shelf with a nod as if satisfied with their work and turned for her room. Though she left the lamp on the table, he felt as if some of the light went with her.

She'd taken only a couple of steps, however, before

she turned to face him. "Thank you for your help, Michael Haggerty. Now if you'll be so good as to answer a question or two for me."

Michael toweled off his hands. "What do you want to know?"

She gazed up at him, the light shining in her dark brown eyes. "Are you involved with the Dead Rabbits?"

Had Sylvie written to her? But no, Maddie had been surprised to see him on the pier. It must have been Ciara's prayer that had raised the question in Maddie's mind.

"I'll have no truck with gangs," Michael promised her.

She seemed to accept that, and he relaxed.

Her next question, however, drove all thought from his mind.

"So, who is Katie O'Doul?" Maddie asked, watching him. "And why would Ciara wish her to regret how she hurt you?"

Chapter Five

Maddie watched as Michael's eyes dilated until the blue seemed as vast as the sky. Did he know that his face gave him away? She could see every thought, every hope on those firm features.

He set down the cloth he'd been using on the dishes and stepped away from the bucket. He must have splashed water on himself at some point, because she could see darker spots on his shirt. He took a deep breath as if determined to give her a good answer. She found herself holding her own breath, waiting.

"I courted Miss O'Doul for a time," he said slowly, as if measuring each word as she might have measured an ingredient for her baking. "She decided we would not suit."

As simple as that. She wasn't sure why she was certain there was more to the story. Perhaps it was the tense line of his body, poised as if ready to escape. It was none of her affair, yet she felt as miffed as Ciara had been about Miss O'Doul's decision.

"Well, then," she told him. "I'll know how to help Ciara pray in the future. Sure-n but it's intelligence and wisdom Miss O'Doul must be lacking to refuse a fine upstanding gentleman like yourself."

She'd hoped for a smile, but he turned away from her. The hurt went deeper than she'd thought, or perhaps it was merely too soon for him to feel comfortable joking about it.

"If there's nothing else you need from me tonight, Maddie," he said, "I'll be turning in."

All at once she wanted more. There was nothing wrong with two people from common backgrounds sitting at a table, swapping tales, perhaps sharing a chuckle. She'd seen her friend Allegra and her husband, Clay, behave that way aboard ship, and Maddie had thought it a shame her father and stepmother hadn't managed that kind of relationship. They'd each put so much time and energy into keeping the family fed and housed that they'd nothing left for companionship. It must be her own hard work that had her thinking about a quiet cup of tea with a friend just then.

Besides, why be companionable with a man who would be in her life less than a month if she had her preferences?

"I need nothing from you, Mr. Haggerty," she said, turning for her room. "I'll wish you good-night and see you in the morning."

A distant thunk woke Michael from a deep sleep. He shifted on the hard planks of the floor, listening. It couldn't be morning. Not a ray of light came through the curtains, and the room was as dark as it had been when he'd blown out the lamp and gone to sleep, bundled in front of the stove.

He'd thought between his sparse bedding and his busy mind he would have difficulty sleeping. Lord knew Katie's betrayal had kept him up more than one night. He still remembered the cold glitter of her green eyes when she'd informed him she wanted nothing more to do with him.

"As if anyone could ask me to be marrying a coward," she'd flung at him from the doorway of her father's flat.

Michael had fisted his hands at his sides, knowing that half the tenement was listening to their argument. "I'm no coward. But a woman who claims to love me wouldn't ask me to make myself a liar and a thief."

"You think only of yourself," she'd complained, delicate chin high with righteousness. "I'll be having nothing more to do with you, Michael Haggerty, until you've begged the pardon of those fine men who asked you for a paltry favor you cannot be bringing yourself to grant." And she'd slammed the door in his face.

Paltry favor. Michael wrapped the blanket closer now. The coals had cooled, leaving the room as chilly as Katie's parting look. Katie's father had asked Michael to lie to the man who'd hired him to keep watch on the ships at shore. Michael was to betray his employer's trust and look the other way while the Dead Rabbits pillaged what they liked from those they found beneath them. Nothing about that was paltry.

How could I ever have looked at myself in the mirror again, Lord? How would I have explained myself to You when I see You face-to-face one day?

He knew he'd made the right choice. But the gang's reaction had put his life in danger and threatened Sylvie and her children as well. He could only hope the gang's tentacles didn't reach across the nation to the frontier.

Another thump had him stiffening on the floor. Turning his head, he could just make out the three doors across from him that led to Maddie's, Ciara's and Aiden's rooms. No one seemed to be stirring, not even the little gray cat. What had caused that sound?

As he eased up on one elbow, he heard more noises—a thud, a creak, a murmur of a voice, all coming from below. Had someone broken into the bakery?

He climbed to his feet, thankful he'd worn his shirt and trousers to bed for added warmth. He had no weapon, but he seized the broom and took it with him as he crossed to the stairs in his stockinged feet.

Whoever was below was making enough noise that the sounds of Michael's footsteps on the stairs went unnoticed. The shop stood empty, waiting for the morning's customers. He crept to the curtain, then whipped it aside with his free hand and sprang into the kitchen with a yell, broom handle raised above his head.

Maddie dropped the pot she'd been holding with a clang. "What!"

She was alone in the room, crouching by the firebox, her black-and-white-striped cotton gown swathed in an apron and pooled about her. Her red hair wilted around her face, like steamed cabbage, and the warmth of the room struck him for the first time. He could hear the heat crackling in the firebox, and the scent of something moist and tangy hung in the air.

Michael lowered the broom. "What are you doing so early?"

She threw up her hands, sending flour puffing in all directions. "My job, if you'll let me."

She pushed off from the floor and swept up to the worktable, which was draped in checkered cloth. Whipping off the material, she nodded to the two dozen mounds of dough, white and puffy, and pans of rolls, cinnamon showing in each swirl. He set the broom in the corner and ventured closer, mouth starting to water.

"Forgive me," he told her. "I heard a noise, and I thought we were being robbed."

She chuckled as she shook out the cloth. "No robbers," she said, folding it up and tucking it under the worktable. "If one stuck his head in the door right now, I'd put him to work."

Doing what? By the dirty bowls and pans stacked on the sideboard and the speckles on her apron, she'd already finished for the morning. How early had she risen?

"What else do you need done?" he asked.

She eyed him a moment as if trying to decide whether he was teasing. Then she raised her flour-dusted hand and began counting off the remaining tasks on her fingers.

"I have to finish preparing the oven, put in the bread and rolls, gather the eggs, brush and turn the bread and make icing for the cinnamon rolls, all before my customers arrive on their way to work."

That didn't sound so daunting. "Then you might as well put me to work," Michael said. "I'm up anyway."

She pointed to a door at the back of the kitchen. "There's a rake and a pail in the shed. Bring them in and muck out the firebox."

Michael frowned. "You want to clear out the fire before you start baking?"

"'Tis the hot bricks that bake the bread, Mr. Haggerty," she informed him. "And don't you be questioning my work like you question the raising of Ciara and Aiden."

Michael held up his hands in surrender and went to do as she asked.

Sylvie had baked from time to time, when she could use a neighbor's oven. He'd never realized there was so much to be done, and all at a rhythm only Maddie seemed to understand. Under her direction, he raked the hot coals into the pail and closed the lid, then swept out the ashes. Taking a long-handled wooden paddle from where it hung on the wall and resting it on the table, she dusted it with flour and then began shifting the rounded loaves onto it.

As she grabbed the handle, Michael stepped forward. "Let me."

Brow raised, she moved aside. "Just you be careful with my peel, Mr. Haggerty."

He had a feeling he was going to hear the name *Michael* from those pink lips only when he'd done something magnificent. He lifted the paddle and was surprised by the weight. With the oven set above her waist, how did she manage?

As if she saw his surprise, she smiled and reached for the peel. "Here, let me. Watch now. There's a trick to putting them in so you can bake the most." She nodded toward the oven, and Michael hurried to open the iron door for her. Heat blasted him, raising sweat on his forehead and neck. With a deft movement, she stuck in the paddle, lifted the end and slid the loaves onto the brick. It took her three trips to transfer everything into the oven. Michael shut the door for the last time, and she closed the damper.

"Now we wait," he guessed.

She laughed. "Now we hurry, Mr. Haggerty."

And hurry they did. While Maddie went outside with a basket to gather eggs, Michael began washing the dishes. She took one of the bowls, then shaved sugar from a cone, pounded it to powder with a pestle and mixed it with water for icing. Next, she mixed dough for cookies, rolled and cut them to lay them on a sheet, and popped them into the oven after she had removed the bread and rolls to cool. She never sat down, never stopped moving, even when he helped her carry her wares out to the shop to set them on display.

The newly risen sun was gilding the signs of the merchants across the street as Michael glanced out the panes of the front window. But what took him aback were the faces pressed against the glass.

"Me charming customers," Maddie assured him. She pointed toward the stairs. "Go on, now. Take some of the cinnamon rolls upstairs for you and Ciara and Aiden. I should be finished here in a half hour."

All that bread, all those rolls and cookies, gone in a half hour? He couldn't believe it. She'd be working for hours to sell all that. As she went to open the latch, he picked up three of the rolls, then headed for the stairs. Glancing back, he saw her throw wide the door.

And every man in Seattle, he thought, stampeded into the shop. Dressed in flannel shirts and rough trousers, caps pulled down over their lank hair, bushy beards bristling, they crowded the counter, the sound of their heavy boots against the wood planks as loud as thunder. Voices rose in entreaty, hands held out coins. They were the happiest gang of rioters he'd ever seen.

One of the men with a deep voice managed to make himself heard over the din. "Whatcha got for us today, Miss Maddie?"

"Cinnamon rolls dripping icing," Maddie assured him, beaming around at them all. "Fresh-baked bread with the steam still rising and gingersnaps to tickle your tongue." She waved one arm down the display counter as if presenting jewels to royalty.

"I'll take one of each," someone declared.

"I'll take two!" another shouted.

Voices rose louder as they surged forward.

How could he leave her surrounded?

Michael wasn't sure how he heard the noise on the stair. Looking back, he saw Ciara creeping toward him. Her brown hair was tumbled into her face, and she hugged a plaid flannel wrapper around her nightgown.

"Is it the mob?" she whispered, face pinched. "Have they come for us, then?"

She must be remembering the violence that had cut like metal through the fabric of life in Five Points, as the Dead Rabbits clashed with other gangs.

"Just some happy customers come to sample your sister's baking," Michael assured her. He handed her the rolls. "Take these upstairs for you and your brother. I'll be up shortly."

Her face brightened as she accepted the rolls. Holding them close, she scurried back up the stairs.

Michael turned to the fray. Maddie was handing out loaves, rolls and cookies at breathtaking speed and grabbing payments even faster. He wasn't sure how she knew which came from whom. He started to wade through the men, but they squeezed closer, frowning at him as if thinking he was trying to reach the food before they did. He was only thankful he could match or better the muscle arrayed against him.

With the liberal use of his shoulders, he managed to reach the counter and slide in next to Maddie. "How can I help?"

"Take their money and give them what they want," she said, turning her smile on the next fellow. The wizened man asked for a roll and a half-dozen cookies, and she named an exorbitant price that would have set the denizens of Five Points to crying with despair or laughing at the sheer lunacy of it. The man piled his silver on the counter, offering a toothless grin.

"How about you?" Michael asked the next fellow.

This man was tall and lean, short-cropped dark hair showing under the edge of a broad-brimmed black hat. His gaze swept over Michael as cold and gray as the Confederate cannon on display in the Battery.

"I'll wait for Miss O'Rourke," he said, voice low and gravelly.

Was he a suitor? She certainly hadn't mentioned a particular fellow. In fact, she'd seemed pretty against marriage last night.

"Suit yourself," Michael told him.

He tried the next man over and the one after him, but the answer was always the same. Even though the food was disappearing by the moment, every man was content to wait until Maddie could serve him personally.

That's when it struck Michael. They weren't here because they loved Maddie's baking. They were here because they loved Maddie!

He wanted to throw wide his arms, shove them all out of the shop right then and there. They had no right to treat her as if she was one of her own confections, available for a smile and some pieces of silver. Yet even as the thought poked at him, he knew it was none of his affair. In the end, the only way he could help matters was to control the crowd.

Stalking around the edges, shoulders thrown back and eyes narrowed, he managed to herd the men into some semblance of a line. At least then they couldn't all rush her at once. He yanked back a few who tried to push ahead before their turn, made one fellow sit down on the floor when he shouted for her attention. One by one, they bought their food and left.

A gentle rain had begun to fall as he opened the door to let out the last two men. The one who had first refused Michael's services paused to glance back at Maddie.

"Hired a man-of-all-work, have you now, Miss O'Rourke?"

Maddie's smile was as sweet as the icing on her rolls. "Mr. Haggerty brought my sister and brother to me on the ship, Deputy McCormick. He's staying with us until he finds a job."

Deputy. So this was the law in Seattle. Michael met his gaze straight on, refusing to be the one to look away first. The deputy's steely eyes narrowed.

"Yesler is looking for another man on his saws," the lawman offered. "Long hours but good pay. And there are rooms at Patterson's boardinghouse by the mill."

Michael nodded, relaxing. "My thanks to you. I'll go by the mill today."

Deputy McCormick touched the brim of his black hat to Maddie, then stalked out.

As Michael shut the door behind him, Maddie collapsed against the counter. "Like ravens, they are, swooping in to devour." She glanced around the empty counter and smiled. "But they are loyal, bless them."

Surely she knew it went beyond loyalty. "They're sweet on you, every last one of them," Michael told her.

She tsked, pushing off from the counter. "It isn't me. They act that way with every unmarried female within miles, all twenty of us."

Michael found that hard to believe. "They'd pay those kind of prices to any woman?"

Maddie shrugged as if the matter were out of her

hands. "There are nine men for every female over the age of twelve here. Before we came on the *Continental*, fellows were paying fathers to hold their newborn daughter to marry when she was of age, just so they'd know they'd have a wife someday."

"That's madness," Michael said, stepping away from the door.

"That's loneliness," Maddie countered, pulling open the curtain to the kitchen. "I suppose they think it's better to have a spouse than live alone. Can't say I agree with them."

Was she so willing to encourage her customers, only to leave the men dangling? He couldn't help thinking of Katie, with her sweet smiles and warm words, until he'd refused to risk his future to help the Dead Rabbits. He'd wondered whether she was the only woman to think her power was more important than her suitor's love. He wasn't sure why he was disappointed to find Maddie O'Rourke might think the same way.

Michael followed her into the kitchen. "With dozens of suitors to choose from, you haven't found one to your liking?" he asked, trying for a light tone. "Are your standards so high, Maddie?"

She chuckled as she pulled a canister from under her worktable and pried off the lid. "Sure-n I could find more than one fellow in that lot to marry, if marriage was important to me." She jingled the coins she drew from her skirts and dropped them into the tin with a clank. "As it is, if I marry I have to share all this. Why would I want to be doing that, when it's my efforts that earned it in the first place?"

He couldn't argue with her there. He knew the law generally granted any money a woman earned to her husband. But to be so coldhearted about it? That didn't make sense.

She cocked her head, watching him. "You look disappointed in my answer. Did you think I should give up my dreams to marry? You never let love get in the way of your goals, did you now? You wouldn't have let your Katie sway you from your intended course."

"I fell in love," he admitted, "but I never lost sight of my goals. If I had been willing to compromise my values, I might be married by now."

"Love is compromise from what I can see," she said, going to the washbasin, wetting a cloth and wringing it out. "You work and work to put food on the table and clothes on your back, until there's no time left for love. Sure-n but we're better off without such heartache." She tossed him the rag, and he caught it in one hand. "Use that to clean off the counter. I'll go up to check on Ciara and Aiden, and then I'll start the baking for this evening."

In the act of pushing back into the shop, Michael paused. "More baking?"

She laughed. "You make it sound as pleasant as the rack. Yes, more baking. That's my job. This is a bakery, and I bake. I was hoping for a lady to come with Ciara and Aiden to help, if you recall."

And she'd gotten him instead. "I'm sorry I can't be more use to you," he said, "but I'll do what I can." Feeling inept for the first time in his life, he went to clean off the counter, wiping away the crumbs and scrubbing at the drips of icing. Yet her words refused to leave him.

He wanted to agree with her that love meant heartache. He'd certainly had his fill. But some part of him whispered that more might be possible, if he would but try once again.

He had been so focused on his task that he didn't see her move into the room. Instead, he felt her hand on his arm.

"Good enough, Mr. Haggerty," she said. "Another minute and you'll rub right through the wood."

He relaxed his hand, feeling her grip soften. She was close enough that he could see a dusting of freckles across the tip of her nose, as if ginger had escaped some of her cookies. Cinnamon-colored lashes fluttered over eyes as dark as fresh-roasted coffee.

Michael mentally shook himself. Working in the bakery must have addled his brain, because all he could think about was that her kiss would taste as sweet as her cooking.

"Are they gone?" Ciara asked from the stair.

Maddie stepped away from Michael, cheeks turning pink as if she'd been the one thinking about sweet kisses.

"For the moment," she told her sister. "There will be another group coming later, when the shift changes at the mill. I aim to have more loaves of bread and dozens of cookies ready by then along with the ones I promised Mr. Horton."

With her chin up, she was all determination, and Michael could only marvel at her energy.

But even more surprising was his reaction to her. He'd given his heart to Katie. He'd never thought to give it to another. And she'd made it clear that, while she might flirt with her customers, she had no interest in marrying.

Why, then, did he want her to reserve her flirting for him?

Chapter Six

Maddie could only be glad for her sister's interruption. For a moment, with her hand on Michael's burly arm, she had felt as if the earth had tilted, pushing her toward him. Why? It was all well and good to talk about true loves and lost hearts, but in the end she'd only be disappointed. She had too much evidence to think otherwise.

So, broad-shouldered or not, charming smile or not, Michael Haggerty would get no further in her affections. She knew her plans, and they did not include forming an attachment to any fellow, no matter how helpful and well-meaning.

Standing at the foot of the stairs now, Ciara scrunched her face. "More work, more noise? What sort of place is this?"

Her sister's complaints were like touching a hot stove with her bare hand—sharp and painful. She'd worked so hard to make a home for Ciara and Aiden. Could her sister not appreciate the effort?

"This is a home with plenty of food to eat," Maddie told her. "That's a blessing."

Ciara shrugged. "The rolls were good. But I'm not

going to sit in my room all day while you have all the fun."

"Fun, is it?" Maddie said, temper rising. "Perhaps I ought to wake you at three in the morning to help knead tomorrow's dough."

Her sister scowled at her.

Michael leaned his hip against the counter. "You seemed awfully pleased with that room yesterday," he reminded Ciara.

The girl eyed him. "It's nice too, I suppose."

What crumbs of affection she offered! Had her sister no understanding? Maddie tightened her lips to hold back a scold.

Michael merely smiled at Ciara. "But you have the urge to wander, is that it?" he teased with a look to Maddie.

Maddie blinked. Of course! That must be the source of today's animosity. Ciara and Aiden had been cooped up aboard ship for months. It was only natural that they'd want to get out, explore their new home. And that was one yearning she could satisfy.

"Let's go see Seattle," Maddie told Ciara. "Make sure you and Aiden are ready for the day. Do your chores as I asked. I'll mix up the next batch of dough. We can take a walk while it rises and I can make a delivery."

"All right," Ciara agreed. "But don't expect me to hold your hand while we walk. I'm not a child, you know." She turned and flounced up the stairs.

"Nicely done," Michael said, straightening away from the counter.

"Thank you," Maddie replied. "But I was only following your lead."

He smiled. "Glad to help. I'll join you on your walk, if I may, so I'll know where to start looking for work."

"Of course," Maddie said. "But perhaps you should be putting on shoes first."

He glanced down at his stockinged feet, the thick gray yarn darkened with grime after he'd traipsed across the floorboards so many times, then rubbed the dark stubble speckling his chin. "And I should shave as well," he said before he pounded up the stairs.

A short while later, the four of them left the front of the bakery. Maddie was careful to lock the door behind her. Seattle was remarkably free from crime, especially compared with Five Points, but she wasn't taking any chances with her livelihood. She could only hope today Michael might find an opportunity for a livelihood of his own.

"What sort of work are you seeking?" she asked, Mr. Porter's shirts tucked under one arm as they strolled down the boardwalk. The bakery was the last shop on the street, but she knew Seattle would only grow from there. Already someone else was building a new store down the block.

Michael eyed her over Ciara's head. "I'll take whatever I can get for the moment. I just want to pay my way."

"Well, you ought to find something here," she said, lifting her skirts to navigate a gap in the boardwalk. Ciara hopped from hump to hump, but Aiden slogged merrily through the puddles. A breeze came in off the water, moist and briny, setting the clapboard signs above them to creaking as she climbed onto the next stretch of boardwalk.

Ahead of them, the door of a mercantile opened and three natives exited, murmuring in husky voices. Hair slicked down and smelling of aromatic oils, colorful blankets draping their sturdy frames, they moved past

Maddie and the children with dignity born of sorrows. Maddie nodded respectfully to them. Aiden stopped and stared.

Maddie put a hand on his shoulder and turned him back the way they were going. "That's enough, me lad."

"But those were Indians," he whispered as if concerned the elders might turn and pounce on him any moment. "Aren't you afraid they'll scalp us?"

"There hasn't been an uprising in over ten years," Michael told him. He must have caught Maddie frowning at him, for he shrugged. "I read it in the newspapers."

How he rushed to assure the children. She ought to be miffed with him taking over her role again, but she found she couldn't be. He'd meant well.

"The natives hereabouts are generally peaceable," Maddie told Aiden. "They have homes and jobs and families, and you'll be treating them with respect just as you would any other adult you meet."

Aiden frowned as if he hadn't thought about things that way before. Maddie patted his shoulder. "I can teach you a few words in their language. We learned some on the way here."

Her brother brightened.

They continued down the street together, Maddie pointing out things she thought might interest Ciara and Aiden. She made sure to show Michael the way to Yesler's Mill, the boardinghouse where she delivered Mr. Porter's shirts and the harbor. She also drew his attention to every Help Wanted sign she spotted in the shop windows.

By the time they returned to the bakery, Ciara and Aiden were talking about all the things that they'd seen. Michael once again was quiet, and Maddie could only hope it was because his mind was full of plans. As her siblings clambered up the stairs, Maddie started for the kitchen, and Michael paused.

"What else can I do to help?" he asked.

"I thought you wanted to get over to the mill about that job," she said.

He nodded. "I will later. Right now, I'm more concerned about you. Did you even sleep last night?"

"For several hours," she admitted, surprised by the question. She stifled a yawn, then dropped her hand. "I'm fine, and there's work to be done."

He raised his head. "Then let me help."

Perhaps she should. Perhaps if he knew just how hard she worked, it would spur him to find other employment.

"Very well," she said. "You can start the laundry."

He followed her through the kitchen to the fenced rear yard. Like much of Seattle, the ground was mostly black dirt, but she'd marked off a spot for a garden next year, beside the chicken coop. Her hens fluttered out of her way now, then went back to scratching and pecking.

Ducking under the lines she'd strung from post to post, Maddie led Michael to the shed and pointed to the burlap sacks piled on the floor. "That's the latest batch, one sack to a customer, so see that you don't mix them up. Mr. Hennessy will not be pleased to receive Mr. Weinclef's shirts back."

"Wrong color?" Michael teased, poking at the lowest sack with his boot.

"Wrong size," Maddie said. She nodded to the wooden tubs hanging from nails on the walls. "Those are for the washing. Set them in the yard, and fill one with water hot from the stove and one with cold water from the pump. You can bring in a load of firewood as well. Call me when you're ready to wash."

He snapped her a salute. "Aye, aye, Captain."

Not sure what to expect from him, she went to check on her dough.

A short while later, Ciara and Aiden came into the kitchen just as Michael called from the yard. Maddie motioned her brother and sister to come with her to see what Michael had accomplished.

He had set the tubs side by side just beyond the doorway. She could see the steam rising from the largest tub into a heavy sky that threatened more rain. She bent to open one of the sacks he'd piled up nearby.

"Sort the clothes by color and material," she explained. "Never wash the red flannels with anything but other red flannels. They turn everything else pink."

Aiden made a face. "Ew!"

"Exactly what my customers say," Maddie assured him with a grin. "Hot first to get out the dirt, like this." She tossed the flannels into the water, took a paddle from the side of the shed and pushed the cloth around in the water. "If you spot a stain, take out the bar of soap and scrub. I've a washboard over there for the worst of it. When you're ready, put the clothes in the cold water to rinse." She tightened her grip and scooped the mass out with the paddle, shoulders bunching with the weight.

Michael took the load from her with ease and swung the sodden clothes into the second tub.

Maddie peered into the first and nodded. "The water's not too dirty. Drop in the next set while the first soaks in the rinse. If the water gets too dirty, dump it on the garden patch and start over. Run each piece through the mangle to press out the water, then hang it to dry on the line. If it starts to rain, bring everything inside and hang the clothes in the kitchen."

Michael wiped damp hair from his brow and drew in a breath as if daunted simply by the thought of all that work. "How often do you do this?"

"Three times a week," Maddie said. "I'd do it more often, but it takes too long to dry the clothes, and it rains so much here that some weeks I can barely find time between storms."

He glanced at the tubs. "I think I have it. Go ahead with your work inside. I'll call if I have questions, and you can check on me when you have a moment."

He could be sure she would. She'd built her list of customers from people she'd met aboard ship; they had become friends over the months at sea. She wasn't about to lose one of them to mishandling, not when she needed every penny.

But as she stepped away from the tubs, she caught Michael watching her as if she was something quite extraordinary, and her face felt as if she'd been the one laboring over the laundry.

Michael heaved a mass of red flannel shirts from the hot water to the cold, leaving a wash of pink behind. How did she do this? Even on a cool day like today, laboring over the steaming water set him sweating. The lye soap burned when he splashed some of the suds against his hand, and he had to plunge his arm into the cold water to clear the pain. And the smell! He wasn't sure what her customers did all day, but he wouldn't have been surprised if it didn't involve shoveling manure for a herd of cattle.

He wrung out the first batch of clothes and laid it over the lines to dry. He was dragging the second tub to the alley behind the shop to dump, having already flooded the garden patch, when he heard a protest.

"Will you be washing me boots now too?"

Michael glanced up with a grin at his friend Patrick, battered top hat on his short, wavy blond hair. The other Irishman leaned against the fence, slender body covered in a brown wool coat and plaid trousers. His green eyes crinkled with laughter.

"Afraid of a good cleaning, are you?" Michael challenged, flipping the empty tub at his friend as if ready to give him a good dousing.

Patrick ducked away, then straightened to shift the sack he was holding over his shoulder. "Afraid of nothing, and you know it." He came to a stop in front of Michael and tipped his clean-shaven chin at the tub. "What exactly does she have you doing to work off your passage?"

"Laundry," Michael said, turning for the yard.

Patrick clutched his chest over his heart. "Oh, the horror of it! Can you not escape?" He followed Michael into the yard and shut the gate behind him, pausing to glance around at the space. At the sight of him, the chickens ran clucking back into their coop.

"It's my duty," Michael assured him. He rummaged through the remaining clothes and dumped them into the hot water before carrying the empty tub to the pump to fill. "And how goes it with you? Any job prospects yet?"

Patrick glanced up at the sky as if gauging how much rain would be falling any moment. "Oh, you know, this and that. I'm making do as we did in New York. In fact, some of the fellows at the boardinghouse gave me a penny to bring over their laundry." He lowered his gaze and tossed the sack onto the pile, then bent to help

Michael position the tub under the iron pump. "What of you? Have you been able to cut her apron strings to look for work?"

"She isn't tying me here," Michael told him, pumping the curved handle up and down until cool water splashed into the tub. "Working was my idea. It's the least I can do after she paid my way."

"I suppose," Patrick said, sounding none too sure of the matter. Then he brightened. "Ah, but I found some of our own."

Michael straightened from the pump. "Relatives or Irishmen?"

"Same thing in my book," Patrick said. "Several fellows at that mill of theirs and one of the shopkeepers, if you can believe it. They haven't been through what we did in New York, but they have possibilities, though none were in a position to offer employment."

Like him, Michael knew, Patrick missed the gathering of friends and family. At times, the camaraderie had been the only thing to make life bearable in New York. Perhaps that's why it had hurt so much to lose it.

"I'm glad you're making friends," Michael said, bending to drag the tub back to its place beside the hot water. "Now all we have to do is find work."

"Looks like you already found plenty." Patrick nodded toward the tubs. "Michael Haggerty, laundress. Never did I think to see the day."

"And what would you be having against an honest day's work, me good man?" Maddie demanded. Michael looked up to find that she'd come out of the bakery, with Ciara and Michael right behind her. She must have caught the end of their conversation.

Patrick whipped the hat off his head, setting his blond hair fluttering in the rising breeze. "Beggin' your pardon, ma'am," he said as Maddie approached. "I never meant to disparage honest work or the fine ladies who launder."

Maddie's look softened as she reached their sides. "Honest work it may be, but hot and hard. I'll be thanking you, Mr. Haggerty, for your help."

She made it sound as if he'd done the work from kindness instead of duty. "No trouble at all," he said, wiping his hands on his trousers. "Maddie, this is my friend Patrick Flannery, the one who traveled from New York with us."

Maddie inclined her head, but Ciara scuttled forward, brown eyes tilted up in delight. "How nice to see you again, Mr. Flannery."

"And you as well, Miss Ciara," he said, though his gaze remained on Maddie. "How is it that in all those long months at sea, you were never mentioning how pretty your sister is?"

Ciara flinched, but Aiden wrinkled his nose. "Maddie's not pretty. She's just Maddie."

"Spoken like a brother," Maddie said with a smile to Aiden. "And I'm not accounted the beauty in the family. Sure-n but I'll leave that place to Ciara."

Ciara blushed as she peered up at Patrick through her long brown lashes, obviously trying to see how he'd take the statement. Michael and his friend had noticed the girl's infatuation with Patrick aboard ship, and Patrick had always been kind but careful to remember she was still a child.

"Very wise of you, to be sure, Miss O'Rourke," Patrick said with a smile to Ciara. "And you, Miss Ciara, you had better watch yourself. I hear they marry young in Seattle. There will be suitors lining up at your door before you know it."

Aiden made a gagging sound.

"I don't need suitors," Ciara said with a toss of her brown braid. "I know who I want to marry." She fluttered her lashes at Patrick, who once more consulted the clouds.

"Have you never heard of biding your time?" Maddie asked, putting a hand on her sister's shoulder. "You've years yet before you must make such a decision."

"Decades," Patrick told the clouds. "Why, you may not know even when you're as old as Michael and me." He glanced at Michael with a laugh.

Ciara sagged, heaving a sigh that lifted her slender shoulders in the blue cotton gown.

Michael had pity on her. "I've been going in and out a lot, Ciara. Make sure Amelia Batterby is safe."

Ciara stiffened. "You better not have let her out!" Lifting her skirts, she ran for the door, Aiden right behind her.

"Another fair lady?" Patrick guessed with a look to Maddie.

"A cat," Maddie confessed. "And one who looks to be greatly spoiled now that my brother and sister are here. It was nice meeting you, Mr. Flannery, but I have dough on the rise, and I should see to it." With a nod to them both, she followed her siblings to the door.

Patrick watched her go. "So that's why laundry suddenly holds such a fascination."

Michael shoved the paddle into the water. "I'm working off a debt, remember?"

"A debt you could pay in good time if you were earning money working elsewhere," Patrick pointed out.

"And abandon Ciara and Aiden?" Michael protested, smashing the clothes around the tub. "They've been through enough."

"And are now safely delivered to their beloved sister," Patrick pointed out. "You can stop your protests. I see the attraction, I truly do."

Michael stepped away from the tub and lowered his voice. "Do you honestly think I'd allow another woman to affect my decisions after what happened with Katie?"

Patrick shrugged. "Katie was directed by her father's ambitions as much as her own desires to prove herself an ally to the Dead Rabbits and earn their favor. I have a feeling Maddie O'Rourke makes up her own mind."

"I make up my own mind as well," Michael said. "I'm working off my debt. Nothing more."

"Fine," Patrick said. "Then you won't mind if I begin paying my respects to the lady."

He shouldn't mind. He had no intentions of courting. Besides, by the way Maddie had held her own against the combined forces of Seattle's most determined would-be grooms, Patrick stood little chance of winning her heart.

Yet the idea that his friend would court the energetic redhead only made Michael's gut churn. It seemed some part of him minded a great deal. And that was not to be borne.

"Suit yourself," Michael told him. "Just remember—she and Ciara and Aiden have been through a great deal, losing their parents, leaving everything they've known to start anew. I'll thank you not to be bringing trouble to their door."

"Me?" Patrick's green eyes were guileless. "And what trouble would I be bringing?"

Michael didn't answer. Truth be told, he thought the most likely trouble would come from Maddie O'Rourke and the feelings she was raising in him.

Chapter Seven

Maddie shut the back door firmly behind her. So that was Michael's friend from New York. Patrick Flannery was a handsome fellow with his thick blond hair as warm as sunlight and his winning ways. What change in circumstance had brought him west? Somehow she didn't think it was a faithless fiancée like in Michael's case. Patrick wouldn't be the one with a broken heart. He'd be the one to break hearts.

But not Ciara's. Maddie had seen how her little sister looked at the brash Irishman. The girl clearly had a bad case of calf love, that wide-eyed admiration that struck so many young ladies her age. By the way Michael had frowned at the pair, he wasn't encouraging it, and neither would Maddie. No matter Seattle's dearth of marriageable misses, Ciara had a lot of growing up to do before she was old enough to start courting.

"She's safe," Ciara declared, appearing in the doorway of the kitchen, arm hugging Amelia Batterby close. The amber-eyed shorthair regarded Maddie, tail twitching, obviously unamused.

"Good," Maddie said, pushing off from the door. "Set her down now so she can earn her keep."

Ciara gave the cat one more stroke on her silky head before depositing her on the floor. Amelia Batterby stalked off, tail high and steps stiff with dignity.

"Go find a mouse to harass," Maddie called after her. "Better yet, find two."

Ciara shuddered. "Poor mice. I hope she doesn't find any."

"Poor us," Maddie corrected her. "Mice eat what I need to be baking."

Ciara wandered past her to the window overlooking the rear yard. "I do hope Patrick finds work."

"Patrick, is it now?" Maddie challenged, passing the mounds of cloth-covered dough on her way toward the stairs. "Sure-n Mr. Flannery deserves more respect."

Ciara sniffed, gaze out the window. "He calls me Ciara."

"He called you Miss Ciara a moment ago," Maddie replied. "That's a sign of respect too. Now come along. I want to see what dresses you brought so we know if you have enough for school."

Ciara brightened as she turned from the window. Maddie guessed it was at the possibility of new clothes, but her sister's words as she followed Maddie up the stairs proved the direction of the girl's thoughts. "I never knew saying Miss was a sign of respect. How sweet of Patrick."

Maddie paused, concern rising like her dough. "So he's given you leave to use his first name?"

Red flared in her sister's cheeks. "No."

She drew in a breath and lifted her skirts to step into the room. "Then it's Mr. Flannery, my girl. And that's that."

She could hear her sister's sigh behind her. "You

don't understand. You're too old. Are there any girls my age in Seattle?"

Though she nearly choked at the idea of being aged, Maddie could almost feel the loneliness seeping out of the girl like mist from the Sound on a cool night.

"Not many," she acknowledged, heading for Ciara's room. "There are only a few families, and most of them have sons and daughters who were big enough to cross the country with them in covered wagons, so they're now older than you. The rest of the children were born here in the last eight or nine years, making them younger than you. But if there are girls your age, you'll meet them when you go to school Monday."

A thump came from the other side of the wall, and Maddie frowned at Aiden's closed door. "What's your brother doing?"

"Finding mice for Amelia Batterby most likely." Ciara shuddered again, then took a step closer. "Really, Maddie, you should give him more chores, or he'll only get himself into trouble."

Very likely Ciara was right. Maddie knew most of the children here had chores; it was a matter of necessity on the frontier. And certainly she could use the help. Only the fact that Michael was doing the laundry now gave her time to be with Ciara. She'd have to thank him for that.

She'd seen the look on his face when he'd spotted the piles of soiled clothes. She was beginning to think he was unskilled at hiding his feelings. And he'd had every right to balk. Doing the laundry was hot, dirty work. Yet he'd made no complaint to her. That was to his credit.

All the same, she hated giving Ciara and Aiden more chores. She'd been working since she was Ciara's age, and there were moments she was tired of it already.

But lacking chores, she wasn't sure what to do with her sister, much less Aiden, while she worked. In Five Points, there had always been another family to look after them, other children with whom they could play games. Even school would take up only a part of their time. How else was she to keep them busy?

"What did you do aboard ship?" she asked, taking down the clothes Ciara had hung on the pegs.

"Oh, Michael always found things for us to do," Ciara said, helping her lay the dresses out on the quilt. "He read us tales of adventure from books in the ship's library. We tried to learn to play the piano, until some lady passengers ordered us out of the salon."

Maddie hid a smile at that. She could imagine even Michael's good looks and kind words hadn't been enough to prevail over children banging on a piano.

"We helped the sailors pick tar out of the ropes," Ciara continued, fingers grazing the torn hem at the bottom of a skirt, "and they taught us how to navigate by the stars. We watched for whales and flying fish. I never even knew fish could fly!"

The glow in her eyes reminded Maddie of the sister she'd left behind, leaving an answering glow inside her. "It sounds like a fine time."

"It was." Ciara sighed. "And then we came here."

Guilt tugged at Maddie. She hadn't meant to make her sister's life more difficult. Perhaps she should ask Michael for suggestions on how to entertain the children now. But no, she'd told him Ciara and Aiden were hers to care for. Asking his advice was admitting she was out of her depth.

Which she very much feared she was.

"I've a book from Mrs. Howard's lending library," Maddie offered Ciara. "You can read that for a time."

Ciara cocked her head. "What's it about?"

"A family of sisters in England," Maddie said, re-membering. "And the mother is keen to marry one of them off to a cousin, but the eldest will have none of it. And there's a handsome rich fellow who treats her poorly, but I think he has eyes for her and is just fight-ing his feelings."

Ciara's eyes widened. "It sounds wonderful!"

"Top shelf of the sideboard," Maddie said. "Don't lose my place."

"I won't," Ciara promised, dashing out of her room.

Maddie smiled. At least she and Ciara shared a love of books. Unfortunately, she couldn't see Aiden en-thralled over a romantic novel. Chores might have to suffice. Perhaps she could involve both of them in her baking. She didn't want them close to the harsh soap and hot water of the laundry.

She quickly counted the dresses and noted their ragged condition, then went to Aiden's room to check his clothes. She found her brother under his bed pre-tending to be a mountain lion in a cave.

"And Amelia Batterby is my kitten," he announced, one arm around the gray-haired cat.

Amelia Batterby's golden eyes glared at Maddie as if her imprisonment was all Maddie's fault.

Maddie was simply glad that her brother's short pants and shirts would do. Ciara's hems, on the other hand, were rising with her height. Maddie resolved to take the clothing to her friend Nora Underhill, another of Mer-cer's Belles, who was a talented seamstress.

But thinking of the clothes reminded her that she should check to see how Michael was doing with the laundry.

She opened the door to the yard in time to see rain

sheeting down, her chickens rushing to the shelter of the coop. Michael was snatching the clothes from the line. Maddie ran to help.

"Take these," he said, handing her the damp flannel. "I'll get the bundles before they're soaked."

Hugging the material to her, Maddie ran for the door.

Michael was right behind. He dropped his armful of dirty clothes on the kitchen floor. Blowing out a breath, he shook raindrops off his dark hair.

"Thanks," he said. "You got there just in the nick of time."

"I was busy with Ciara and Aiden," Maddie explained, "or I would have come sooner." She piled the flannels on a clean spot on the worktable and went for the rope she used when drying clothes indoors. "Here," she said, handing him a looped end. "Hook that over the nail by the window."

As he went to do as she bid, she looped her own end over a nail by the larder, stretching the line from one side of the room to the other. Michael ducked under it to retrieve a flannel and set about draping the wet material over the line. Maddie started from her end with another of the clammy shirts.

"That's very likely all the laundry that can be done today," she told him, fingers working. "As I've no need for other help, you can go look for a job if you like."

"Good." He finished the last flannel and bumped her shoulder as they met in the middle of the line. He was solid enough that the movement set her to wavering on her feet. His hand shot out to steady her.

"If you're sure you don't need me," he murmured, gaze on hers.

She must have put too much wood in the firebox, for it was suddenly entirely too warm in the kitchen. His look was warmer as he studied her face. What was he looking for? What did he see?

Why did she care?

Maddie stepped back. "I'm certain I've no need for you, Mr. Haggerty. Off with you, now."

He looked almost disappointed, but nodded before turning and heading out the door. Some of the warmth went with him.

Maddie sagged against the table. What was she thinking? She was more than twice Ciara's age, and she'd never been one for fawning infatuation. She had work to do, debts to pay, dreams to realize. No more mooning over Michael Haggerty!

She had three-quarters of an hour before the dough would be ready to bake. Time enough to visit Nora. She collected Ciara and Aiden, and hurried down the hill.

Her friend was happy to lengthen some of Ciara's gowns and remake one of Maddie's for the girl.

"And, someday I hope to make your wedding gown," she told Maddie as she accepted the clothing.

Of all people, Maddie would not have expected Nora to harp on that note. Though she was a plain woman with rosy cheeks, coarse black hair and wise gray eyes, Nora had received no less than six proposals of marriage since arriving in Seattle and had turned them all down.

"Perhaps you should be making a wedding dress for yourself instead," Maddie said, eying the bolt of creamy silk propped up against the rough wood wall. Nora's skill with a needle had made her popular with the ladies as well as the gentlemen. She'd been content to serve her customers from the back of one of the mercantiles, which profited from the sale of its fabric and notions.

While Aiden poked around the shop, Ciara leaned on

a pile of fabric. "Maddie might need a wedding gown soon. She's going to marry Michael Haggerty."

Nora raised her brows as she took her measuring tape from the pocket of her neat gray gown. Maddie hurried to stop any rumors from flying. "Mr. Haggerty was kind enough to escort Ciara and Aiden out to me," she explained to her friend. "We will not be marrying."

Ciara made a face as she straightened. "You better watch out. You'll end up an old maid."

"And who would be caring?" Maddie told her.

Nora nodded, then bent to run her tape up Ciara's frame. "Who indeed? Nothing says you must marry the first man who asks. Or the first six." She covered her mouth with her hand and giggled.

The sound buoyed Maddie as well. "No indeed, me darling girl," she assured her friend. "As well as your work is going, you needn't marry at all if you like."

Ciara looked appalled. "You'd be all alone."

Living alone didn't sound so bad to Maddie, some days. No siblings to worry about. No strapping handsome lad standing in the doorway as if waiting to steal a kiss. Just her and her baking.

What a hollow existence, all work.

She shook off the inner warning. "You're never alone so long as you have friends beside you," Maddie told Ciara with a brisk nod.

"And the Lord," Nora agreed, straightening. "I'll have one of the dresses ready by tomorrow. You can pick it up after services. And if you leave your jacket, Ciara, I'll add red cording to it. That color will bring out the roses in your cheeks."

Ciara stammered her thanks, and Maddie added her own. Yet as they all walked back to the bakery, Maddie couldn't help thinking about what her friend had said.

How odd to consider the Lord as close as a friend, a source of comfort and companionship. Her father and the ministers at the churches they had attended had always acted as if God was someone majestic and magnificent, seated high on a throne and busy directing kings and governments, seasons and oceans. What made Nora think He even cared about someone as insignificant in the grand scheme of things as herself and Maddie?

Ciara obviously had other matters on her mind.

"I still think you should marry Michael," she declared as they reached the bakery. "It would be terrible to be the last one of Mercer's Belles to be a bride."

"Why?" Aiden asked, following her through the door. "Is it a race?"

"No," Maddie said. "And there are opportunities here an unmarried lady never had in New York."

Ciara gave her an arched look. "There's an opportunity right here, if you'd just open your eyes." She started up the stairs.

Aiden hesitated. "Are you sure you don't want to marry Michael?" he asked, face turned up to hers.

"Certain sure," Maddie promised him, but even she could hear the doubt in her voice.

Later in the afternoon, Michael trudged back up the hill from Yesler's Mill. The job Deputy McCormick had mentioned earlier had already been filled by another fellow who had come on the boat with Michael. The foreman had promised to let Michael know if anything else opened up.

He'd tried at the harbor as well but had found things in disarray. Seattle had only one pier, owned by Mr. Yesler, and no paid group of longshoremen for offloading. The crews from the ships generally did much of the work, along with two or three men with wagons. Occasional help from shore was solicited for pennies a task. He couldn't live on pennies, much less pay Maddie back what he owed her. He'd have to look elsewhere.

"You're welcome to join my crew," one of the mates had told him as the fellow stacked crates on the pier. "Every time we reach Seattle, we lose a half dozen or more seeking land of their own."

He might have accepted the offer if it had been made in New York shortly after Katie's cruelty. Escape had been welcome then. Now he wanted to remain in Seattle long enough to make sure Ciara and Aiden were settled.

A shame he couldn't just stake his claim on a strip of land. He simply couldn't see that as a good idea. He was city born and bred—what did he know about farming or logging? He'd likely starve the first winter!

Yet he couldn't help wondering why he'd landed in Seattle. He'd thought it the Lord's providence when the ticket had arrived just as the Dead Rabbits were planning to make good on their threats. He'd refused their invitation to help them. That made him the enemy in their books. And no enemy of the gang lived for long.

If it had been only himself at risk, he might have fought through. But he thought of Sylvie as his mother, her children as his little brothers and sisters. How could he take the chance that the gang might lash out at him and strike them instead?

So, here I am Lord. Just what is it You want me to do now?

He sensed no answer. Funny—Seattle was claimed by some to be the end of the earth, but he still expected God to be present.

He was nearly to Maddie's bakery when he saw the crowd. She must not have opened yet for the afternoon, for men waited six deep by the front door, scrambling over each other to be first inside. He detoured around the back.

The rain had stopped for the moment, so he wasn't surprised to find Ciara and Aiden outside in the rear yard. What did surprise him was their behavior. They were scurrying about, chasing the chickens, and he was certain Maddie would have heard the cackling cries if she hadn't been so busy preparing to be besieged by her customers.

Michael caught Aiden as he dashed past. "Easy, now. What's this about?"

Ciara stopped in front of him. Her face was red from her exertions, and some of her hair had come undone and hung in steamers down her cheeks. "Maddie's busy in the bakery, so it's up to us to figure out how to have fun around here."

"It was my idea," Aiden declared, wiggling in Michael's grip.

Michael released him. "Your idea to do what?"

Aiden's eyes shone. "Hold chicken races."

Michael frowned. "Chicken races?"

From inside came a clang and a cry. Had they broken down the door and overwhelmed Maddie? Backing away from the boy, Michael shook his head. "Bad idea. Stay here. We'll figure out something better when I'm done inside." Turning, he ran for the kitchen.

He found Maddie down on her knees, picking up cookies from the floor. He could hear the voices rising in demand from beyond the shop.

"What happened?" he asked, crossing to help her.

"I turned too fast taking them out of the oven and tangled with a flannel," she said, face flushed and fingers flying. "Blow the dust off them now. Maybe my customers won't notice."

He thought her customers would be too busy looking at her to notice any dirt on the cookies. But she was evidently concerned, for she cupped a set of the ginger morsels in her hand and blew, pink lips pursed as if for a kiss. Michael found himself leaning closer, then jerked upright.

Cookies. He was supposed to be rescuing cookies.

A few minutes later, they had all the gingersnaps lined up with the loaves of bread on the counter. Taking her place behind the display, Maddie nodded to Michael to open the door. He let in the ravenous hordes.

It was a repeat of the morning's performance, every fellow shoving coins at her for a cookie or a loaf of bread, so long as the sweets came with a smile from Maddie. Even Mr. Horton battled his way to the counter for the cookies Maddie had promised him yesterday. Within a half hour, nothing was left but crumbs.

Maddie counted the silver. "Enough to buy more ingredients."

Michael stared at her. "Surely at those prices you made a profit."

She lifted her gaze toward the ceiling as if using it as a slate to calculate the right amount. "Two dollars and fifty cents, give or take."

Michael shook his head. "That can't be right."

She lowered her gaze to meet his. "I wouldn't be judging where I have no knowledge, Mr. Haggerty. Flour and sugar come at a premium here on the frontier. Every ingredient is hard-won. But if I make two dollars of profit a day, six days a week, that will be enough to support my family and begin to pay Clay Howard what I owe." She clutched the money close and headed for the kitchen. A moment later, he heard the clanking as she must have dropped the coins into her canister.

Michael shook his head again. Maddie O'Rourke had a grand vision—a successful bakery, a family for her siblings. But he didn't see how she could sustain this relentless pace and still give Ciara and Aiden the time and attention they needed. They were all heading for heartache, unless he could find a way to stop it. And that would mean breaking his promise to Maddie and interfering.

Chapter Eight

Ah, Sunday! Maddie heaved a deep sigh as she woke the next day. Sunday was the one day she didn't have to bake in the morning or do laundry. It was the one day she had all to herself.

Well, not to herself anymore. Now she had Ciara and Aiden to think about as well. And Michael.

He was asleep on his pallet as she came out of her room dressed for the day. She woke so early the other days of the week, it was difficult to sleep past dawn on Sunday, so light was just glimmering through the curtains. He seemed to be an early riser as well, for he stirred at the squeak of a board under her boots. His dark hair was plastered to one side of his face, and stubble peppered his chin.

"Good morning to you," she murmured as he looked her way. "I'll be making tea and frying eggs. Would you like some?"

Those blue eyes blinked as they focused on her face, and she felt warm despite the cool morning air.

"Thanks," he murmured before gathering himself to rise.

She'd gone downstairs before him the other morning,

so she hadn't realized he was sleeping in his clothes.
Now his rumpled shirt and trousers reminded her of
the flannels hanging on the line downstairs. Perhaps
she would have to do a little laundry today, at least to
fold what was dry.

As he rolled up his blanket, she busied herself with
taking down the teakettle from the top shelf above the
sideboard. "We'll start no loads of laundry today," she
told him. She reached for the cast-iron fry pan as well,
only to realize it wasn't hanging from its usual hook.
Glancing around, she spied the handle sticking out of
a lower shelf.

"Good," he said, straightening. "I know it's only been
one day, but I won't miss it. I don't know how you do
it, Maddie. That's backbreaking work." As if to prove
it, he pressed a hand to his lower back.

She set the fry pan on top of the potbellied stove and
frowned as the iron wobbled. Lifting the pan, she saw
that the bottom was dented and scraped.

"Something wrong?" Michael asked as if he'd noticed her look.

She set the pan down again and watched it rock back
and forth on its uneven bottom. "Something happened
to my pan."

"Let me see what I can do," Michael said, reaching
for it. His arm came around her like an embrace, making her all too aware of his strong body behind her.
Maddie stepped carefully away from him.

"And stoke up the fire, if you've a mind," she said.
"I'll go gather the eggs." She snatched up her basket
and fled.

She didn't catch her breath until she had reached the
kitchen. She'd flirted with half the unmarried men in
Seattle and never felt so flustered. Why was Michael

any different? Certainly he had hair that begged to be stroked back from his face, shoulders a girl could lean on. And that smile!

Enough of that now! She was a businesswoman, with plans for her future that did not include a partnership of any kind. She squared her shoulders and marched herself out into the rear yard.

The hens didn't come running at her, clucking, so she bent to peer into their house. Her chickens lay like old rags on their perches, eyes glazed.

No! They couldn't be sick! She counted on their eggs for her baking, for food. There were only so many of the precious birds in the area, and she'd paid a pretty penny for these. She couldn't lose them.

She ducked out of the henhouse and ran to the kitchen. Dropping her basket on the floor, she dunked a cup in the bucket of water waiting by the oven and returned outside. Crooning to the hens, she slipped into the house.

"There now, me beauties. What's troubling you?"

She offered the water to each in turn, stroked feathers, checked for bugs or sores. The hens seemed healthy, just tremendously tired. Had some threat kept them awake and agitated last night? She hadn't heard them cackling in fear.

By the time she returned upstairs, Ciara and Aiden were awake and dressed and waiting at the table, Amelia Batterby watching them with questionable approval from the doorway to Aiden's room. Michael had poured them tea and offered Maddie a cup as she joined them. She nodded her thanks. His dark brows raised in question as he glanced at her empty hands.

"I'm afraid there will be no eggs for breakfast this morning," she told them all. "Something's ailing the chickens."

Ciara and Aiden exchanged glances, and Michael stiffened. Maddie narrowed her eyes in suspicion.

"And what would you three be knowing about the matter?" she challenged.

Michael set his cup on the table and looked to the children. "You didn't."

Ciara nudged Aiden. "It was your idea, remember."

"You helped!" Aiden protested.

Maddie swallowed, though she had yet to take a sip of her tea. "What have you done?"

"It was only for fun," Aiden said, wide brown eyes begging for her understanding.

"You didn't give us enough to do," Ciara accused her, face as militant as usual.

Michael held up his free hand. "Don't blame your sister for this. I told you it was a bad idea."

"Someone had better be telling me the whole of it," Maddie warned, "or there will be no breakfast at all."

Aiden flinched, then straightened. Amelia Batterby wandered closer and began twining herself around his hanging feet as if she supported anything he had to say.

"The chickens kept running all over the yard," he explained to Maddie. "I thought they liked to run. So I had the idea we could race them."

"Race them," Maddie repeated, trying in vain to picture it.

"It was clever, really," Ciara said, nose in the air with obvious pride. "They kept trying to fly, so I had the idea it would be best to weigh them down so they wouldn't escape."

"And be caught by a fox," Aiden agreed, as if weighing down a chicken was an act of kindness.

"We pulled some loose thread from a shirt in the laundry and tied the chickens' legs to the frying pan,"

Ciara continued. "But they were stronger than we'd thought." She shook her head, clearly impressed.

"So we filled the pan with rocks," Aiden supplied.

"And they still ran?" Maddie asked, not sure whether to be shocked or exasperated.

"We had to chase them a little at first," Aiden admitted. "But then they ran very well. And my chicken won!"

"The first time," Ciara reminded him. "The little red one won the second."

She shouldn't laugh. Her poor chickens were exhausted, and she wasn't sure when they'd lay again. No eggs meant she couldn't practice the fancy cakes she was hoping to make for the wedding. But the picture of the hens scurrying around the yard dragging her frying pan made a smile tug at her mouth. She pressed her lips together to keep Ciara and Aiden from seeing it.

"That wasn't kind to the chickens," she said, voice stern. "How would you like me to tie a cart to you and chase you down the road?"

"It might be fun," Aiden protested. Amelia Batterby hopped up on his lap as if ready to go with him, and he laid a hand on the cat's fur.

Ciara made a face. "You needn't get so high and mighty, Maddie. They're just silly birds."

Michael took a step closer to Maddie, but to stop her from reacting or to offer his advice, she wasn't sure. She also wasn't sure why she took comfort from the gesture.

"Silly they may be," she told Ciara, "but their eggs feed us and help in my baking. From now on, you will give them the respect they deserve."

Ciara sniffed, avoiding Maddie's gaze, but Aiden nodded.

"And breakfast will be tea and toast," Maddie said.

"Again?" Ciara complained.

Maddie cast her a look. "Be thankful there was bread left over from yesterday."

Aiden's face fell, and Amelia Batterby leaned against him in support.

"You could just go buy eggs from the grocers," Ciara said with a huff.

Maddie opened her mouth to tell her little sister exactly what she thought of the idea. As if Michael sensed her intentions, he laid a hand on her shoulder, kind.

"Perhaps later we could go by the mercantiles so Ciara can see what's available," he suggested with a look to Maddie.

He was right. If Maddie protested the cost and scarcity of eggs, Ciara would just scoff. If her sister saw the prices in the shops, she'd realize how precious eggs could be.

"Delighted," Maddie said. "Right after services. And thank you, Michael, for the suggestion."

His smile was slow and pleased, and something fluttered in her stomach at the sight of it. Oh, yes, she would be glad to visit every mercantile in Seattle, if for no other reason than to encourage the owner to hire Michael Haggerty. No matter how helpful and kind he was, the sooner she got him out from underfoot, the better.

Michael took his bag down to the kitchen to shave and change while Maddie finished getting the children ready for services. He might not own anything that wasn't currently wrinkled, but at least what was in the bag was clean.

Still he had to admit they made a fine group heading for church that morning. Maddie was once more in the russet dress she'd worn when she'd met them on the pier, her velvet hat perched atop her red hair. A light rain was falling, so she'd brought an umbrella of green-and-orange plaid, handing it to Michael to hold up over all their heads. Ciara in her blue gown and white collar—the only dress that hadn't gone to the seamstress—looked as proper as a young lady might be. Even Aiden had his hair combed for a change as he loped along beside them in shirt and trousers held up by green suspenders.

They made their way through the business district on the boardwalks that ran along the buildings, aiming for the white steeple to the north that pointed heavenward. The worst part came in crossing the skid road, which was a rutted bog of black mud.

Michael handed the umbrella to Maddie. "Stay here." Before she could protest or question him, he swung Aiden up on his shoulders and scooped Ciara up in his arms. Aiden whooped from his perch, clinging to Michael's shoulders as Michael slogged across the mire and deposited them on the other side.

Ciara arranged her skirts and ignored the amused looks of the other people on the street, as if such conveyance was commonplace. "Wait for your sister and me," Michael instructed them before going back for Maddie.

"Look at your pants, now," she said with a tsk as he joined her. "Sure-n Mrs. Bagley, our reverend's fine wife, will be dismayed at the dirt you're bringing into her church."

"Better my pants than your skirts," Michael countered. He bent and scooped her up.

Brown eyes met his, amused. "Many a time I've managed these streets without your help, Mr. Haggerty."

"You forget, I'm in your debt, Miss O'Rourke," he replied, and he set off across the street once more.

She was heavier than she looked, though not nearly as heavy as the loads he'd borne on the docks in New York, and he didn't think it was the weight of the dress. Maddie O'Rourke might appear to be a frail, petite thing, but he now knew the physical burdens she had carried. Muscle born of hard work strengthened those arms and legs. He was proud to be of assistance to her.

And the feel of her in his arms wasn't half-bad either.

He set her down beside Ciara and Aiden, appreciating the pink that tinged her cheeks. She busied herself settling her skirts about her, then slanted a glance up at him through her cinnamon-colored lashes. Michael smiled.

"Miss O'Rourke?" Another fellow hurried to meet them. He was slight and gangly, every feature sharp on his narrow face. Dressed in a gray wool suit, he looked to Michael as if he might blow away like mist in a good wind.

Maddie, however, beamed at him. "Mr. Weinclef. And how are you this fine morning?"

He whipped off his narrow-brimmed hat, gripping it with both long-fingered hands. His sandy hair was slicked back with pomade, and the scent of lavender made Michael's nose itch.

"Fine, fine," Weinclef murmured. "Did you remember we were to sit together today in church?" He cast Michael a quick glance as if to draw her attention to the extra gentleman in the group.

Though Michael didn't remember Maddie mentioning anything about company this morning, she fluttered her lashes at the man. "Well, of course, Mr. Weinclef. And I intend to visit your fine establishment afterward."

As the fellow colored in obvious pleasure, she put a hand on Aiden's shoulder. "Ciara and Aiden, this is Mr. Weinclef who works at the Kellogg brothers' store. He's been a great help in outfitting the bakery. Mr. Weinclef, this is my sister and brother who have come to live with me." She glanced back at Michael. "And our good friend Mr. Michael Haggerty, who was kind enough to escort them on their journey from New York."

Once more she made it sound as if she owed him a debt rather than the other way around. But Weinclef glanced at Michael again as if considering how Michael had come upon such an honor as befriending Maddie. The man had to wonder what place Michael held in Maddie's affections.

He must have decided not to ask, for he turned his attentions to Ciara and Aiden, offering them a weak smile.

"Children. How pleased you must be to see your sister. She's quite the famous lady in Seattle. One of Mercer's Maidens, you see."

Maddie raised her chin. "Sure-n but I hope I'll be more famous for my bakery than for coming with Asa Mercer to Seattle, sir."

Weinclef blanched as if realizing he'd blundered. "I meant no disrespect, Miss O'Rourke. You know I hold you in the highest esteem."

Another moment and the fellow would be stammering out a marriage proposal. Michael stepped forward. "As I'm new to town, Mr. Weinclef, perhaps you'd be so good as to lead the way to church."

Weinclef's Adam's apple bobbed as he looked up at Michael. "Certainly, sir," he said, voice squeaking. "This way." He seemed to remember his purpose, for he held out his arm to Maddie. She took it, and the man escorted her toward the church.

Michael knew he could have found the church easily enough. Maddie had already pointed it out to them, and the steeple would have made it obvious in any event. Now a steady stream of people was winding toward the chapel on the hill. The Brown Church, Maddie had told them everyone called the building, to distinguish it from the other church in town, which was painted white.

Inside, pews of carved dark wood stretched on each side of a center aisle, beams open above them. Already a goodly portion of Seattle's citizens filled the space, voices stilling, bodies settling.

Weinclef led Maddie to a box pew about halfway back from the altar and let her enter first. Ciara and Aiden squeezed past him, putting themselves between him and Maddie. Weinclef heaved a resigned sigh as Michael took up his place on the end.

The service followed the typical pattern of prayers and readings. When they sang the familiar hymns, Michael heard Maddie's alto rising over Weinclef's tenor. Then the minister, Mr. Bagley, came to speak. A small man, his bushy hair and eyebrows gave testament to the energy inside.

"We often speak of the Lord's condemnation," he said, gazing at them all over his spectacles. "There are right ways to live, following His commands. Thou shalt not lie. Thou shalt not steal. Thou shalt not covet."

"Thou shalt not race your sister's chickens," Michael heard Aiden whisper to Ciara, who poked him into silence.

Maddie shook her head at the pair of them, and Weinclef shifted on the pew. Michael wondered which made the fellow uncomfortable, his Creator's expectations or the children's whimsy.

"But today," the reverend continued, "I want to speak of His unfailing love. The scriptures say there is no greater love than this, that a man should lay down his life for a friend."

The words echoed through the church, and something rose to meet them inside Michael. Glancing down the pew, he saw Maddie regarding the preacher as if drinking in every word as deeply.

He'd suspected her of going off to escape her responsibilities to her siblings, but she'd done exactly what Mr. Bagley said. She'd laid down her freedom, jeopardized her financial security, to make a better life for them. That was love.

What had he felt for Katie O'Doul, then? When she'd encouraged him to do as her father demanded and help the Dead Rabbits rob the port, Michael had never considered sacrificing his career or his honor. He still thought the request wrong, but what if she'd asked for something else? What if she'd wanted to head west and make a new life? Would he have left family and employment for her? He was no longer certain of the answer.

All he knew was that Katie's love had been untrue. She hadn't been willing to change anything about her life for him. He'd merely been one piece in her plans, a piece she could discard at will.

Was Maddie O'Rourke truly so different? She flattered her bakery customers, had obviously given Weinclef leave to join her today for all she paid him only polite attention now. Was she merely being kind or feathering her own nest?

How was he to know the truth about Maddie O'Rourke? For only when he was sure about her could he trust her with Ciara's and Aiden's futures.

And perhaps his own.

Chapter Nine

Maddie walked out of the church, hand on Mr. Wein-clef's arm, thinking that Mr. Bagley had the right of it. Love meant sacrifice and sorrow. Her father and step-mother had worked their fingers to the bone for Ciara and Aiden. They'd had nothing left for each other. Sad to say, but she simply didn't have it in her to offer a fellow a chance at making her life worse. She would save her love for her brother and sister.

Her siblings strolled beside her now on the board-walk, eyes wide at the things on display as well as the people on the street. Once again Maddie was struck by how different things were here. Back in her part of New York, seeing a horse was a rarity, never mind a cow traipsing along the cobblestoned streets. Here oxen trudged the mud, pulling rattling farm wagons laden with goods destined for outlying farms or the last of the harvest from those farms to the local shops. The stores were short wood buildings, only a few painted, instead of the stone and brick edifices of the city. The dry scent of fir mingled with the salty perfume of the tide flats instead of the clogging smoke from coal fires.

But as much as she saw the differences around her,

she found herself more aware of the towering shadow behind her.

She could see Michael's reflection in the windows of the businesses they passed. She'd glanced at him from time to time in service. He seemed to be paying the preacher heed, which was commendable. She'd seen him stiffen when Mr. Bagley had mentioned love. Had Michael been thinking about his Katie? Did he wish he'd stayed in New York and fought for her hand?

Once more she'd felt that urge to scold the woman. Good thing Miss O'Doul wasn't likely to venture west.

Now Michael sauntered along as well, glancing at the stores with interest. Perhaps he was choosing which next to approach about employment.

"A great deal of work to be done in Seattle," she commented with a look of encouragement back at him.

She caught his smile before she faced front again. "There must be someone needing a worker," he agreed.

"I hear they're clamoring for fellows out at the coal mines across Lake Washington," Mr. Weinclef offered.

All the way out across the lake? She might never see him again. Ciara and Aiden would be so disappointed.

"Surely there's work here in town," Maddie insisted. She smiled at her would-be suitor. "A fine upstanding citizen such as yourself must be knowing who needs help, Mr. Weinclef."

He flamed. "You give me too much credit, Miss O'Rourke. Besides, I believe the local employers are becoming quite particular as to whom they hire."

Did he imply there was something wrong with Michael? Michael must have thought so, for his reflection showed dark brows dipping down over his nose.

Maddie decided not to judge Mr. Weinclef so strongly. "I'm not taking your meaning, sir," she said sweetly.

He tugged at his high collar, which she noticed was in need of a good washing. "There have been rumors recently that some people distrust the Irish. Though not me," he hurried to add.

Her temper flared at the old insult. "The country of a person's birth has less to do with their actions than their character, I find," she told him, twitching her skirts out of her way.

"Oh, agreed, agreed," Mr. Weinclef said with a hasty glance back at Michael. "No offense meant, Mr. Haggerty."

"None taken," Michael said. "Though you might remember that I'm not the only Irish person in your company."

As if to prove it, Ciara and Aiden glared at the clerk.

Mr. Weinclef swallowed, Adam's apple bobbing in his throat again. "Indeed, indeed. My words were not well chosen. Oh, look, here we are at the store." He hurried ahead to open the door for Maddie.

Trying to put a damper on her response to the prejudice, she ushered Ciara and Aiden inside, with Michael right behind. Still, it was hard to forget. New York had been a swamp of despair for so many people of her heritage. She still remembered caricatures in the papers showing Irishmen as drunken apes, Irishwomen as grasping pigs. Shops had posted signs saying No Irish Need Apply. That hatred had only fueled the fury of the Dead Rabbits. She didn't want to see such things happen here. Surely Seattle was different.

"Look, Maddie," Aiden called. "Eggs."

Maddie followed him to a crate set up along the wall, where he and Ciara were gazing at six tan shells nestled in wood shavings. Ciara pointed to the price written in black on the white card beside them.

"Well, no one will be paying that," she declared.

"On the contrary, Miss Ciara," Mr. Weinclef said, joining them. "We generally sell out before noon."

Ciara frowned, but Maddie was glad her sister stopped short of accusing the man of telling tales.

"And look here," Aiden said, tugging on Ciara's arm. "Five pennies for a lemon!"

"Brought from California at great expense," Mr. Weinclef said, chest puffing. "As are most of the goods in this store. We trade with the British forts to the north too, and all the way to China and the Japanese Islands."

Ciara's eyes widened.

"With so many goods to stock," Michael put in, "you must need someone to uncrate and shelve them."

Mr. Weinclef scowled at him. "That, sir, is my job."

"And very good you are about it too," Maddie assured him. "Why, I wouldn't have found half the things I needed for my bakery but for your help. Sure-n a fine enterprising lad like yourself deserves an assistant."

Mr. Weinclef nodded, head jiggling on his neck. "That I do, Miss O'Rourke, and no mistake."

Maddie seized Michael's arm and dragged him forward. "And aren't you fortunate that Mr. Haggerty is looking for just such a position?"

Michael's eyes narrowed as if he wasn't too keen on being named Mr. Weinclef's underling, but the clerk reacted even more strongly. He stumbled back and adjusted his bow tie with trembling fingers.

"I am not in a position of authority to be interviewing staff," he sputtered. "No, no, it is simply too much to ask, even for you, Miss O'Rourke."

"Might there be a manager I could talk with instead?" Michael asked.

As if accepting his fate, Mr. Weinclef sagged. "This way." He waved a hand toward the back of the shop.

With a wink to Maddie, Michael followed him.

Maddie sent Ciara to the back of the store as well to pick up her dress and coat from Nora's corner. While they waited, Aiden darted about the store, examining everything from a wide-mouthed bear trap on the rough wood wall to the bright bolts of calico stacked in a corner. Spices and fruits vied with men's cologne to scent the air.

Maddie followed her brother more slowly, peeking around boxes and displays to check on how Michael was faring. She could see him at the rear counter, nodding to something one of the Kellogg brothers, who owned the store, was saying.

She had to admire Michael's tenacity. He seemed to be making a good case for himself. Still, for all she'd championed his cause, she had a hard time seeing him threading his way through the crowded store on a regular basis. Why, those shoulders of his would never make it past the first display!

"Here for more supplies, Miss O'Rourke?"

Maddie turned at the question to find Charles Terry standing in the aisle. Mr. Terry was accorded one of the finest fellows in Seattle, having been among the first to arrive in the area and lend a hand in building many a business. Tall and slender, with a mass of dark hair and bushy beard and mustache veined with silver for all he was a few years shy of forty, his keen gray eyes always drew Maddie's attention.

That and the fact that he owned the other bakery in town.

"Good day to you, Mr. Terry," she said with a nod.

"Thank you for asking, but I have all the supplies I need at the moment."

"Ah," he said with a smile. "And here I was sure you must have sold out, considering the number of customers that have been flocking to your door."

How did he know? It wasn't as if the two establishments were within eyesight of each other. His Eureka Bakery was down on the bluff overlooking the Sound, hers higher on the hill.

"We've been blessed to do well our first few weeks," she acknowledged.

"Seattle ever rushes to the new and interesting," he agreed. "A word of caution, if I may, one owner to another?"

Maddie couldn't imagine what advice he might have for her, but she nodded for him to continue.

He leaned closer as if imparting a secret. "A pretty face may sell all manner of goods in this town, but will your avid followers still support you when it becomes known you favor a certain gentleman?"

His gaze ventured past her to where Michael was returning.

Maddie's temper flared once more. "In the first place, Mr. Terry," she said in ringing tones, "don't be making the mistake of thinking my products inferior because they were made by someone with a pretty face. In the second, I have no favorite gentleman. If I hear rumors to the contrary, I'll be knowing where to place the blame."

Unlike Mr. Weinclef, Mr. Terry did not look away or beg her pardon. He merely inclined his head, smile still pleasant. "Words to the wise, Miss O'Rourke," he said congenially before strolling away.

What, did he think to frighten her with his thinly

veiled threat? She knew the quality of her work. That it was served with a smile was only icing on the cake. Seattle's bachelors were hungry for home cooking, and she met that need. It was as simple as that.

But if rumors began circulating that she was sweet on Michael Haggerty, she'd have more trouble on her hands than starting a new bakery or raising her sister and brother. Her friends Catherine Wallin and Allegra Howard would be all too happy to aid Ciara in matchmaking, and, by Nora's comment the other day, the seamstress wasn't far behind. Maddie wasn't about to admit that she felt anything other than pity for the out-of-work Irishman.

Even though her heart called her liar.

Michael slowed as he approached Maddie. Once more her look was as fiery as her hair. What had upset her now?

"Something wrong?" he asked as he reached her.

"Nothing fresh air won't cure," she promised. Calling to Aiden, she swept for the door. Ciara hurried after them, clutching her folded clothes to her chest.

Weinclef was right behind her. Michael's irritation rose. The clerk had gone out of his way to assure his employer that he needed no help after all. Michael had used every argument he could think of—his experience with the many goods coming in to the Brooklyn docks, his willingness to work for low wages to start as he learned the position, his ability to come in any hours needed—all to no avail. And every time he'd glanced toward the store, he'd seen Maddie gazing at him with such hope in her eyes that he'd wanted the job more than ever, if only to keep from disappointing her.

"You sound like a shopkeeper's best friend, Mr. Hag-

gerty," Kellogg had assured him. "Unfortunately, Weinclef doesn't seem to need help, and there are no other
positions available."

"Must you go, Miss O'Rourke?" the clerk asked now,
darting around her before she could open the door. "I
thought we might go for a walk, just the two of us." He
glanced back at Michael as if to make sure he knew he
was not invited.

"That's very kind of you, Mr. Weinclef," she answered. "But it's raining again, and I should be getting the children home for an early dinner. They didn't
have much breakfast." She smiled at Ciara and Aiden
as they joined her.

"No eggs," Aiden said with a heavy sigh. "Chickens
don't like racing after all."

Weinclef blinked as if he didn't follow, then brightened. "No eggs? Why then, you must take some of ours.
My treat."

There he went again, falling all over himself to do
Maddie a favor. Under the same circumstances, Katie
would have accepted anything the clerk had offered and
thought nothing of it. Ciara's reaction wasn't far off.

"Oh, thank you!" she cried, hugging her clothes,
brown eyes glowing with gratitude.

Maddie, however, shook her head, velvet hat slipping
with the movement. Michael had to clench his fist to
keep from reaching out to right it.

"Very thoughtful of you, Mr. Weinclef," she said,
"but I can't be accepting."

Ciara deflated. Aiden gazed up at Maddie. "Why
not?"

Michael found himself waiting for the answer.

"It isn't right to be taking Mr. Kellogg's only eggs

when we know others may be needing them more," Maddie told her brother.

Aiden frowned. "What others?"

Michael didn't know whom she meant either. But he had a feeling she was simply trying to find an excuse that wouldn't hurt the clerk's feelings. She probably wouldn't thank him for it, but Michael felt compelled to step in.

"Your sister has told you the way of it, Aiden," he told the boy. "Leave be."

Aiden pinched his lips together, but his scowl spoke for him.

"Thank you again for your escort today, Mr. Weinclef," Maddie said with a smile that set the man blushing. "Be sure to stop by the bakery next week. I'll have something sweet waiting just for you."

Stammering his thanks, Weinclef opened the door to allow her to leave. The fellow looked so happy with the crumbs she offered him that Michael felt disgust growing inside him.

"Do you like him?" Ciara asked her sister, scrunching her nose.

Maddie kept her head high as she snapped open the umbrella. "Mr. Weinclef is a fine fellow, and I'm glad he's my friend."

Michael snorted, and she narrowed her eyes at him.

"Then why not take his eggs?" Ciara whined, glancing back at the store.

"Because he's a fine fellow, as I said," Maddie replied. "I won't be impinging on his generosity. But I see no reason to slight him just because people will gossip if they see us together." She angled the umbrella to try to cover Michael. He took it from her and held it over them all. She strode down the boardwalk so fast Ciara and Aiden had to scurry to keep up.

Who was gossiping? He'd noticed her talking to that curly-haired fellow in the store, but the man had left before Michael had heard any of the conversation.

Ciara and Aiden seemed to accept her word, for they fell to arguing over who had sung better in church. Michael leaned closer to Maddie, catching a whiff of cinnamon.

"If it's gossip that concerns you," he murmured, "I probably provide more fodder than Mr. Weinclef."

"Nonsense," she said, so forcefully that a strand of red hair flew up to tickle his nose.

"The truth," he promised. "You must have seen how your customers reacted to me yesterday. They didn't seem too pleased to find me in your employ."

"You are not in my employ, Mr. Haggerty," she said. "You are a friend of the family who's helping while you look to establish yourself here. That's all anyone needs to know."

Surprised at her vehemence, he hesitated, and she reached out to pull Ciara and Aiden closer.

"Come with me," she told them. "I want to show you something." She turned the corner and started up the hill, lifting her skirts out of the mud. Michael lengthened his stride to keep up.

The rain stopped as they climbed the hill above the shops, away from the harbor. But the lack of precipitation didn't mean anything would dry out soon, he was learning. From what he'd seen, Michael was amazed Seattle didn't just wash itself down into the Sound. The entire town was built on a hillside, and every stretch of land that wasn't covered by a building seemed to be covered in mud. Here and there, single-story whitewashed houses popped up like mushrooms. But the higher they climbed, the nicer the houses became.

Maddie stopped in front of one. The lovely two-story house had bric-a-brac dripping from the eaves and broad shutters framing every window. The wide front porch beckoned the weary traveler, as did the golden light shining from the parlor window. He'd never imagined anything so fine out in the wilderness.

"This is where Mr. Terry and his wife live," Maddie told Ciara and Aiden. "He came to Seattle when he hadn't even reached his majority. He worked hard, saved his pennies and now he has this and a farm on the Duwamish River."

"It's a castle," Aiden said, eyeing the peaked points over the second-story windows.

"It's not a castle," Ciara scolded him. "Castles have moats. But it is a fine house." She turned wistfully to Maddie. "Could we have something so nice one day?"

Maddie hugged her closer. "Someday, me darling. You see, Mr. Terry owns a bakery, just like me. I figure if he can rise so far, why can't I? If I can make a success of it, we'll have all this and more."

Michael wished he could believe that. Once he'd thought that hard work and integrity would make his fortune. Then circumstances had pulled all his dreams from his grip. Maddie's bakery was on shaky footing as it was, if the loss of a day's worth of eggs could set her back. He'd seen how hard she worked just to make ends meet.

If this was what she really wanted, a fine house on the hill overlooking Puget Sound, how much harder would she have to work? And what would she have to sacrifice to make her dreams come true?

Chapter Ten

Maddie returned to the bakery with Michael, Ciara and Aiden, head high. Walking past the fine houses on Third Avenue always raised her spirits. On a sunny day, she could see Mount Rainier in one direction, and Puget Sound and the Olympics in the other. But most of all, she caught a glimpse of what she might become: prosperous, comfortable, safe. It was all up to her.

She could tell she'd made an impression on her sister, for Ciara had kept glancing back at the Terry house until it was out of sight, and now she nearly skipped into the bakery. That was hope. Perhaps faith in the future would help them past this rough patch.

Michael was more pensive, head bowed and hands deep in the pockets of his trousers. She supposed it was a fussy house for a man like him, all that fancy trim and pointy spires. But it seemed to her that something more was bothering him than Mr. Terry's taste in homebuilding.

"Change out of your good clothes," she told Aiden as her brother and sister started up the stairs. "And see that you hang up your new dress, Ciara. I'll find something in the larder for dinner."

Aiden heaved a sigh as if even climbing the stairs was too much. "What can you make with no eggs?"

Perhaps he'd learned his lesson. "I'll bake the ham in a pie with a nice flaky crust," she told him. "You'll like that."

Aiden's lack of reply disagreed with her.

Foot on the stair, Michael hesitated.

"Is there a problem, Mr. Haggerty?" Maddie asked.

"So all this—" his hand swung to encompass the bakery and the flat above "—is for a pretty house on a hill."

Heat pulsed through her. "You don't understand."

He turned from the stair and approached her, gaze searching hers. "Then help me understand."

Maddie sighed. She owed him no explanation, yet she longed to give him one. "You were raised in Five Points. Do you truly see so little value in a clean and comfortable place to live?"

Again he waved his hand. "You already have something clean and comfortable."

"And what's wrong with wanting more?" Maddie challenged him. "Perhaps just once in my life I'd like to wake up without feeling the burdens on my shoulders, to know that me and mine will be fed and sheltered, even if I spend the day reading or visiting friends. To feel as if I'm safe from the whims of others, unlike me mother, father and stepmother, who wearied themselves working and worrying. Is that too much to ask?"

His face looked sad. "No," he said. "If that's what you want."

Maddie threw up her hands. "Name me one person who doesn't want that!"

He caught one of her hands and held it. "That wasn't what I meant, Maddie. Many people in the world have all those things and think nothing of them. I doubt Mr. Weinclef or the Kellogg brothers lay awake at night listening for the next shot of a pistol, the shouts and screams of fear from the neighbors that tells you trouble is just a door away. I see how hard you're working. How can you take on more?"

His hand was warm, the touch gentle, but she felt as if someone was standing behind her, prodding her with a stick. She pulled away from him. "I'll take on as much as need be so Ciara and Aiden and I don't have to worry about the future. And that will be soon, if this wedding is the success I'm hoping it will be."

He shook his head. "You already serve every man in Seattle from what I can see."

"But not many of their wives." She hated to point it out to him lest he accuse her of selling her smile. "If this bakery is to prosper, I need the patronage of my own gender—the Denny ladies, Mrs. Maynard. They are the future of Seattle."

At last his brow cleared. "So, along with security, you want respect."

She nodded. "Now you have the right of it. Security for my family, respect for my work and my character. There's nothing wrong with that."

"Nothing at all," he agreed, but his tone was turning darker again, and she realized that was exactly what he'd left behind in New York. Shame on Katie O'Doul for crushing his heart, making him think he was less of a man!

Maddie put her hand on his arm. "It's early days yet, Michael. You'll find work, and the security and respect that go with it."

His smile was less sure than hers. "From your lips to God's ears."

For some reason, the statement made her look to his lips, so firm above hers. The slightest upturn had a way of making her heart beat faster, her body sway closer.

This time, he pulled back first. "I better check on Ciara and Aiden," he said before turning to climb the stairs.

She opened her mouth to remind him that that was her responsibility and thought better of it. At the moment, she needed a little distance, even at the expense of letting him take her role again. Baking a pie would keep her mind focused on something other than Michael's smile.

So she went to the bakery kitchen and took out her pie pan, rolling pin and apron. Wrapping her apron around her gown, she headed for the larder. She'd fold the remaining laundry later, perhaps do one or two more pieces for delivery on Monday. Michael could take them. She smiled, thinking of how her customers would react when they found him at the door of the boardinghouse instead of her.

Well, perhaps she should deliver the laundry.

Opening the larder door, she reached up for the ham. It wasn't there.

Neither was her sugar. And there, where her precious bottle of rose extract should be, was nothing but an empty spot.

She blinked, touching the shelf, feeling the rough wood scrape her fingers. That extract had been brought for her from San Francisco. She'd done no more than open the cap and sniff the sweet scent. It was the special ingredient she needed for the wedding cakes. She couldn't have misplaced it!

She took a step back. It had to be a mistake. Perhaps Michael had wanted to be helpful and moved her ingredients somewhere he thought would be more handy. Yes, that had to be it. She'd find them all piled up in a corner like the laundry. She scurried from the sideboard to the worktable, looked under and over the display counter, panic rising with each step.

"Michael Haggerty!" she shouted at the ceiling. "I need you. Now!"

Feet thundered on the stairs, and he careened into the kitchen, broom handle once more up and at the ready.

"What is it?" he demanded, blue eyes wide. "What's happened?"

Maddie threw out her arms. "The ham, my sugar and extract, gone." She took a step closer and laid a hand on his tensed arm. "Please tell me you moved it somewhere for safekeeping, or I think I'll go mad."

Maddie's fear radiated out of her like heat from her oven, and Michael had to struggle not to take her in his arms. Instead, he leaned the broom against the worktable and shook his head. "I haven't touched anything but the laundry."

She sagged against the table, face crumpling. "Oh, but we're lost, then. Everything gone, and I haven't the funds or the time to replace it." She choked and pressed her hands to her mouth as if to hold in her cry.

That did it. Michael wrapped his arms around her, held her close. "It must be a mistake," he murmured against her hair. "Perhaps Ciara or Aiden moved things. Maybe they thought the chickens needed more exercise."

She gulped, a sound that was half laugh and half sob. "No, it couldn't have been them. I would have seen them. I'm always in the kitchen, it seems."

Except this morning, he realized. He held her back from him. "Show me."

She pulled away to point to the open door of the larder. Even from here he could see that it was emptier than when he'd last looked in. His heart sank.

"You've been robbed," he told her.

She stiffened. "Robbed?" She spun and crouched beside the worktable, reaching underneath it to draw out her canister. Her hands shook as she twisted off the lid, and he heard the chime of coins before she tilted the tin to peer inside.

She rocked back on her heels, drawing in a breath. "It seems to be all there."

"At least we can be thankful for that," Michael said.

She rose, frowning. "But why didn't the thief take it too? He'd have to search for the larder. The door isn't obvious. He wouldn't have had to look very hard for this, and one shake would have told him what was in it."

"Perhaps our thief preferred food to money," Michael said, though he agreed it odd to have left the canister behind. Even if the thief had been starving, why not take the money for more food later?

Maddie stiffened. "If he was after food, did he take the chickens?" She ran past him for the door, and Michael followed.

But over her head he immediately spotted her hens wandering about the yard, scratching and pecking. Recovered from the children's races, they clucked at the sight of Maddie, ruffling their feathers and rushing toward the door in obvious hopes she'd come to feed them. She turned to gaze at Michael, dark eyes troubled. "I don't understand."

Neither did he. If the thief could carry off the cones

of sugar, why not grab a chicken or two as well? Unless he'd been too burdened.

"Look for Amelia Batterby," Michael said, stepping into the yard. "He might have let her out."

She darted back inside, calling for the cat.

Michael checked the latch on the door first. The scrapes and scratches showed where the thief had broken the lock. He crossed next to the gate and peered over. Boot prints were gouged deep in the mud of the alley behind the bakery, but they quickly disappeared on Washington Street. It wouldn't have been so hard to tuck what was left of the ham and the cones of sugar under a long coat and hurry off. The closest businesses to the bakery were all closed on a Sunday.

He met Maddie in the kitchen.

"Amelia Batterby is fine," she reported. "Ciara found her shut up in my room. I didn't see her there when we left, but she's small enough to have hidden under the bed."

Either that or the thief had shut her in. But that made even less sense. Why would a thief care about a cat?

"Nothing's missing upstairs," Maddie continued. "Did you find anything outside?" Her tone begged him for good news.

He wished he had some to give her. "Looks like our thief made off through the alley. Very likely he knew you'd be at church, along with a good number of Seattle's citizens. He must have thought a bakery would have plenty of bread."

Maddie started. "He wasn't after bread. He wasn't hungry. He wanted to keep me from baking!"

Michael frowned at her logic, but the fire sprang to life in her eyes again, and she stormed about the kitchen as if heat fueled each step.

"Oh, the rat! I don't care how much the rest of Seattle admires him. 'Here for more supplies?' he says." She stopped to point at Michael. "He knew my supplies were gone before I did."

"Who?" Michael asked. "Weinclef?"

She waved a hand and resumed pacing. "No, Mr. Terry."

Michael stared at her. "The man who owns the castle?"

"The man who owns the other bakery," Maddie corrected him. "He stopped me at Kelloggs', asked how my supplies were holding out. Why would he do that if he didn't know they'd gone missing?"

Michael didn't want to accuse someone without cause. "Perhaps he saw the long line of customers at your door."

"So he said," Maddie replied, coming to a stop by the worktable. "But how was he to know? Oh, but I never thought he'd be so devious! Sure-n he built that house of his on lies!"

Michael still wasn't convinced. "We should call for Deputy McCormick." Another fellow who was sweet on Maddie, if Michael didn't miss his guess. Very likely McCormick would rush to do her a favor. "Tell me where to find him, and I'll go for him right now."

"I didn't see him at services this morning," Maddie said, "so he may have been called elsewhere in the county. But I'll tell you how to find the sheriff's office."

Michael listened to her instructions, then headed for the door. "Put a washtub to block the back door behind me, and lock the front," he told her. "I doubt the thief will be back, but I'm not taking any chances."

"Neither am I," Maddie said. The look on her face almost made him feel sorry for the thief.

* * *

Deputy McCormick was in his office and on his feet before Michael finished his story. Michael wasn't sure whether to be pleased or alarmed that he buckled on his gun belt before heading for the door.

The sun had come out from behind the clouds, setting the muddy street to steaming, as Michael and the deputy started for the bakery. In the golden light, Michael could see that the man was only a little younger than Michael's twenty-eight years. What made him look older was the coolness of his gunmetal-gray eyes.

"And they didn't take money or valuables outside the food?" he asked as he strode down the boardwalk, gaze constantly roaming ahead as if he was expecting trouble to come pouring out onto the street from the shops they passed.

"Not that we could find," Michael admitted. "We're simple people, Deputy. There aren't a lot of valuables to be had."

McCormick grunted as if he didn't like Michael's answer. Michael wished he had more information to offer. How could he protect Maddie and the children from a nameless threat?

"Seems odd Miss O'Rourke never had any trouble until you arrived," McCormick said.

Michael pulled up short, forcing the lawman to stop as well. "This was none of my doing. I was in church with Maddie and the children. There will be more than a dozen witnesses who can testify to that."

McCormick stuck out his lower lip. "Interesting. Why assume you need witnesses for me to believe your word?"

He could give the man a casual answer, laugh off the implied accusation, tell McCormick it was none of his affair. But Michael had come west to escape schemes and intrigue. Why bring them with him?

"Do you know much about New York City, Deputy?" he asked, starting forward once more.

McCormick fell into step beside him. "Never been there. No interest in going. But that's where you and Miss O'Rourke hail from, isn't it?"

Michael nodded, shoving his hands down deep in the pockets of his trousers. "I was born and raised there. She and her father eventually made their home there after they came over from Ireland. The Irish tended to congregate in an area called Five Points."

"I've heard of it," McCormick gritted out, and the scowl on his face said nothing he had heard had been good.

"I'm not surprised," Michael told him. "There's been a lot of trouble there over the years, most recently when an Irish gang called the Dead Rabbits decided to take the upper hand. I worked offloading cargo at the docks in Brooklyn. I was told to look the other way while the gang robbed a ship. I refused and warned the ship's captain. They threatened my life for turning traitor, as they saw it. A lot of ugly words were said to me before I came west. So, you'll pardon me for expecting to need witnesses to prove myself."

McCormick nodded. "These Dead Rabbits sound like the type of fellows I like to hunt. Any of them follow you west?"

He sounded almost eager for the confrontation, but all Michael felt was cold. Could it be? Had he brought trouble with Ciara and Aiden to Maddie's door?

No! Surely he was far too insignificant now that he'd lost his place in New York. What good would it do for the gang to make him a martyr where no one could see?

"Not that I know of," Michael said. "No offense, but Seattle is a little small for their ambitions."

McCormick shrugged. "Guess that's something to be thankful for."

They reached the bakery, and Maddie opened the door to Michael's knock. Deputy McCormick tipped his hat to her.

"Miss O'Rourke. I hear you had trouble."

She showed him to the larder. Michael could see Ciara and Aiden peering through the curtain, a frustrated-looking Amelia Batterby clutched in Ciara's arms like a rag doll. He waved them out of sight.

"Do you think it could be Mr. Terry?" Maddie was asking the deputy when Michael joined them. "He knows his customers prefer my baking."

"Your baking wins hands down," McCormick agreed, turning from the empty shelves. "But I wouldn't be so quick to assume. Terry is well liked, well respected. He doesn't strike me as the type to sabotage another business. He has enough money to simply start another of his own."

Maddie's lips tightened as if she couldn't believe him, but McCormick glanced around the kitchen.

"We've had complaints the last two days around Seattle," he told her. "Food disappearing, clothes taken off the line. Sheriff Wyckoff wonders whether we have some down-on-their-luck types trying to raise a stake without paying for it." He glanced at Michael.

He could look all he liked. Michael was done protesting his innocence. "They probably don't have friends or family to support them until they can get on their feet," Michael said with a look to Maddie, who managed a smile.

"Few here do," McCormick agreed. Michael was glad to see his heavy gaze return to the room at large.

McCormick spent the next little while poking about the kitchen, rear yard and alley. Maddie followed at his heels, interjecting supposition, asking questions. Michael was content to stay in the background and watch, waiting for the deputy to tell them more. He could see that Maddie trusted the fellow by the way she listened, head cocked so that the little velvet hat she'd had no time to remove slid on her hair.

She didn't deserve this, Lord. She's worked so hard. Isn't there something You can do? Isn't there something I can do?

What he felt in response was the urge to fight. But whom?

As the lawman returned to the building, Michael straightened away from the door and made room for the deputy to join him in the kitchen.

"Nothing conclusive," he told Michael and Maddie. "But I'll ask around and send word if I learn anything."

That was it? Michael wanted him to go riding off after the thief, bring the fellow to justice, recover Maddie's supplies. For all they knew, the things could be eaten by morning.

His frustrations must have been written on his face, for the deputy's eyes narrowed.

"A word with you, Haggerty, before I go," he said as he moved to the front door.

"Is there a problem?" Maddie asked, glancing between the two of them.

McCormick paused to touch the brim of his hat to her. "Nothing that need concern you, ma'am." He jerked his head toward the door, and Michael followed him out.

"I appreciate you telling me about New York," he

said as they stood on the boardwalk in front of the bakery, the street quiet and nearly deserted on a Sunday afternoon. "Let me return the favor. I was raised in an orphanage in Saint Louis. When I escaped, I ran with a gang for a while. They're trouble, pure and simple. If there's one thing I learned during that time it's that family comes first."

He poked a finger into Michael's chest. "We protect our own out here, Haggerty. Miss Maddie O'Rourke is one of us. If trouble's coming, I aim to stop it."

Michael met the man's hard gaze. "Don't concern yourself, Deputy. Maddie and those children *are* my family. If trouble's coming, I'll be standing between it and them."

Chapter Eleven

Maddie looked up from counting her coins as Michael returned to the bakery. She wasn't sure why Deputy McCormick had wanted to speak to him privately. Very likely it was one of those male whimsies, but she didn't like being left out, particularly when her livelihood was at stake.

"Everything all right?" she asked as he came to join her at the display counter.

He nodded. "Fine. Deputy McCormick and I are agreed that the bakery is under our protection."

Maddie nearly laughed at that, but the serious look on his face stopped her. His head was high, his blue eyes narrowed, his shoulders tensed and hands fisted. She might have thought the building held the crown jewels of England instead of breads and cookies for hungry loggers and miners.

"I counted my savings," she told him instead with a nod to the stacked coins glinting silver in front of her. "At best I can buy a cone of sugar, some food for the children and a few eggs until the hens start laying. That will be enough for a day or two of baking and eating, if I choose my recipes carefully. I'll still be able to pay

Clay Howard what I owe this month, but I won't have enough for the wedding supplies, especially with the loss of the extract."

"Extract?" he asked, fingering a silver coin as if he hadn't touched one in a while.

"Like perfume, only for cakes," she offered.

He looked as if she'd asked him to drink perfume instead. Maddie couldn't help a laugh.

"It tastes very nice," she assured him. "But it's costly and hard to come by out here. I had a bottle brought up from San Francisco as soon as James asked me to bake for his wedding. I don't know if there's another bottle in all of Seattle."

"What about this James?" he asked. "Can he pay in advance? There must be a fast ship that could bring you a bottle."

"Perhaps, but I'll not ask it of him," Maddie replied. "Sure-n he's nearly family, he is. No, I'll have to find another recipe. And I'll need a way to raise capital quickly. Normally, I wouldn't deliver laundry on a Sunday, but we could use the payment for services rendered."

"I'll finish the rest today and deliver it by evening," he promised. By the fierce look that remained on his face, she pitied the flannels.

"We'll work together," Maddie told him. "We can hang the things to dry in the sun. The more we can get done the better."

"We'll help too," Aiden declared, coming out of the stairwell. Ciara followed more slowly. Like Michael, she wore a look of resolution, brows gathered, lips tight.

"No thief's going to get the best of our family," she said with a stomp of her foot.

Maddie's heart gave its own little leap. "You're right. I'll not let this setback get the better of me." She plucked two coins from her hard-won pile and held them out to Ciara. "The Kellogg store closes early on Sunday. Hurry back and buy us the makings for dinner. I'll purchase the rest tomorrow. I'll not be able to have bread for the morning rush, but we'll make do with the laundry money. Go with her to help carry, Aiden."

"Yes, ma'am," Aiden said, so eagerly she could only hope he wouldn't return with nothing but candy for dinner.

As the children left, Maddie turned to Michael to find him watching her. She offered him a smile with a determination she hoped matched his.

"Set the water to boiling, Mr. Haggerty," she said. "I'll change my clothes and join you shortly."

By the time Maddie returned downstairs, Michael had the tubs out in the rear yard and was pouring a kettle of steaming water into the first. Maddie's gaze was drawn to the double line of rope stretching across in front of the oven. "What have you done with my drying line?" she called out to him.

He straightened to grin at her. "Your oven can put out a lot of heat. I figured why not use it to help dry the clothes faster. You won't need the space for baking today."

Maddie grinned back. "Why, Mr. Haggerty, you're a right smart fellow, you are. Let me sort the first batch of clothes, and I'll bring it out to you."

She closed the door to keep Amelia Batterby from escaping and bent over the sacks still piled on the kitchen floor. In his haste to retrieve things yesterday, Michael had tumbled a few items together. Tsking, she retrieved some shirts.

Odd. They weren't from her usual customers. She felt

as if each shirt was an old friend these days, from Mr. Hennessey's broad plaid to Mr. Porter's battered blue flannel. Had Michael added some of his own clothes to the washing? She wouldn't have blamed him for getting some of his work done in the process of doing hers. She knew how hard it had been to wash aboard ship.

The last piece of clothing on the floor was a pair of trousers, wadded into a ball. Maddie shook them out and draped them over the remaining sacks. Then she froze, staring.

Running down the side of the dark blue pants was a red stripe, sewn into the seam. She straightened, swallowing. Michael had claimed he had no use for gangs like the Dead Rabbits, talked about them with disdain.

Why then was he hiding the one thing that marked members of the dreaded gang—blue trousers with a red stripe?

The door banged open, and she nearly jumped. Michael set the kettle on the sideboard. "Ready?"

Maddie nodded, shoving the trousers into the nearest sack. "Take these shirts now. I'll be right behind you."

And determined to get answers from him.

The laundry didn't seem so tiresome today to Michael. Perhaps he was getting used to the rhythm of it: wash, rinse, wring and hang. But he thought the ease had more to do with the company.

Maddie worked beside him at her usual brisk pace. She'd changed into a green gingham gown that fluttered about her frame in the breeze. The sunlight set her hair aglow.

Sleeves rolled up, he handled the first tub, Maddie the rinse. Over her shoulder, he caught sight of Amelia

Batterby peering out the kitchen window before disappearing to more interesting pursuits.

"You said Sylvie had the raising of you," Maddie said as he lifted the first batch and dumped it into her tub with a splash. "I don't recall seeing you at her flat."

"I moved to Irishtown to be closer to the Brooklyn docks," he explained as he straightened. Together they peered down into the water of his tub, heads so close together he could smell the cinnamon that clung to her. Maddie made a face at the filthy water. With a chuckle, Michael bent to heave up the tub and take it to the garden patch to dump. He caught sight of her watching him before she turned away with a blush.

He knew he shouldn't be pleased by her reaction to his strength. He'd been born with a sturdy body, and his work on the docks had only honed it like a knife to iron. Still, it was nice to be admired for a change instead of derided for cowardice for failing to support the gang.

As if she knew he'd seen her staring, she hurried to the bakery for the kettle and returned a short time later with the hot water to pour into the tub. But her next statement proved she hadn't forgotten their conversation.

"So you labored on the docks in Brooklyn," she mused as they worked to the sound of clucking hens. "That's a far piece away from family."

He dumped some cool water in with the hot and swirled the mixture with a paddle. "Not so far away," he said, bending to retrieve the next set of clothes. "It's only a ferry ride to Manhattan. You might say it's far enough away from Five Points to be civilized."

Maddie finished rinsing her clothes and began putting them through the tall metal wringer, cranking on the handle as water streamed back into the tub on one side and damp clothes trickled out on the other. "Sure-n I can't be arguing with you on that," she told Michael. "There was nothing civilized about Five Points."

He'd be ahead of her soon. Best to help with the wringing. He left the paddle in the tub and took one of the flannels from the rinse. "I can only hope they raze that place someday, once Sylvie has found somewhere else to live." He twisted at the material, sending water cascading down into the rinse and wishing he could wash away his past as easily.

"Thankful I was that she agreed to take in Ciara and Aiden," Maddie said. "I couldn't have come west otherwise."

He knew that, and he knew what he'd originally thought of the matter—that she'd abandoned her family for greener pastures. He tossed the shirt over the line beside them, then turned to eye her. "I owe you an apology."

Maddie glanced up at him, brows raised. "Whatever for?"

He ducked down to retrieve another shirt and wring it, taking the time to choose his words carefully. "When Sylvie told me where you went, who you went with, I thought you'd left Ciara and Aiden behind with your worries."

Maddie's gaze returned to the iron wringer in front of her as if to avoid meeting his gaze as he straightened. "I'll not deny there were moments I thought about doing just that," she confessed. "I was struggling on my own before Da and their mum died. How could I care for two more? But they're family, my own flesh and blood. I could no more abandon them as stop breathing."

Something inside him unfurled like a shirt freed from the wringer. "I'm glad. For your sake and theirs."

She took the shirt she'd wrung out and slipped it over the line. It was still damp enough that the movement sent a shower flying. Michael wiped a drop from his cheek.

"Sorry," Maddie said, gaze on his face. She lifted a hand as if she wanted to touch his skin. Would her caress be as soft as her look?

Disappointment bit as she grabbed the next shirt instead and shoved it into the wringer.

"But what of you?" she asked, cranking the handle for all she was worth. "No brother, no sister? Was Sylvie all your family?"

"All I needed," he replied, finishing with that shirt and hanging it out to dry. "But there's something else you should know about me, Maddie. I was offered a chance to help the Dead Rabbits and I refused. That's why Katie O'Doul broke off the engagement. That's why I used your ticket to come here. It was either escape New York or stay, face their wrath and see Sylvie and her children harmed."

He heard the bitterness creeping back into his voice, felt it in a hard kernel inside him. She had to hear it too.

"'Tis a sad tale," she murmured, smoothing the wrinkles from the shirt in front of her. "But if what you say is true, why did I find the Dead Rabbits' striped trousers in your wash?"

Michael felt as if she'd slapped him. His hands froze halfway to the paddle. "Not my wash."

She darted around him to retrieve the sack she'd brought from the kitchen and reached inside.

"These," she said, straightening to hold a pair of trousers out to him.

He ducked under the line and came to stand in front

of her, staring down at the red stripe. He knew the meaning. The sight of them made his stomach knot.

"Those aren't mine," he promised her, gaze meeting hers. He could see the doubt in those deep brown eyes.

"Whose, then?" she demanded.

He shook his head. "I don't know. But someone connected to the Dead Rabbits is here, and he isn't afraid to show it."

Maddie wadded up the pants, eyes tightening with obvious worry. "Could they have followed you here, intent on revenge?"

"I'm not that important," he assured her. He put a hand to her elbow. "I haven't brought trouble to your door, Maddie, I promise. There has to be another explanation for why those trousers showed up in the wash."

"And I'll be glad to hear it," she said, bending to stuff the offending article back in the sack.

Michael reached down to take the burlap from her. "Who owns this?"

She examined the sack. "Mr. Hennessy. But those trousers can't be his. Sure-n he's a mountain of a man. His neck must be as big as my waist!"

"Then someone must have slipped them into his laundry," Michael reasoned.

She shrugged. "I only found them near his sack, but it's possible. He lives in that boardinghouse, and the manager allows the boarders to leave their sacks in the parlor for me to collect."

"Someone might have put the trousers into the sack unnoticed," Michael mused. "How many men live in that boardinghouse?"

"Perhaps a dozen," she answered, "including Mr. Hennessy and Mr. Weinclef."

Weinclef didn't seem likely, worse luck. Michael

wasn't sure why he felt the need to show up the scrawny clerk. But Maddie's would-be suitor couldn't be a member of the Dead Rabbits. He wasn't Irish, which was the main requirement for joining the gang.

Maddie lay her fingers on his arm, her touch comforting.

"Maybe a red stripe is the uniform of some sailing ship or a foreign army," she said, though the frown on her face betrayed her doubts. "All nations are flocking to the West."

He nodded, though he could not make himself believe the answer was so simple. "You're probably right. But just to be sure, I'll deliver the clean laundry this time."

She withdrew her hand. "But..." She bit her lower lip as if trying to halt the rest of her words.

Michael cocked his head. "But?"

She was turning pink. "Well, I have to collect my pay."

Why was that cause for concern? "I'll collect it," Michael said, watching her. "Unless you think I'd cheat you."

"No! Never!" Her blush was deepening, and she turned for the tubs as if to prevent him from seeing it.

Michael followed her. "Then what's the trouble, Maddie?"

"It's just that sometimes they give me a little extra," she said, grabbing his paddle and shoving it under the sodden clothes. "For a smile or a kind word. I'm not thinking they'll treat you the same way."

So she wasn't above flirting for profit. He wasn't sure why that thought disappointed him. Even Sylvie wasn't above batting her eyes at the grocer if it meant an extra potato for the soup.

"They won't," he said, taking the paddle from her and using it to heave up the clothes and slide them into the second tub. "Just like they won't buy bread from me like they buy it from you."

She stiffened. "I bake a good bread, Michael Haggerty. It's not my smile that makes it so tasty."

"But it is your smile that helps sell it," he replied, stirring the clothes in the rinse water.

The breath she puffed out was thick with vexation. "I'll not be arguing with you over the point. Right now, we need every penny we can scrape together. So, I'll be delivering the laundry, and smiling, and asking any questions that need to be answered."

He couldn't like it. If there was a gang member in town bent on trouble, he didn't want Maddie anywhere near the fellow. For all Michael knew, the Dead Rabbits could be behind the theft of her supplies, though why they'd care whether Maddie baked was beyond him. Unless they thought her pain was his. They wouldn't be wrong.

"We'll deliver the laundry together," he compromised, giving the second batch a final swirl in the clean water. "You can smile and collect your money, and I'll ask the questions."

She narrowed her eyes but stopped short of arguing.

They finished the second batch and hung it up to dry, removing the pieces that had already dried with the heat of the oven. Maddie set about ironing the shirts on the worktable. She kept glancing at Michael as if more questions pressed against her lips as surely as her flat iron pressed the wrinkles from the shirts. He forced himself to focus on their task.

Someone rapped on the rear door as they began folding the clothes for delivery. Maddie wiped the steam from her brow and went to answer as Michael straightened from the worktable.

In the yard, the Kellogg brother who had interviewed Michael at the store tipped his tall hat to Maddie.

"Good afternoon, Miss O'Rourke," he said with a smile that lifted his bushy blond mustache. "I believe you know these charming children."

Ciara and Aiden darted around him for the kitchen. Ciara was smiling, her brown eyes twinkling like Maddie's, and Aiden grinned from ear to ear. Michael couldn't help smiling with them.

Maddie looked less certain of the situation. "And what have you two been up to?" she asked, arms akimbo.

Kellogg put a hand on each of their shoulders, his black coat and trousers dark behind their clothes. "They were telling me all about your troubles," he confided with a fond look to the children. His blue gaze rose to Maddie's face. "We can't have Seattle's finest bakery in jeopardy of closing."

Was he smitten with Maddie like every other man in Seattle and thus willing to donate to the cause? Or was he planning on extending credit that would ultimately put Maddie in debt so deep she'd be forced to concede her dreams?

Michael edged closer as Mr. Kellogg stepped aside and nodded toward the yard. Mr. Weinclef waited just beyond, bearing a cone of sugar wrapped in blue paper in his slender arms. Over the fence, he could see the head and shoulders of another man, who must be sitting on the bench of a wagon in the alley.

"What's all this?" Maddie asked with a look to her siblings. "I sent you for dinner."

"And they returned with enough for breakfast too," Mr. Kellogg said with a laugh. "Seattle's breakfast, that is. Miss O'Rourke, the Kellogg mercantile is pleased to extend you credit. You may pay it off within the quarter at twenty-five percent interest per month. All you have to do is say yes."

Chapter Twelve

Credit? That would meet Maddie's needs in the short-term, but oh, how it could sap her future. Yet Mr. Kellogg stood there smiling at her as if he wanted to grant her every wish. Ciara and Aiden gazed up at her almost as eagerly.

Only Michael beside her wore a frown. She wasn't sure what he was thinking, but even if he had urged her to accept the offer, she would have refused. She wasn't about to change her mind to please him. She struggled to change her mind even when she thought it might be God's will for her.

But she thought she knew His will in this instance.

"It's very kind of you," she told Mr. Kellogg, including the two men beyond him in her smile. "But I can't accept."

She thought Michael drew in a breath. Mr. Weinclef sagged.

Aiden's face fell. "But Maddie," he protested. "It's free!"

"It's not free, me darling boy," Maddie explained. "Mr. Kellogg is allowing me the use of it until I can pay him back with interest. But if I use my profits to pay his interest, I'll have nothing to buy food for you next week."

"Then I'll merely extend you further credit," Mr. Kellogg assured her, smile never wavering.

She'd seen too many people go down that road to their sorrow. Her father and stepmother had owed the grocer nearly one hundred dollars when they'd died. It had taken her months to pay off the debt.

"I appreciate the offer," she said to the shop owner, "but I must refuse. I've enough to buy one cone of sugar. That's all we'll be taking. Excuse me while I fetch the money." She turned and went for her savings, which she'd left in the front of the shop.

Ciara followed her. "Why did you say no? We could have had lamb for dinner! Eggs for breakfast!"

"And been forced to sell our own chickens to pay for the privilege a month from now," Maddie countered. She took out her savings can and opened the lid.

Ciara stood on tiptoe to peer inside. Then she gasped. "You have lots of money!" she accused Maddie. "You just didn't want to spend it on us!"

Anger forced a response. "This money is for sending you and Aiden to school," Maddie told her. "And for paying back Mr. Howard for building this bakery for us, all the pots and pans, the supplies, even the bed you're sleeping on. I'll not be cheating him or go further into debt because you want more than you need."

"You want more!" Ciara cried. "You want a fancy house. You said so."

"And I'll have that house," Maddie told her. "When I've earned it. If you want to help, get up in the morning, work in the bakery and stop questioning everything I do!"

Ciara's face crumpled. Pulling away, she turned and ran up the stairs.

Maddie sagged against the counter. There, she'd made a mess of things again. Surely she could have found a better way to discuss the matter with her sister. She was supposed to be the adult!

Yet how was she to counter Ciara's logic? Mr. Kellogg's seemingly kind offer was nothing but a slippery slope, and if she started down it she very much feared she'd never make it back to the top again. She wanted the best for her brother and sister, but they all had to make do with what they could afford. She was simply grateful the bakery was doing so well that they could afford more in Seattle than they had in New York.

Prayer bubbled up inside her. If God really did care about the little people such as her, maybe He'd hear it.

Help me find a way to explain it to her, Lord. Bridle my tongue if You must. And please, give me patience!

No majestic voice thundered an amen, but for some reason she felt better. Drawing in a deep breath, she returned to the kitchen.

Mr. Kellogg and his clerks were gone, the rear door shut. Michael and Aiden were loading the last of the supplies into the larder. She counted two cones of sugar, a haunch of venison and a fine ham. The anger she was working so hard to master leaped up again like a dog on a chain.

"What have you done?" Maddie demanded, clutching the coins so hard the metal bit into her palm. "I refused his credit, and you took his supplies anyway! Why can't you understand I can't afford this? Do I have to fight the lot of you?"

Aiden glanced between Michael and Maddie. "Michael said it would be all right."

Fury wrapped around her like a howling hurricane, setting her arms to shaking. "Michael Haggerty is not the authority in this house," she spit out. "I am. Go upstairs, Aiden."

Aiden took Michael's hand and gave it a squeeze. "If she puts you on bread and tea, you can have some of mine," he whispered. Then he scurried past Maddie for the other room.

Michael would have to have been blind and deaf to have missed the fire blazing out of her. She felt as if she might char to a cinder from the heat of it. Blue eyes drawn down at the corners, he spread his hands in supplication. "Let me explain."

"No." She couldn't listen to another calm word. She wanted to throw over the worktable, order him from her sight, somehow take back her life from all the demands that had been placed upon her. She strode up to him and grabbed his hand, shoving the coins against his fingers.

"You take this and anything it won't pay for back to the store. And find yourself somewhere else to stay while you're at it. It was bad enough you took my place with Ciara and Aiden. I'll not be having you make financial decisions for me."

He did not so much as blink, his blue gaze holding hers. "I didn't make a decision for you. I made one for me. I don't hold with debt either. That's why I was so set on working off my passage. I told Mr. Kellogg that I'd restock for him at night to pay for the supplies. That way, you can keep baking."

He'd offered to work nights as well as days here, for her? Doubling the burden on himself? No one had ever done so much for her.

All the fire washed out of her, leaving her drained, lost. "You didn't have to do that."

He shrugged as he handed her back her money. "Maybe not. But I didn't do it entirely to help you. I thought that if Kellogg saw my good work he might think again about hiring me."

It was a brilliant solution, like the line he'd stretched by the oven to hasten the drying, like the way he handled squabbles between Ciara and Aiden. She felt small for not realizing his intentions sooner.

"I'm sorry," she said, dropping her hand. "You've been nothing but kindness. I shouldn't have assumed the worst."

"You've had to be on your own for a while," he said. "It's understandable that you don't like others interfering."

Understandable, perhaps, but not the person she wanted to be. This feeling of helplessness, of crushing weight, had been why she'd run away from New York to begin with. She'd thought things would be different in Seattle, that she could make a fresh start, make something of herself. She refused to fall back into the old pattern.

"There's interfering and there's being helpful," she told Michael, "and I'm not very good about seeing the difference. I fear I was no better with Ciara. She thought I was selfish for refusing to go into debt for her." Just remembering her sister's behavior and her own brought tears to her eyes.

"She doesn't understand," Michael said. "You and I saw how debt can hurt people. She's too young to have realized the cost. But what you did today will save her and yourself years of heartache later."

She wanted to believe that. "I'll talk to her, once I've calmed myself." She shook her head. "I've a terrible temper, Mr. Haggerty. Sure-n someone should have warned you before you stepped into my life."

He smiled. "I've seen worse."

So had she. But at least they were free from the gang violence in Five Points.

Unless, of course, it had followed them to Seattle.

Maddie squared her shoulders. "It seems we have work to be doing. I'll start that meat pie for Aiden, then you and I can deliver the laundry. And I'll try to smile for me customers."

He reached out and wiped away the tears that had started down her cheek. "You could frown, and they'd still come flocking to your side, Maddie. You're beautiful even when you don't smile."

For some reason, that made the tears start all over again.

He gathered her close, held her gently, let her sob against his chest. When was the last time someone had cared enough to listen to her fears, offer support? Her friends Allegra and Catherine had been wonderful aboard ship, and Rina had been a kind friend since, but none of them had known the truth about her. She'd been ashamed to admit that she'd abandoned her own family for Seattle.

Michael knew the truth, and he still was willing to hold her, encourage her.

"I just want the best for Ciara and Aiden," she murmured, resting her cheek against the rough wool of his waistcoat. "They deserve more than I had—a roof that doesn't leak when it rains or shake when the neighbors fight. Food that isn't half-rotten. A family that isn't falling apart from work and weariness. Am I selfish for hoping I won't have to go into debt for all that?"

"No," Michael murmured against her hair, arms

tightening as if he wanted to protect her. "There's nothing selfish about you, Maddie. You work harder than anyone I've ever met and you're being clever about it, if you ask me. You're building a business to support you and Ciara and Aiden, and maybe even their children when they're grown. That's something to be proud of." As if to prove it, he bent and kissed her on her forehead.

Maddie shuddered at the gentle pressure. Raising her head, she stared at him. In the expanse of blue she thought she saw a question. For once, she was sure of the answer. She needed that comfort, and, she thought, so did he. She lifted her lips, and he met them with his own.

The warmth, the sweetness of it set her to trembling. She wrapped her arms about his neck and kissed him back. The turmoil and conflict of the day disappeared in his touch. All she wanted was to stay like this forever.

A warning rose inside her, insistent, demanding. She had a future all planned, and it didn't include falling in love. That way led to sorrow. She knew that.

Why, then, had she offered Michael a chance to stake a claim on her heart?

The warmth of the kitchen seemed to fade as Maddie pulled away from Michael. Her lips were as pink as her cheeks, her cinnamon lashes fluttering. All he wanted was to pull her close again.

Good thing she was smarter than that.

"That's entirely enough," she said, turning away from him. "Sure-n there are more ways to comfort a lady than to kiss her, Michael Haggerty."

Comfort. Yes, that's what he'd intended. She'd had such a difficult afternoon, with the robbery, Kellogg's offer and Ciara's reaction to her refusal. He'd only wanted to bring back the smile to those soft, sweet lips, not feel them warm beneath his.

Maybe there was something in the air in Seattle, to make him want to kiss her. He was hard-pressed to explain himself otherwise. He'd already had one pretty Irish lass knock a hole in his heart. He wasn't about to give that chance to another.

"Just doing my duty, ma'am," he said, knuckling his forehead in salute. "As you said, we have work ahead of us."

Maddie drew in a breath as she visibly gathered her composure around her like a shawl. Had the kiss affected her as much as it had him? Why did the thought make him smile?

She went upstairs to check on Aiden while Michael finished with the clothes. Something soft brushed his trousers, and he looked down to find Amelia Batterby gazing up at him with wide eyes as bright as copper pennies.

"I agree," Michael told her. "That wasn't my finest moment, but I was only trying to help."

Her tail in the air, she turned and stalked back into the shop. It seemed even Maddie's cat didn't believe his excuses.

The sun was disappearing behind the Olympics as Michael and Maddie went to return the laundry. Lights spilled from houses, laughter and music from the rougher establishments on the skid road. The mud squelched under Michael's feet, and he lifted the sacks higher to keep them safely out of it.

"We should come to an understanding, you and me," Maddie said beside him, one hand on the lantern.

Was she talking about the kiss this time? He wasn't

ready to put words to those feelings yet. He wasn't sure he'd ever be ready. Better to focus on her earlier accusations, that he was still trying to usurp her place in the house.

"I thought we had," Michael said, pausing to thump the mud off his boots. "You are the authority. I'm the hired help."

She grimaced, but whether because of the mud she shook off her skirts with her free hand or his assertion, he wasn't sure.

"You're more than the hired help and you know it," she said, heading down the block toward the two-story whitewashed boardinghouse. "Ciara and Aiden look up to you."

He noticed she didn't include herself in that statement. "From habit," he said, following her as she approached the door. Overhead, a sign read Rooms for Rent—Gents Only. "They knew me in New York and on the ship."

"And they miss Da," she acknowledged. "Sure-n but you're the first fellow to pay them any mind since the fire. That has to mean something to them, especially Aiden. You're important to them. I see that. But you can't go around protecting us without asking. Sometimes it's best if we protect ourselves."

Funny, but he'd never thought of protection as a bad thing. He'd done all he could to support Sylvie—giving her part of his pay, coming by the house several times a week to fix things, playing with the children. In his mind, that's what made a man a man, that he protected those he cared about.

Those he loved.

But he didn't love Maddie. Not yet, and not ever if he had his way about things. He could not deny, however, that thought and emotion were as tangled as a lose bowline inside him, and he wasn't sure how to straighten them out.

Lord, could You be helping me on this? I feel all at sea.

Maddie lifted her hand, but paused short of knocking. "Listen, now," she said, looking to Michael, eyes narrowed. "Let me do the talking inside. And we can discuss this matter of Ciara and Aiden more on the way back."

So she wouldn't even let him question the men? Was he good for nothing but fetching and carrying? It went against everything he believed in, but she clearly needed to be the one in charge. Michael forced himself to nod.

That must have satisfied her, for she turned to rap on the wood. A moment later and a slender man with a gray goatee opened the door. He frowned at Michael.

"We're full. Try French's two doors down."

So much for hospitality.

Maddie stepped forward. "Sure-n but my customers will be sad to find their shirts somewhere else."

"Ah, Miss O'Rourke." He nodded at her, breaking into a smile that revealed a gap between his two front teeth. "I didn't see you there. You may come in and bring your—" he looked Michael up and down "—fellow."

"Mr. Michael Haggerty," Maddie supplied as she walked past him into a narrow parlor crammed with wooden benches and chairs along with a few bright brass spittoons. "A fine gentleman newly arrived on our shores. He's looking for better work while he helps me."

"Lucky man," the boardinghouse owner muttered as Michael passed.

In the parlor, men in cotton shirts over flannel, with

suspenders holding up their trousers, rose from their seats. Others came clambering down the stairs, smiles broadening at the sight of Maddie. But as soon as they spotted Michael, their smiles faded, their heads came up and they crossed their arms over their broad chests.

Michael refused to acknowledge their hostility. If he could let the angry taunts and threats from the gang members roll off him in New York, he wasn't about to let a little old-fashioned jealousy prick his pride. He stood beside Maddie, scowling at anyone who got too friendly, and handed her a sack at a time to call the owner. And he looked each customer over carefully for size and demeanor, seeking anyone who might smell of Five Points and the Dead Rabbits.

The first two fellows were far too beefy to own the red-striped trousers, the next two either too short or too tall. Others were too slender. In fact, not a single man the size of Michael came forward. He began to see why Maddie had assumed the pants must be his.

The last sack was for Mr. Hennessy, and Maddie had certainly been right about his size, for a behemoth shuffled forward when she called his name. He took the sack from Maddie's grip, glanced down at it, then brightened into a smile.

"That's my name," he said loudly enough for the entire room to hear him as he pointed to the word someone had stitched on the burlap in colored thread. "I can write it now as well as read it."

Maddie beamed at him. "Sure-n but Miss Fosgrave was telling me what a fine student you are, Mr. Hennessy."

This fellow attended classes? He seemed tremendously pleased about the matter, for his cheeks darkened, and he shifted on his massive feet. "She's a good teacher. Mr. Wallin is lucky to be marrying her."

Maddie was nodding. She'd told Michael to keep his mouth shut and let her do the talking, but she wasn't talking. She'd found the trousers near Hennessy's sack. Didn't it follow that Hennessy might know something more about them, even if they weren't his?

"Did a friend of yours order a new pair of trousers for the wedding?" Michael put in.

Hennessy frowned at him. "No." He glanced down at his stained pants. "Do I need new trousers to go?"

"You'll be fine," Maddie assured him with a look of warning to Michael. "It's just that we found an odd pair of trousers in your wash—blue with a red stripe down the sides."

He shook his head. "They're not mine. I'm no fancy man."

As if just as determined to get to the bottom of things as Michael, Maddie lowered her voice and leaned closer to her client. "Might you be knowing a fancy man here in the boardinghouse?"

Michael thought she waited as expectantly as he did for the answer.

"No," Hennessy said, scratching his grizzled chin with one hand.

Maddie sagged, but Michael gave her credit for not giving up. "Not even one?"

Hennessy's frown grew, as if he was putting every effort into thinking about the matter. "Maybe that new Irishman who came on the boat this week from New York," he offered.

Maddie glanced at Michael, brows raised. But Michael felt as if Hennessy had reached out and flattened him with his broad hand. Maddie clearly thought the man meant Michael, but he knew the truth.

The only other Irish passenger on the boat from New York had been Patrick.

Chapter Thirteen

Maddie wasn't sure what to say to Michael as they walked home. She'd received fewer bonuses than usual, but more than she'd hoped with him standing beside her. She was certain the comments her customers had made about him being "Miss Maddie's fellow" had not sat well with Michael.

But more important, she was certain he knew the owner of those trousers. Why was she afraid to ask? She'd never been one to run from a fight.

The streets were dark and nearly abandoned as they slogged their way toward the bakery. Though she'd refused his help in other ways, she could not deny that she was glad for his solid frame beside her. The golden light of the lantern bathed his face as he turned from side to side, ever watchful for trouble.

Maddie drew in a breath and plunged in. "Who else from Five Points or Irishtown came on the boat with you and Mr. Flannery?"

"No one." He bit off the words as if the fact troubled him as well. "But those pants can't belong to Patrick. He left New York to escape the violence just like I did."

She didn't like to think about the dapper Mr. Flannery as a member of the vicious gang. Yet the only other answer would be what she'd originally feared—that Michael was a member instead.

"And you're certain of Mr. Flannery's background?" she couldn't help asking as piano music echoed from one of the houses they were passing.

"I'm certain," Michael said, so firmly she wondered if he was trying to convince her or himself. "I had it from his own lips, and on the ship he often talked about the need to protect ourselves from them. If he spoke the same way in New York, I'm sure he didn't endear himself to the Dead Rabbits. They liked to be the ones claiming to provide all the protection."

All that did make it sound as if he hated the gang as much as Maddie did. "Perhaps it was a mistake, then," she said, trying to take heart in the thought. "Perhaps we were right that the trousers hold some other meaning."

"Perhaps," he allowed, but his hesitation told her he thought otherwise.

They had little opportunity to continue the conversation for the next while. When they arrived at the bakery, they found that Ciara had set the table and laid out the blackberry preserves to go with the meat pie. Hoping the gesture was a peace offering, Maddie made sure to compliment her on her work.

Though Michael seemed too pensive to eat, Aiden tucked in.

"Isn't it nice to have all the food we want?" Ciara said.

Maddie tried not to bridle at her sister's smug smile. The girl seemed all too pleased to have gotten her way about the food and supplies.

"You should be thanking Mr. Haggerty for our dinner," Maddie told her sister and brother. "He'll be breaking his back to pay for it, starting tomorrow night."

Michael chuckled, but Aiden frowned.

Ciara cocked her head. "Why are you breaking your back?" she asked.

"My back will be fine," Michael assured her. "What your sister means is that I promised Mr. Kellogg I'd work in his store to pay for the supplies he brought today."

Ciara's look darkened as it swung to Maddie. "So you wouldn't even let go of a penny to help Michael. I know what Da would say about that."

Heat flushed up Maddie. "So do I. He'd say good on Michael for taking the initiative." She nodded to him.

Michael, however, turned his look on Ciara. "I never met your da, but I know what mine would say. He'd say every member of a family needs to contribute, and those who choose otherwise don't get to complain."

Now Ciara reddened, dropping her gaze. She leaned slightly to one side, and Maddie was pretty sure she was reaching down to take comfort in Amelia Batterby's soft fur as the cat strolled beneath the table. Maddie knew she shouldn't take equal comfort from Michael's support, but she couldn't help the swell of thanks inside her.

"Dessert?" Aiden asked as if that would make everything better.

Maddie patted his shoulder. "Not tonight, me darling boy. I've not had time to bake today. But soon I'll be testing some of my recipes for the wedding. I'll need you to taste every one and tell me what you think."

Aiden's eyes lit. "Yes, ma'am! Can I help bake them too?"

"And make a mess?" Ciara scoffed. "You'd fall in the cake batter and poison it."

Could she never be kind? "I imagine I can find work for a fine young man like yourself," Maddie said with a smile to her brother. "But you'll have to get up early."

"I will! I promise." He hopped off his chair. "Michael can wake me."

"If your sister wakes me first," Michael said with a glance at Maddie. "After all, you'd have to get up anyway. School starts tomorrow, doesn't it?"

Maddie nodded.

Ciara dropped her fork on her plate with a clatter. "Tomorrow! I forgot. I have so much to do!" She pushed back her chair, ran for her room and slammed shut the door.

Aiden frowned after her. "What do you have to do to be ready? Don't you just walk up the hill and sit down at a table?"

Maddie shared a wink with Michael. "Indeed you do, me darling boy. But I'm guessing Ciara wants her clothes and shoes to be just right."

Aiden glanced down at his shirt and shorts. "Aren't my clothes all right?"

"They're fine," Maddie promised him. "But if I were you, I'd leave your sister alone this evening."

Aiden agreed. He even went so far as to request a rag from Maddie to shine his shoes. Michael moved closer to Maddie as she watched the boy rub the worn leather, his tongue poking out of one corner of his mouth.

"They're coming to realize they can rely on you," Michael murmured. "I'll watch the shop in the morning if you want to walk them to school."

"And scare off me best customers?" Maddie asked, giving him a nudge with her shoulder. "No. I'll handle the morning rush, then we'll shut things up and both walk them to school."

"Does that mean you're not kicking me out tonight?" he asked.

His question brought her harsh words from earlier rushing back at her. "You can stay," she told him. "Sure-n but you're a part of this family, Michael Haggerty. Just see that you find work for yourself. I think we'll all set better with that resolved."

She turned for the table to gather up the dishes only to find Michael's hands blocking hers.

"Let me clear this away," he said with a smile. "You've done enough today."

There he went helping again, but so charmingly she didn't have the heart to tell him no. And perhaps this too was a way to apologize for any differences between them. She nodded, and he stacked the plates and set the cups teetering on top, winking when he caught her watching.

"Why don't you ask Aiden what he learned aboard ship?" he suggested.

"Are you trying to keep me from seeing how poorly you wash, Michael Haggerty?" she challenged.

He chuckled. "I wash well enough." He nodded toward Aiden's open door. "You saw how excited he was to help you. Now his sister has him wondering about school. You can ease his mind by making him realize he knows something you don't."

Maddie stared at him. "How do you understand them so well? I've known them their whole lives and still I struggle. I'm just thankful I've seen no sign of the crying at night like you did aboard ship."

"How old were you when Ciara was born?" he asked, pouring some of the water from the bucket by the stove into the washtub.

"Fourteen," Maddie remembered.

He shrugged. "There you are, then—you were nearly grown before you were a sister, and out on your own a few years later. I can barely remember a time when I wasn't someone's big brother, bound by love, not blood."

She didn't think that was entirely the answer. His parents had died, just like hers, and when he was far younger than she'd been. He had to have been hurting. Perhaps helping the other children deal with their wounds had helped him deal with his own.

"Now," he said, "ask Aiden."

Maddie raised her brows at his insistence, but turned to eye her brother's door. "Aiden!" she called. "I hear you learned something important aboard ship."

Her brother rushed out of his room, and she heard the snick that indicated Ciara had turned the knob on her door as well as if to listen.

"The sailors taught me knots," he said, chest puffed out in pride. "And how to find the North Star to steer the boat."

"Ship," Ciara corrected him, wandering out of her room. Amelia Batterby took the opportunity to dart around her and head for Michael. Even the cat knew who the protector was in this family.

"Ship," Aiden acknowledged. "And they taught me how to whistle. Want to hear?"

Maddie nodded. "Please."

She thought he'd merely purse his lips, but he ran back to his room and returned carrying a thin wooden barrel with holes in it.

Maddie grinned. "Ah, a penny whistle."

"A *feadóg*," Ciara insisted, using the Gaelic word for the little flute. She came to a stop near Aiden and waited expectantly.

Aiden began to play, the high notes dancing around

the room even as he tapped his toe in time. Maddie clutched her skirts to clear them from the floor and swayed back and forth to the bright sounds. Michael set aside the dishes to join them, clapping along.

Ciara went one further. She brought her feet together, then gave a little skip. Soon she was hopping in circles around Michael, the sound of her shoes against the boards beating time to the rhythm.

Michael bumped into Maddie, and she looked up at him, surprised.

He winked again. "Come along, me lass," he said, voice heavy with the lilt of home. "Let's be showing them how it's done."

Grinning, Maddie curtsied to him, and he bowed. Then they both began moving to the music, skipping and hopping together, Maddie following his lead. When he stopped, arms poised over his head, she took up the challenge, spinning around him, skipping back to her spot. Hands on her hips, she waited.

Michael stood tall, proud, hands dropping to his side. His legs moved, feet beating a mighty tattoo against the floor, nearly drowning Aiden's piping. The strength and power of it made her breath catch.

Ciara darted in front of him. "Now me!" She wove her way between the pair, giggling as Michael reached out as if to catch her. "Now, Maddie!" she cried as she reached her sister's side.

Maddie danced between Ciara and Michael, joy bubbling up as laughter. Then Michael reached out once more, and she found herself caught in his arms.

His gaze locked with hers, breath coming quickly. She couldn't move, couldn't think. Ciara's call to Aiden seemed to come from a million miles away.

"Stop playing, you loon. They're going to kiss."

"Oooh," Aiden taunted as he lowered the pipe. His voice was as singsong as his playing. "Maddie loves Michael. Maddie loves Michael."

No, no she didn't. Just the thought was enough to force her back from him, out of his embrace. She focused on her little brother, red-faced and beaming.

"That's some fine whistling, me lad," she assured him. "Sure-n but we'll have to have you play for us more often."

Aiden ducked his head, obviously pleased by the praise.

"And maybe we can dance more too," Ciara said, glancing between Maddie and Michael.

"You're the finer dancer, Ciara," Maddie said. "I'll leave the floor to you."

To her surprise, Ciara looked disappointed. A similar look flitted across Michael's handsome face, only to be replaced with a polite smile. She hadn't meant to hurt him, but she couldn't afford these feelings for him any more than she could afford Mr. Kellogg's supplies. In fact, caring for Michael could impact her future even more.

Michael's pulse refused to return to normal as Aiden accepted Maddie's praise for playing. For a moment there, he'd forgotten everything—his reason for coming to Seattle, the tensions between him and Maddie, his promise not to interfere. Once again, the world had narrowed to her smiling face, her bright eyes, the cinnamon scent of her as she swayed closer.

Hadn't he learned the dangers of such feelings by now?

Yet something inside insisted that Maddie wasn't Katie. She sincerely loved her brother and sister, was concerned for their welfare and future. Still, she'd dictated Michael's role in the family and offered her approval only when he behaved according to her rules. Was that behavior so very much different from the relationship he'd had with his former fiancée?

The best thing he could do was find a job and somewhere else to stay. That's what she'd said she wanted from him, and that certainly would keep a rein on these feelings that popped up whenever she was near. He thanked Aiden for playing, then turned to finish the dishes. He had a debt to work off, and he refused to incur a new one.

So, he rose when Maddie did in the morning and helped her bake bread and rolls with the supplies for which he'd indentured himself. He kept his promise to Aiden and woke the boy just after sunrise, but he made himself scarce before the customers arrived. The cacophony of voices told him when Maddie started selling. He used the time to shave and dust off his clothes. She and Aiden came to find him and Ciara a short time later.

"Maddie's the best baker in Seattle," her brother bragged, climbing into a seat at the table. "Everyone came to buy her bread today." He bit into one of the rolls she'd saved for them, honey dripping off his fingers.

"It was a good morning," Maddie agreed. "Now let's make it even better."

Together they left the bakery. Michael had wedged a log of firewood against the back door to prevent further break-ins, and Maddie locked the front door behind them. Then they headed across town.

The day was once more bright; birds called from the wood, swooping low over the brown autumn grass that dotted the hillside. Ciara in her refitted dress of blue cloth walked with her head high, hand clasping Aiden's.

From shops and homes, other children joined the trek up the hill until they all converged before the building. Michael had to own it was impressive—tall columns supported a white cupola, windows looking toward town like the eyes of wisdom. He noticed a girl about Ciara's age smiling shyly at Maddie's sister, and two boys, twins by the looks of them, thrust a pail at Aiden. By the way all three boys' faces brightened as they gazed down into it, he thought it contained something significantly more interesting than bread and cheese. He'd have to pack lunches for Ciara and Aiden tomorrow. Perhaps he should bring them something later.

Michael grimaced. There he went interfering again!

A tall, slender woman, hair wound up tight in a bun, came out of the building, gray skirts brushing the wood of the entry.

"That's Miss Reynolds," Maddie whispered. "She traveled with me on the *Continental*."

Another of Mercer's Belles. This one certainly looked intrepid enough to brave the wilderness.

"Good morning," she said, voice carrying in the cool air. "I see we have some new students today." She smiled at Ciara and Aiden, and every eye turned their way. Ciara kept her head high even though her face was turning red. Aiden waved at them all.

"Come inside now," Miss Reynolds said, and all the children streamed past her into the school.

Maddie heaved a sigh.

Michael put a hand on her shoulder. "They'll be fine."

"They will," she said with conviction. By the height

of her head, Michael thought one part of her burden had lifted. For some reason, so had his.

Thank You, Lord. The Good Word says You've a soft spot for widows and orphans. I know You'll watch over Ciara and Aiden today, and Maddie too. Show me how I fit in this new picture You're painting.

"I'll keep looking for employment today," he told Maddie as they walked back to the bakery. "And I'll be working at Kelloggs' tonight. With the robbery yesterday, I hate to ask you to leave the door unlocked."

"I'll likely be up anyway," she said.

Most likely she would, because he had come to Seattle instead of the woman who was to help her. He still wondered how she could keep up this pace.

You could stay here, work beside her.

As soon as the thought entered his mind, he dismissed it. She'd made it plain she saw his help as interference. Besides, though Patrick might tease him about being a laundress, Michael felt as if he was meant for something more than hard, unthinking work. Maddie baked; the results of her work fed people, satisfied a need. She made a difference in people's lives whether she knew it or not. That's what he wanted for himself. There had to be work in Seattle that applied.

Yet something told him he'd already found the work most important to him—making Maddie, Ciara and Aiden his family.

Chapter Fourteen

For the next three days, Michael canvassed Seattle, determined to find a way to start over. The area boasted so much industry—from logging to mining to more shops than he had expected. Surely there was a place for him.

But as he moved from shop to shop, the story was always the same. No work was to be had, or a position had been promised to a friend or family member. One shop with a Help Wanted sign told him the sign was old, but he noticed the clerk did not rush to remove it as Michael left.

He broadened his search, trying new businesses that might be more eager for workers. The recently built Occidental Hotel turned him away. Even the funeral parlor refused his offer to dig graves in the black mud. He was almost glad he saw so little of Maddie, so he didn't have to tell her how dismally he fared. As it was, when he rose in the morning and when they ate dinner together with Ciara and Aiden, she always gave him a smile of encouragement.

He was about to leave the ironworks on Wednesday, having failed yet again to secure a position, when the door opened to admit Patrick. His friend's smile widened as his gaze met Michael's, and he came forward to clap Michael on the shoulder.

"Have you won the job before I could apply?" he joked.

"No position to be had here," Michael said with a glance back into the cavernous building. The foreman ducked out of sight as if to avoid further conversation.

Patrick's face fell. "No position to be had in all of Seattle, it seems. The land of opportunity, yet no opportunity for the Irish."

Michael didn't want to believe the old prejudice was alive here. He took Patrick's arm and drew him outside. As if the sun had no answer for him either, it had disappeared to be replaced by a sharp drizzle. The icy drops pricked Michael's skin. He started down the block.

"I've seen no sign of trouble here," he told his friend as Patrick joined them. "People with names like Hennessy and O'Rourke seem to be doing all right."

"For now," Patrick said darkly. "But all that could change tomorrow, as we both know."

Michael nodded. Motioning to his friend, he led Patrick to the end of the block, where the town petered out onto a clear-cut just waiting the next round of building. Stumps stuck up amid dusky ferns. Seed pods of wild flowers rattled in the breeze, their husks nearly gold. A shame there was no other gold to be had.

Turning up his collar against the chill, Michael looked to Patrick. "I need you to help me solve a mystery, Pat. Was there another Irishman on the ship out besides us?"

Patrick rubbed a hand along the plaid of his trousers. "No. You'd think he'd have made himself known to us."

"Unless he refused to be seen with the likes of us,"

Michael said, "because he was a member of the Dead Rabbits."

Patrick stiffened. Then he ducked his head and lowered his voice as if suspecting the gang members to be hiding among the stumps surrounding them. "You saw a Dead Rabbit here?"

"Not saw," Michael assured him. "Maddie found a pair of red-striped trousers in someone's laundry. She thought they were mine."

"And a royal donnybrook that started, I imagine," Patrick said, straightening.

"We argued," Michael admitted, "but not about the trousers. It seems I may have appeared a bit too high-handed."

Patrick clutched his chest. "Ah, say it isn't so!"

Michael cuffed his shoulder. "Enough of that, now. We reached an agreement, though I've no liking for it. I'm to find work and keep myself out of her hair."

Patrick sighed. "And such lovely hair it is too."

Michael shook his head. "I'll not deny that. But the important thing right now is to figure out what the Dead Rabbits want with Seattle."

"Maybe it's nothing they're wanting," Patrick mused, scuffing his boots against each other and rubbing off the wet grass. "Those pants could be years old, used only for rough work now, their original purpose long forgotten."

"They didn't look old or all that worn," Michael told him, gaze rising to the trees on the ridge as he remembered. "And when we talked to the man whose sack we thought they came from, he denied all knowledge."

Patrick threw up his hands. "Well, there you are! He's lying."

"He wouldn't fit one leg in those pants," Michael

said, gaze returning to his friend. "They weren't his, Pat. I fear someone's starting trouble. That's why no one will hire us."

Patrick's face darkened. "It won't just be us hurt, then, but every Irishman in Seattle."

Not just Irishmen but Irishwomen. It could easily affect the success of Maddie's bakery.

She'd told him not to help her anymore. Even his minor assistance the other day with the supplies had put him on shaky ground. But surely finding and stopping the danger benefited him and Pat as much as it did Maddie. He wasn't really helping her for her sake.

"Is there a way to find out if others have been affected?" he asked his friend.

"I can ask the fellows I've become acquainted with on me rounds," Patrick offered. "But if trouble's starting here, we can't sit idly by. I'd call everyone to a meeting one evening, but I have no place to offer."

Neither did he. Then he realized he knew a spot that was unfrequented and easily accessed.

"There's the alley behind the bakery," Michael said. "No one but Maddie uses it, with no businesses beyond hers yet. It has no place to sit, but the meeting shouldn't take long. I'll invite Hennessy."

"Is he the big fellow at the main boardinghouse?" Patrick asked. When Michael nodded, he waved a hand. "Save yourself the trouble. I'll ask him myself. He's only two doors down from me."

"Fine. Tell them to come by Sunday afternoon at two. Most of them should have time off then. In the meantime, keep your eyes open. If there's a gang member in Seattle, I want to know who it is and why he's here."

Before danger came anywhere near Maddie and the children.

* * *

Maddie knew she should be pleased. Ciara and Aiden had returned from school with stories of new friends and new things they were learning. She'd figured out how to send them lunches in pails like the other children carried. The bakery and her laundry business were doing well enough that she could afford to have the lock fixed on the rear door. And Michael had been diligently seeking work for the past few days.

She saw little of him during the day, and he spent the evenings at the Kellogg store working off the cost of the supplies he'd accepted without her approval. The only time their paths crossed was when they rose in the morning and when they all ate dinner together.

But she had to admit those were her two favorite times of the day. For one thing, he made her tea every morning.

"And shouldn't you be focusing on your own needs, Mr. Haggerty?" she'd asked as she'd accepted the cup from him in the dim light.

He'd shrugged. "I have to make it for myself. Adding a bit more isn't any bother."

He'd assisted at dinner with a similar excuse. "Everyone is pitching in. Why not me?" He'd winked at Maddie. "I have to keep my right to complain, don't I?"

Really, the man could be exasperating. Adorable, but exasperating.

"Don't you like help?" Aiden asked as he stirred the batter for the cake she was trying that day. True to his word, her little brother rose with her every morning and supported her where he could after school while Ciara kept busy with chores, reading and visiting her new friends. Aiden swept the floor, brought Maddie ingredients from the larder and scrubbed the pans. Some of the customers had even taken to giving him pennies when he held the door open for them. Maddie knew he was squirreling away the money under his bed for something special.

"I like your help," Maddie told him, pulling out the pan she'd need for baking. "You've a quick mind and a willing heart."

"So does Michael," Aiden pointed out, stirring so hard he splattered creamy batter on his cheek. "And he's a lot bigger, so he can do more."

"But Michael has his own life to be living," Maddie protested, setting the pan beside the bowl and wiping butter along the bottom and sides. "We can't be holding him back. It isn't fair to him."

Aiden stopped stirring with a frown. "Will he leave us, then?"

He sounded so worried Maddie had to give him a hug. "He'll find himself a job and move into a house all his own. You want such good for him, don't you?"

"Yes," Aiden said, spoon slowly starting to move again. "I guess so. But I like having him around."

So did she. Too much. And that would never do.

Still, she was congratulating herself on her success and preparing to take her first month's payment up the hill to Clay Howard when Michael put his foot down.

They'd been eating an early dinner so she'd have time to deliver the money and return before dark, but when she told Ciara to watch Aiden in the meantime, Michael straightened over his split-pea-and-ham soup.

"You can't go alone."

Maddie chuckled, dipping her spoon to catch a fat piece of ham. "I most certainly can. This is a free country, so it is."

Ciara and Aiden glanced between the two of them.

"Have you forgotten the robbery?" Michael countered. "You shouldn't wander around Seattle carrying large sums of money. That's asking for trouble."

"As if anyone would suspect me of having large sums of money," Maddie scoffed. "Besides, this isn't Five Points, you know."

A shadow crossed his face, and she wished she hadn't brought up home. She knew he was trying to forget that time.

"That doesn't mean there's no crime," he insisted. He set down his spoon. "If you're going, I'm coming with you."

"And what about your work for Mr. Kellogg?" Maddie argued. "I won't be putting another burden on you."

"It's not a burden," he said, that gritty tone creeping back into his voice. As if he heard it too, he took a deep breath and forced a smile. "I can work at Kelloggs' after we're done. It doesn't matter when the shelves are stocked so long as they're ready for customers in the morning."

"I think you take too much on yourself, Mr. Haggerty," Maddie said with a shake of her head.

"Perhaps I do," he replied, smile growing. "But, as a wise woman said, it's a free country. If I decide to stretch my legs and happen to be going the same direction you are, that's no one's business but my own."

Maddie laughed.

Ciara giggled. "Maybe it would do you both good to take a walk together. In the moonlight." She wiggled her eyebrows.

"Ew," Aiden said, but he returned to his soup nonetheless.

In the end, Maddie decided to accept Michael's escort up the hill. He might be worried about creatures of the two-footed variety; she was more concerned about the four-footed. It wasn't unknown for bears and cougars to be spotted along the edges of the city, and deer often still wandered down the streets in the evening and early-morning hours. Michael looked a great deal more intimidating than she ever would.

It was a nice evening, as if Seattle clung to a few warm memories of summer before winter's chill breezed across the Sound. As they reached the top of the hill, the mountain rose in the distance, white snow turning pink in the setting sun.

Michael stopped and gaped at it. "What is that?"

"Mount Rainier, they call it," Maddie told him, smiling at his obvious surprise. "Though Clay told us the natives named it Tahoma, meaning mother of waters. Sure-n but every major river in these parts has the mountain to thank for its birth."

Michael shook his head. "Why haven't I seen it before?"

"She likes to hide behind the rain and clouds," Maddie explained. "You never know when she'll pop out."

He chuckled as they started forward again. "Who'd think a little rain could hide that?"

"Or that," Maddie said. She nodded toward the house at the top of the hill and had the satisfaction of seeing Michael stop once more in his tracks.

Clay and Allegra had both been raised in Boston society, so it had come as no surprise to anyone who knew them that they'd built one of the finest homes in Seattle. Unlike the Terry house that Maddie admired, the Howard house was less ornate, with a single story capped by a low roof and a massive porch that wrapped around three sides of the house. The glass windows spilled light out onto the stone-paved walk as Maddie and Michael approached, and she could hear the tinkling sound of a spinet piano from inside.

The housekeeper let them in.

"Miss Maddie," the older woman said with a benevolent smile. Her brown-eyed gaze drifted over Michael and widened. "Mrs. Howard will be so pleased that you called."

"Thank you, Mrs. Adams," Maddie said as the woman turned with a swish of her black skirts to lead them deeper into the house. Maddie had considered applying for the position of housekeeper before her friend Rina had encouraged her to pursue her dream of baking. She found herself thankful that the tasks of polishing the fine wood floors and dusting all the furniture Clay had had brought up from San Francisco were not hers.

The housekeeper led them into the parlor, where a crimson rug and roaring fire added warmth to the whitewashed walls.

"Maddie!" Allegra's daughter, Gillian, slid off the bench of the spinet. The five-year-old ran up to Maddie in a flurry of petticoats and hugged her fiercely. "I missed you!"

Maddie hugged her back. "And I missed you, me darling girl. Ask your Mama to bring you down to the bakery one day soon. I have a surprise for you."

Gillian released her to gaze up with wide dark blue eyes. "A cake?" she guessed.

"A new friend," Maddie answered with a smile.

Gillian glanced over at Michael with a frown. "He's kind of big."

Michael laughed and crouched beside her, putting his head still a good foot above her golden hair. "Better now?"

She smiled at him. "You're funny."

"And you are incorrigible," her mother said, coming into the room. As always, Allegra Banks Howard moved with grace and dignity, black hair swept back from her oval face. Maddie was surprised to see her press a hand to her back and grimace as she joined them. "Forgive me. I'm not moving very fast right now and probably won't for a good five months more. That's why I missed services this week."

"Mama's making me a sister," Gillian announced.

As Maddie beamed at her friend, Allegra blushed. "Or a brother," she reminded the girl.

Gillian shook her golden curls. "A sister. There are too many boys here."

Allegra put a hand to her daughter's shoulder as Michael rose. "And speaking of boys, why don't you go help Mrs. Adams tell your father we have company?"

Gillian beamed, obviously pleased to have been given such an important task, and hurried out of the room.

"Allegra Howard, allow me to present Mr. Michael Haggerty, late of New York," Maddie said with a smile to her friend. "He brought me my sister and brother."

Allegra held out her hand before her amethyst-colored fine silk skirts as if greeting royalty. "Mr. Haggerty, a pleasure. Did your wife not come with you?"

Michael shook her hand and his head at the same time. "I'm a bachelor, Mrs. Howard."

Allegra glanced around him, midnight brows raised at Maddie. "Oh, really. How interesting."

Oh, no! She'd been afraid of just such a reaction. The last thing she needed was for her friend to start matchmaking.

"Mr. Haggerty came west for a fresh start," Maddie told Allegra. "He's been helping at the bakery only until he can find other work."

Michael glanced at her, brows down, as if he wondered why she had phrased things so carefully. She wasn't about to admit her fears for her friend's intentions.

Allegra tapped her chin with one long finger. "Clay might know of places with positions open. He's acquainted with every business owner in Seattle." Her smile broadened as she looked to the door. "Clay, come meet Mr. Haggerty. He's a friend of Maddie's, and he's looking for work."

Clay Howard came into the room, Gillian up in his arms. Maddie had always found Clay a presentable fellow, but now she couldn't help comparing him with Michael. Both men were tall and well built, with broad shoulders and strong legs. But the blond-haired Clay stood relaxed, confident in his character and accomplishments. Michael's shoulders came up as the man joined them, his stance widening as if he was determined to prove himself. The two men shook hands.

"Pleased to meet you, Haggerty," Clay said. "There's always room in Seattle for a fellow looking to make good."

Maddie leaned forward, hoping to hear of a likely position for Michael, but Allegra put her hand on Maddie's arm and tilted her head.

"A word with you?" she whispered.

Maddie nodded and turned aside, leaving the men to discuss various opportunities in the area while Gillian toyed with the silver button on Clay's waistcoat.

"Is this fellow from your past?" Allegra continued in a whisper, dark blue eyes so like her daughter's shining with possibilities. "Is he why you don't talk about New York?"

She had to put a stop to any such thoughts. "I never met him before he arrived on the pier," Maddie assured her. "And there is no gentleman in my past. I don't like talking about New York because my father and step-mother died there."

"And you had to leave your sister and brother behind to come west," Allegra remembered. "I'm so glad Clay was able to help you bring them out. I just didn't realize you were paying for a fellow to join them."

Maddie grimaced. "I didn't pay for a fellow. I paid for a woman to help me with the bakery and laundry. He had a spot of trouble in New York, so his aunt sent him instead."

By the way Allegra twisted her head to look at Maddie from the corners of her eyes, her friend was certain there was more to the story.

"That's the truth!" Maddie protested. "He's merely paying off his passage while he looks for other work. I don't like to encourage the gentlemen, and you know it."

"You never do more than flirt," Allegra agreed, relaxing. "But I find this fellow intriguing. He's handsome, eager to work and, by the sound of it, good with children."

"He's also bossy, determined and likely to put his nose into other people's business with the excuse that he's being helpful," Maddie countered.

"Sounds like someone else I know," Allegra said with a smile. "You!"

Maddie humphed. The sound was so much like Ciara's that she felt a smile forming. "Oh, very well. So I like to help my friends. And I'll not deny it's handy hav-

ing him around from time to time. He insisted on coming with me this evening."

Allegra sobered. "I'm glad he did. More and more
people arrive every week, Maddie. Not all of them are
as brave and hardworking as the first settlers. Several
of the businesses Clay supports have seen troubles
recently—supplies stolen, property defaced. He's trying to determine who's behind it."

"We've had a spot of trouble at the bakery as well,"
Maddie admitted. When Allegra stiffened, she hurried
on. "Nothing we cannot handle, so you don't go worrying for me."

Allegra frowned. "And how can I not worry? You're
my friend, Maddie. I want the best for you."

Maddie couldn't help glancing to where Michael
was laughing over something Clay had said. He wanted
the best for her and Ciara and Aiden, that much was
clear. And, as she'd told Aiden, she wanted the best for
Michael—a fine job, a home. Surely as good as he was
with the children, he'd want a family of his own one
day. That thought left a lump in her throat.

Worse, though, was the next thought. If trouble was
coming to Seattle, did she want him anywhere else but
at her side?

Chapter Fifteen

Michael made way for Maddie and Allegra to rejoin him and Clay by the stone hearth, as Gillian wiggled to be set down. He hadn't been sure of the tall steely-eyed businessman, for all the fellow was married to a dear friend of Maddie's. He'd half expected Clay to offer him a loan, at exorbitant interest.

Instead, the man had given him several leads on possible jobs as well as permission to use him as a reference. It was clear to Michael the clever entrepreneur had his hand in a dozen enterprises all over town. Very likely he'd be well respected by the other local business owners, several of whom it seemed owed him their start here. Surely his support would go a long way toward convincing an employer to hire Michael.

As Gillian returned to the spinet, Allegra settled herself next to her husband and laid a hand on his arm, purple skirts reflecting the light from the fire. "Clay, I was telling Maddie about the troubles your businesses have been having, and she said the bakery has been plagued too."

Clay frowned, glance going to Maddie first, and then to Michael. Michael stood up straighter under it.

"That makes the fourth, then," Clay said as Gillian's music rose from the other side of the room. "I've had reports from Butler's stamp mill, Disney's newspaper and Aherne's tailor shop as well, but I can't see the pattern. None of my other shops have been harmed, so the troublemaker isn't lashing out at me."

Michael frowned. Why would the Howards expect someone to target them?

As if she'd seen his look, Maddie nodded to him. "Allegra and Clay had trouble from their relatives on the way out," she explained. "The scoundrels threatened to take Gillian away."

Clay glanced to where the little girl was running her chubby fingers up and down the keys, golden-haired head cocked as if she listened to every note with approval.

"That's been settled," Clay said, and by the firm tone of his voice, Michael was sure the matter had been finished to the businessman's satisfaction. "It's not the Howard family troubling us this time. And it can't be something between the owners. They never met before they came to Seattle. The buildings are in different parts of town, of different types, with different clientele."

"You said the owners' names were Butler, Disney and Aherne," Michael put in, feeling as if the room had chilled. "That's a pattern, all right. They're all Irish."

Maddie paled even as Clay stiffened.

"But what would anyone have against the Irish here?" Allegra asked, glancing around at them all.

At the spinet, Gillian hit a wrong chord, the sound as jarring as Michael's assumption.

"There was prejudice aplenty in New York," Maddie told her. "Why should we be surprised it followed us here?" She wrapped one arm about the waist of her green gingham gown, and Michael had to force his hands to his sides to keep from putting his own arm around her shoulders.

"Because it's Washington Territory," Allegra said. Michael had thought her the calm and cool lady of the house with her black hair and midnight-blue eyes. Now those eyes snapped fire. "People came here to escape such nonsense," she insisted, "not perpetuate it."

"That's true enough, Allie," Clay said. "But just in case Mr. Haggerty has the right of it, I'll tell all my partners to remain alert." He looked to Michael. "I assume you've talked with Sheriff Wyckoff."

"Deputy McCormick is aware of the problem," Michael assured him.

Clay nodded as if confident in the lawman's ability to solve the problem, but Michael couldn't feel so certain. It was quite possible the trouble could escalate, especially if the Dead Rabbits were behind it.

Talk turned to other things then, polite, civilized. But Michael couldn't help wondering what lay beyond the golden light of the house on the hill. Were there really men in Seattle intent on harming all those who claimed any allegiance to Ireland? Or was he letting his own fears get the better of him?

Before they left, Maddie took Clay aside. She pressed the money into her benefactor's hand, and Michael saw the man smile at her with obvious pride. He felt his own chest swelling with pride for her as well.

"She's the most hardworking, caring person I've ever met," Allegra volunteered as she stood beside Michael.

"You won't get an argument from me," Michael replied. "She rises in the middle of the night to start work and doesn't stop until after sundown, all so her brother and sister will have a better life than she had."

"And all without asking for help," Allegra told him. "I'm not sure what made her decide to approach Clay for a loan, but I'm pleased she trusted us to that extent." She smiled at Michael. "Everyone loves her baking."

"Everyone loves her," Michael answered with a chuckle. "She has a loyal following."

"And yet she has never introduced me to a gentleman or invited him to our home," Allegra informed him. "I suspect you are special to her, Mr. Haggerty."

Michael shook his head. "If I am it's only because I can help her with Ciara and Aiden."

"I think you are too humble, sir," she said. "But I am glad we agree that Maddie is a dear. She deserves a gentleman who appreciates that."

Though her tone remained kind, Michael could hear the iron under the words. Allegra cared enough for her friend to warn him that if he didn't appreciate her he ought to leave her life before any damage was done.

Maddie returned to their sides then, and she and Michael said their goodbyes and headed back to the bakery.

They'd stayed long enough at the Howards that night had fallen. Allegra had pressed a lantern into Michael's hand, and now he held it up to light their way. A tart breeze from the Sound brushed his face as he and Maddie walked down the hill. Insects chirped from the forest, and something with wide wings soared across the moon. It was hard to believe violence stirred on so peaceful a night.

Maddie puffed out a breath as if her thoughts were as dark as his. "I'm not liking this idea that the Irish are being chosen for attack," she said, one hand on Michael's arm as they negotiated the bumps to cross the skid road. "Allegra's right. We all came here to get away from such things."

"At least you and I did," Michael agreed as they reached the other side. "Some may have brought their prejudices with them."

As if to prove as much, raucous laughter echoed from one of the buildings near the mill.

Maddie hastened around the corner onto Washington Street. "You may be right," she murmured. "And though I told you I had no need for help, I was glad you were there tonight, Michael."

Something inside him warmed at her words. It seemed like a long time since he'd felt truly useful.

They turned onto Second Avenue, and he took her arm to help her step up onto the boardwalk. They reached the door of the bakery, putting out a hand for the latch at the same time, fingers brushing. Michael clutched her hand and held it a moment, unwilling to part.

"You should be proud of yourself, Maddie," he told her. "I'm sure Ciara could have suggested any number of ways to spend that money. Instead, you paid down your debt."

She gazed up at him, red hair turned pale in the moonlight. "We have that in common, you and I. We don't allow a debt to stand for long."

Another moment, and he'd kiss her again. Indeed, the urge to do so was nearly overpowering. Overhead, he heard a penny whistle playing in tune with his heart.

Something flew past them to hit the lantern with a clang. The vibration rattled up Michael's arm, sending the lantern tumbling. Out snuffed the wick, wrapping them in darkness. Before he could react, he felt Maddie grab his arm and tug him down even as another missile grazed his cheek. The tinkle of breaking glass told him the troublemaker had hit the bakery window.

"Get inside," Michael told Maddie, reaching up to

twist the latch with one hand and push her forward with the other.

She scrambled past him into the bakery, making way for him on the floor beside her, but Michael turned for the street, trying in vain to make out a darker shape among the shadows.

"Who's there?" he demanded. "You've no call to be harassing innocent folk."

In the silence, he thought he heard ragged breathing. A moment later, and feet pounded on the boardwalk across from him, running away.

Michael surged to his feet, ready to give chase, but something caught his pant leg.

"Don't you be going out there, Michael Haggerty," Maddie begged. "I've already lost three people in my family. I'll not be losing another."

Maddie clung to the rough wool of Michael's pant leg, feeling as if her breath had disappeared with her courage. Who was out there? Why attack her bakery?

How could she keep Michael safe?

He crouched down beside her, a darker shape in the night. "It's all right, Maddie," he said. "Whoever did this is gone. I heard him leave."

Bunching her skirts in one hand, she let him help her up. Her boot crunched on glass as in the front of the shop.

She nearly grabbed him again as he turned toward the boardwalk. Then she saw him bend to retrieve something. A shiver shook her.

"What was the meaning of that?" she demanded as Michael came inside and closed the door, lantern in one hand. "He could have started a fire, striking the lantern that way. Or hit one of us."

Michael placed the lantern on the display counter and set about relighting it. As the glow filled the shop, Maddie could see the jagged edge that was all that remained of one of the panes of glass in her window.

She blew out a breath. "And now I'll have to be fixing that."

"This only proves that the Irish are being targeted," he said, lifting the lantern higher. The light glittered off the hunk of granite sitting on the counter. So that's what the villain had been throwing.

"This proves *I'm* being targeted," Maddie corrected him. "And I still say Mr. Terry is a far more likely suspect than some nameless fellow on the outs with anyone Irish. Mr. Terry owns other businesses, you know. Perhaps he's Clay's competition in every area."

"Perhaps," Michael said, voice doubtful. She glanced his way, then gasped.

"Your cheek!" she cried, hurrying forward.

His fingers flew up to his face even as she converged on him. She cupped his chin and turned him to the light. Below the sweep of black hair an angry red line welled.

"Oh, the villain!" Maddie dropped his chin, hands fisting. "He could have put out your eye!"

Michael shook his head as he lowered his hand. "I was facing away from him, Maddie. The worst he could do was give me this scratch."

"A scratch, he calls it," Maddie muttered, snatching the lantern and stalking for the kitchen. He followed her in and watched as she wet a rag and returned to apply it to the red mark.

"You just hold that in place, now," she told him. "The cold will help the swelling come down."

His blue gaze twinkled over the rag. "Yes, Dr. O'Rourke."

Maddie humphed at his teasing, but a thump overhead reminded her of her duty. "I'll see to Ciara and Aiden. By the sound of it, they were too busy playing to pay any heed to the creature at their door, but I'd like to make sure."

He nodded. "I'll put a patch over the glass for now."

She opened her mouth to protest, but he raised a brow and she decided not to fight over the matter.

"Where do you keep the hammer and nails?" he asked.

"I've a few nails left from the building of the bakery," Maddie told him. "Top shelf of the larder. I've no hammer, but I make do with my frying pan."

He laughed and headed for the larder. Amelia Batterby streaked out of his way and zipped up the stairs.

"And a fine watch cat you are," Maddie called, following her. "Couldn't you be meowing to warn us?"

Ciara and Aiden hastily righted the chairs as Maddie entered, standing with eyes wide and mouths tight and looking nearly as worried as the cat.

"And just what were you two doing?" Maddie asked, eyes narrowing.

"Testing ourselves," Aiden said. "In case we get lost in the wilderness."

"Which I told him would never happen," Ciara put in with a look to her brother. "You're not going to catch me in the woods alone."

Maddie decided the less said the better at the moment. "Michael and I had some trouble coming in. Did you see anyone, hear anything?"

Ciara and Aiden both shook their heads.

"Did they steal the cakes?" Aiden asked, face stricken.

"As far as I know, they didn't enter the building this

time," Maddie told him. "They were throwing rocks at it instead."

Ciara rolled her eyes. "How childish."

"How vindictive," Maddie countered. "A rock nearly broke the lantern we borrowed from Mr. and Mrs. Howard. Another took out a pane in the window and scratched Michael's face."

Now Ciara looked stricken.

"I didn't see anything," Aiden said with a look to Ciara, who nodded again.

"I didn't hear anything either," she said. "Aiden was playing his *feadóg*."

"Not that loud!" he protested.

"No need for concern," Maddie said. "Michael and I will see to the matter. Go and get ready for bed now, and I'll hear your prayers."

Her sister and brother did not argue with her for once.

A short while later, she came back downstairs. Both Ciara and Aiden had asked God to stop the people who were bothering the bakery, her sister going so far as to ask the Lord for a hero, like one of the Dead Rabbits. Maddie still struggled to believe the Lord cared about such things. But He had kept her and Michael safe. Surely that was enough to ask.

She could not deny, however, that she had her own hero for whom to be thankful. Michael had taken a shingle of wood and nailed it in place to cover the hole. He'd also swept the glass from the boardwalk and shop floor, piling the three heavy rocks that had been their attacker's ammunition in a corner as if for evidence. The scratch on his face had faded from a fiery red to a blushing pink.

"You're a good man to have about, Mr. Haggerty,"

she told him as he leaned the broom into the corner of the kitchen.

He grinned at her. "And you're a sweet woman to allow me to help, Miss O'Rourke," he answered.

She didn't feel sweet. The injustice of the attack was like a coal inside her, burning red and hot. She wanted to lash out, demand answers. But there wasn't any reason to bother Deputy McCormick at this time of night. She could tell him about the trouble in the morning. For now, she had work to do and so did Michael.

"You best be going," she said. "I know you have to help Mr. Kellogg tonight."

"The shelves can wait a while longer," he assured her. "Are you all right?"

"Fine." She stalked to her worktable. "I didn't have a chance to prepare the trough before we left for the Howards. I'll just sift the flour now before I turn in."

He eyed her. "You usually go to bed by now."

Maddie whipped her apron about her and settled it into place. "And I'm usually ready for bed. Right now, I need to be doing. If you've a mind to help, join in."

In answer, he peeled off his coat.

Maddie sent him to the larder for the cask of flour while she pulled out the wooden frame she used for sifting and positioned it over the trough. When they'd been outfitting the building, Clay had been amazed by the size of the wooden box where she would mix her dough. Michael looked nearly as impressed as he returned to her side.

"You pour the flour, I'll agitate it," she said.

He hefted the wooden cask into his arms, muscles showing through the fabric of his sleeves. Maddie barely noticed the creamy-colored flour flowing.

"Shouldn't you be shaking that?" Michael asked, gaze amused.

Of course she should! Maddie rattled the wooden knob, and the frame shook back and forth, turning lumps into finer powder. Normally, she had to fill the sifter, then shake out the flour, repeating the process many times before she had enough in the trough. With Michael's help, they filled the trough in record time.

He returned the half-empty cask to the larder, then retrieved his coat, leaving white fingerprints on the blue fabric. "Get some rest. I'll see you in the morning."

Maddie reached up and brushed off the marks. His look caught hers, held her captive. She stood on tiptoe and pressed a kiss to his cheek. "Thank you, Michael, for everything."

Skin turning pinker than his scratch, he nearly fled the room. If she hadn't known better, she'd have thought something had scared him.

She knew the feeling. When the rocks had started hitting, her heart had jumped, but she hadn't feared for herself or the bakery. She'd been afraid something might happen to Michael.

And that fact scared her most of all.

Chapter Sixteen

It was a long night for Michael. After helping at the bakery, he went to Kelloggs' and finished stacking the latest goods in the right places. He thought maybe the busy work would keep his mind off Maddie, but it seemed as if he felt that kiss against his cheek through the entire evening.

She'd only meant it in thanks. He knew that. Why dwell on it? He wasn't willing to take the matter further and begin courting again. She'd made it clear she was not interested in marriage.

Still, he pushed himself hard to make sure he returned to the bakery before dawn, just in time to make tea for him and Maddie.

She yawned before burying her face in the rising steam. "Sure-n but I'll miss you when you move out, Michael Haggerty," she murmured, eyes half-closed.

And he'd miss this, he realized. These quiet moments, before Ciara and Aiden or most of the people in town were awake, had become precious to him. Maddie stumbled out of her room each morning, hair braided tight and dress clean and tidy even though her eyes were heavy. Breathing deep of the fragrant steam, she straightened her shoulders, smile curving up. It was like watching the rising sun paint the sky gold.

Still, he had a life to reclaim. He couldn't stay here forever, for all a part of him wanted to do just that.

"Today I'll be contacting those businesses Clay suggested," he told her as she sat across from him at the table, sipping her tea. "Depending on how long that takes, I may go straight to Kelloggs' afterward. Don't wait dinner for me."

She nodded, setting down her cup. "I'll be saying a prayer for you, but I know you'll find work today. You're too clever a lad to be left dangling."

"Thank you," he said. "You're sure you'll be all right?"

She rose with a chuckle and went to set her cup on the sideboard. "I'll be fine. I'll send word to Deputy McCormick about the incident last night. Perhaps we'll both have good things to report when next we see each other."

He rose to intercept her. "Here's hoping." Returning her gesture from the night before, he bent and kissed her cheek. She pulled away quickly, but he saw her touching her face with a smile as she hurried out, her shoes clattering on the stairs.

And once again, Maddie remained on his mind as he set out.

The first three business owners had excuses for not hiring, all logical. One had just filled the opening, another wanted someone with experience specific to the job and the third had decided to expand his offerings a bit more before hiring. The fourth, however, made no bones about his opinion.

"I don't hire the Irish," he said, beefy body blocking the doorway of his shop as if to prevent Michael from entering. "Not even on the recommendation of Clay Howard. Go work with your own kind, if you can find one honest and sober enough to do a day's work."

Michael felt his fists bunching, but he bit back harsh words and left. A mind that closed wouldn't have been persuaded no matter how eloquently he presented his case. The good Lord had said not to throw pearls to pigs.

He wasn't hopeful for the last business Clay had suggested. Michael had no experience working as a blacksmith, and he knew he was much older than the lads usually taken on as apprentices. He ducked out of the rain into the wide wooden building near the waterfront. Darkness and heat wrapped around him, the sharp smell of smoke poking his nose. He made out a number of iron tools lining the walls, surrounding a forge of rough stone with a chimney blackened by smoke.

An older fellow with a brown leather apron tied around his broad frame straightened from the anvil and lifted a pair of tongs that held an ax blade fading from a glowing red. "Is this good enough for your brother?"

Another man stepped out of the shadows. He wore a fine brown suit, bow tie at his throat, and Michael could not imagine why he would be in Seattle or what he could do for a living here. The dandy cocked his head, golden-brown hair spilling to one side. "Better. But perhaps it needs a little more of a curve. Drew tends to swing hard."

"And why wouldn't he, big fellow that he is?" the smith grumbled, running his free hand back through his thinning hair. By the amount of soot on his fingers, Michael couldn't tell whether his hair was gray or merely coated with the by-products of his work.

He must have caught sight of Michael just then, for

he lowered the ax and jerked up his double chin in greeting. "Can I help you, mister?"

Michael took a step forward, nodding to both men. "I hope so. My name is Michael Haggerty. I'm looking for work, and Clay Howard thought you might need someone."

The smith shoved the blade back into the coals. "I might. Do you know anything about smithing?"

"No," Michael admitted. "I worked the docks in New York. But I'm good with my hands and I'm willing to learn."

The smith humphed. He pulled a different piece of iron from the fire with his battered tongs, set it on the anvil and hammered, the metal chiming with each blow.

The other man eyed Michael and raised his voice over the din. "You aren't looking to log, are you?"

Michael smiled. "I'm looking for any job that will allow me to support myself and pay off my debts."

"Debts, eh?" The smith held up the iron, then plunged it back into the fire. "Gambling man?" he asked Michael as the ax blade started glowing again.

"No, sir," Michael said. "Someone here funded my passage from New York, and I want to pay her back."

The other man started. "Her? I know who you are! You're Maddie's fellow."

Michael nearly cringed at the name. The smith set down his tongs, red-rimmed eyes narrowing.

"You're the man who's been helping Miss O'Rourke at her bakery," he said, tone like an accusation.

Michael refused to lie. "I am. Though I'm no baker either."

"No, but you must be a hard worker if Maddie puts up with you," the other man said. He came to nudge the smith with his shoulder. "What do you say, Smitty? You know you can't keep up with the volume, even with the new fancy ironworks opening. It's taken a week for you to fix Drew's ax as it is."

"Maybe if your brother wasn't such a demanding fellow, I might have gotten it done faster," the smith complained. He eyed Michael. "Come closer, if you've a mind to work. You saw how I used the tongs. Pick up a piece of iron from the fire and cut it through on the hardy there." He pointed to a triangle of metal embedded in one end of the anvil.

Michael moved to the fire. Up close, the heat pushed at him like a live thing, the smoke singeing his face. With two pairs of eyes on him, he knew better than to flinch. Taking the tongs, he squinted to peer into the flames, then reached in, skin heating.

Father, guide me now.

Feeling as if his breath burned in his lungs, he drew out one of the iron bars that glowed nearly yellow. He used the tongs to hold it steady on the point of the hardy, then took the smith's hammer and brought it down once, twice. The ring of metal echoed in his ears, followed by the soft thunk of the iron dropping to the dirt floor.

The smith's customer started laughing. "Maybe I better take my business to Mr. Haggerty in the future."

The smith scowled at him a moment, then turned to Michael. "No experience, eh? What made you pick that piece?"

"It was glowing brightest," Michael admitted, not knowing whether it was a good reason. "I thought that meant it might be softer and easier to cut."

"Did you now?" The smith let out a cackle. "Smart fellow. You're hired. You can start this minute. There's wood that needs chopping for the fire and fresh water to be brought from the pump for cooling."

Michael stared at him. "You're hiring me?"

The smith spat on his dirt floor. "Didn't I just say so? Now, hop to it, fellow, before I change my mind."

"Give him a moment to catch his breath, Smitty," his customer chided him. He held out a hand. "Congratulations, Haggerty. Glad to make your acquaintance. I'm James Wallin."

Michael nodded, accepting his hand. So this was the man throwing the elaborate wedding Maddie thought would make her famous in Seattle. "Maddie's spoken of you."

"All good, I'm sure," he said with a grin Michael couldn't help returning. "Just don't work too hard for Smitty here. Maddie's going to need your help baking for my wedding. I wore out my brother's ax clearing off my property and getting things ready for my bride. Now I mean to throw the biggest party Seattle has ever seen, and you're all invited."

Smitty snorted. "Always the best for James Wallin."

"Always the best for Rina," James corrected him. "She was raised as a princess, and I intend to show her she's queen in my books."

His bride must be wealthy if James could liken her upbringing to that of a princess. Michael had heard of such families in New York. The newspapers were full of news about the Astors and Vanderbilts.

"You spoil her at the start, you'll have to spoil her the rest of your life," Smitty predicted, bending to lift his water bucket. He threw it at Michael, who caught it. "Tell him, Haggerty."

James eyed him, but Michael shook his head. "I'd be the last one to tell you how to treat your betrothed."

"Why?" Smitty demanded. "Miss O'Rourke leading you in a merry dance?"

"Miss O'Rourke and I are not betrothed," Michael said. "She paid the passage for someone to bring her sister and brother out to her. I happened to be the one available."

"So now you're a nursemaid too?" Smitty looked so shocked that Michael wouldn't have been surprised to hear him make good on his threat and rescind his offer of employment.

"What a man won't do for love," James teased.

Love? No, what he felt for Maddie couldn't be love. After what had happened in New York, he wasn't ready to fall in love again, certainly not after knowing a woman only a week or so.

Still, the question remained—what exactly did he feel for Maddie O'Rourke?

The day flew by faster than usual for Maddie. She had Aiden and Ciara take word to the sheriff's office on their way to school and received a visit from Deputy McCormick shortly thereafter. The lawman examined the rocks, window and boardwalk, face set and eyes narrowed as if he didn't like what he'd found.

"Well?" Maddie asked as he straightened away from the rough planks. "Any idea who might have done this?"

"Not at the moment," he said. "But I'll ask around."

Maddie threw up her hands. "That's what you said last time, and you never found my rose extract."

"I found the empty bottle," he said, voice rougher than usual. "Someone poured the contents out behind the university. One of the male students complained of the smell."

Maddie lowered her hands. "But that makes no sense. That extract was costly and hard to come by here. Why steal it to throw it away?"

"Maybe he didn't know what he was stealing," Deputy McCormick reasoned. "Those patent medicines all look alike to me. Or maybe once he discovered what it was, he realized he couldn't sell it here without someone asking questions."

Maddie bristled. "Or he never intended to sell it at all. Now do you see what I was saying about Mr. Terry?"

He held up a hand. "Terry is one of the most well-liked fellows in the territory. I'll keep an eye on him, but I can't see him being so petty as to throw rocks at your bakery in the middle of the night."

In truth, neither could she. But the alternative left her even more angry, for it meant someone else in Seattle had something against her.

She was glad for the hustle and bustle of work because it kept her too busy to ruminate about either her adversary or a certain handsome Irishman who had stolen a kiss that morning. She was so busy serving her starving customers that afternoon, in fact, that she didn't immediately notice Michael's entry. It wasn't until she was shutting the door behind the last of the gentlemen buyers that she could turn and smile at him as he stood in the shadows of the stairs.

And then she rushed up to him.

"What have you done to yourself now?" she demanded, taking his arm and dragging him into the light from the front window.

He touched the red patch on his cheek and grimaced as if it hurt. "I got a little too close to the forge, but I'll know better next time." His smile turned up as his gaze met hers. "I did it, Maddie. I found work. You're looking at Seattle's newest blacksmith."

Joy bubbled up inside her, and she threw her arms

around him. "Oh, congratulations, me darling boy! I knew you could do it!"

She leaned back to look at him, and the warmth in his eyes robbed her of speech, of breath. She knew if she didn't move right then, he was going to kiss her.

She couldn't seem to budge.

"Are they gone, then?" Aiden asked, coming down the stairs. He stopped and stared at the pair of them, face scrunching. "Are you going to kiss her?"

"It had crossed my mind," Michael said, but he stepped back from Maddie.

"Did you need something, Aiden?" Maddie asked, feeling as if she'd stepped too near a fire as well.

Her brother glanced between the two of them. "No, that's all right. I was just wondering if you had any cookies left."

"I saved some just for you," Maddie told him. "I'll go fetch them." With a bob of her head in farewell to Michael, she fled for the kitchen.

What was wrong with her? She'd actually encouraged him to kiss her, throwing herself in his arms that way. Of course she was happy for him, but she knew that wasn't the entire reason for her reaction. Despite all her intentions, despite all her misgivings, she'd developed feelings for Michael Haggerty.

And why wouldn't she? He was a steady rock in the mad swirling river of her life, someone she could always count on. But that was an illusion. Sooner or later the stress of life would prove too much, turning warm feelings into cold ash that blew away in the wind. She'd promised herself she wouldn't live the way her father and stepmother had lived, the way so many families lived in Five Points. She refused to pass on such heartache to Ciara and Aiden. They deserved better.

So, for the next few days, she focused on her work and her siblings. She picked up, washed and delivered another batch of laundry. She did her usual baking, managed to add sugar cookies and her father's *barmbrack* loaf to her offerings and finished testing the last of the recipes she would need for James and Rina's wedding, to Aiden's satisfied delight.

She also made sure to stop by Nora's corner, pick up the rest of Ciara's clothing and pay her friend for her work.

"Tell Ciara she can dye that skirt," Nora said as she folded the clothes for Maddie to carry home. "Use the blue paper that covers your sugar and mix it with a little vinegar and alum in a kettle." A bolt of fabric slid off one of the haphazard piles behind her, and she stopped to lift it back into place.

"That will give her something useful to do," Maddie said. "I'm struggling to know how to deal with her, Nora, for all Michael Haggerty seems to have discovered the secret."

"If you want, I can teach her to sew," Nora offered, giving the pile one last shove and a glare that dared it to move again. "That's one of the ways my brother kept me out of mischief."

Maddie had a hard time imagining her friend as a troublemaker. "I'll think on the matter." She took one of the dresses to fold while Nora folded the other.

"You must have a lot to think about lately," Nora said, hands busy and gray eyes downcast. "About your sister, about the bakery, about a certain gentleman from New York. What exactly do you intend to do with the fellow?"

She made it sound as if Michael was a dress Maddie had outgrown or a hat that had gone out of style. "It's not up to me," Maddie said. "He's found work with the blacksmith. When he's saved enough money, I expect he'll move into his own lodgings, and that will be that."

Nora glanced at her out of the corners of her eyes. "And will you be glad to see him go?"

She couldn't say that. She'd come to enjoy his company. "Ciara and Aiden and I will all miss him," she told her friend. "But he came here to start over, and we shouldn't hinder that."

"No indeed," Nora agreed, laying the last dress on the pile. "I hope your sister enjoys these. She seems to have very high standards." She smiled, broadening her already broad cheeks. "Almost as high as your standards for a husband."

"I've no such thing," Maddie declared. "Do you?"

Nora's gray gaze turned misty as she looked out over her small corner of the shop, as if she saw much farther than the dark wood walls and wooden spools of thread massed by color. "I doubt I'll ever marry, but if I can tell you the qualities I'd want in a husband—kindness, intelligence, creativity, determination and unswerving devotion to me and his Savior." She sighed as if the picture she saw in her mind was nothing short of perfection.

"Sure-n but I wonder how you can find such a paragon," Maddie said with a smile.

Nora lowered her gaze, cheeks darkening. "Oh, I haven't. Most likely he doesn't exist. But it's nice to dream." Humming to herself, she lifted Ciara's clothes and handed them to Maddie, then gave her a hug and sent her on her way.

Maddie walked back to the bakery, deep in thought. Funny how Nora had that effect on her. Her friend saw the world so differently. This idea of a perfect husband, held up as a comparison with all gentlemen, sounded like a recipe for disaster. Small wonder Nora had refused all suitors. Who couldn't help but be found lacking?

Still, Maddie couldn't help wondering what she would consider the perfect husband, if she were ever to convince herself to take a chance on marriage. Someone patient and kind, certainly. He would have to keep a civil tongue in his head the way Michael did. Definitely a man who was good with Ciara and Aiden, a man they could look up to like Michael. Someone who'd laugh with her in the good times and hold her through the bad the way he did. Someone who wouldn't grow cold in trouble.

She stopped on the street and hugged the clothes closer. Several bachelors hurrying past eyed her, then kept walking, as if they didn't want to deal with whatever had put that shocked expression on her face. She couldn't blame them. She wasn't sure she was willing to deal with it either.

For while Nora might not be able to envision the fellow she wanted to marry, Maddie had a real picture, and the man in her mind wore Michael's face.

Chapter Seventeen

Michael finished his first two days at the smithy feeling older and wiser. Muscles he hadn't known he never used ached. The red mark on his cheek was fading, but he'd singed the hair off his arm and burned a hole through the chest of a shirt before realizing he had to wear the apron at all times.

Still, Smitty was pleased with him, going so far as to offer his grimace of a smile as he counted out Michael's wages on Saturday afternoon.

"And a little more for your effort," he declared, dropping the coins into Michael's outstretched palm. "You're a good worker. I'll bless the day Clay Howard sent you to me."

Michael felt blessed as well. Working the forge was far hotter and dirtier than shifting freight on the docks, yet each time he finished a piece, something warmer than the forge wrapped around him. Out of a black, shapeless thing, he'd created something useful. There was satisfaction in that.

Perhaps that was why his head was high as he escorted Maddie, Ciara and Aiden to church on Sunday. The day was bright and clear, with the mountain gleaming above the trees on the ridge. Maddie was wearing her russet gown, hat perched on her curls, smile playing about her pink lips as she watched her brother and sister cavort. He couldn't help thinking he was leading the prettiest girl in town to her spot in the box pew.

You've brought me to a good place, Lord. Let my life reflect Your glory, not my own.

As if Maddie knew his thoughts and supported them, she took his hand. He looked at her askance, but her gaze was focused on the curly-haired minister stepping up to begin his sermon. Did she even know she had reached out? He should probably pull away, but the touch was warm, encouraging. He held her hand through the rest of the service.

Clay, Allegra and Gillian were waiting for them outside. The Howards had also dressed for services, Allegra in a blue gown with white piping along each scalloped edge of her collar and skirts, and Clay in a suit of fine brown wool. The little girl, in her frilly white frock with a sash as blue as her eyes, stared at Aiden, and he returned the considered look. Allegra and Maddie exchanged amused glances over their heads.

"I know where there's a black rock that turns red in the rain," Gillian said. "Want to see?"

Aiden nodded, and the two scurried off toward the side of the churchyard together.

"Don't go far," Allegra called after them.

"They won't listen," Ciara complained. "I'll go with them." She hurried after her brother and his new friend.

Clay took a step closer to Michael and lowered his voice as if mindful of the parishioners exiting around them. "I checked with my other partners. You were right. Everyone who's been robbed or had buildings damaged has been Irish."

Maddie met Michael's gaze, and he could see the concern darkening her brown eyes.

"Tell them about the sign," Allegra urged, taking his arm.

Michael leaned closer and felt Maddie doing the same.

"In the last week," Clay told them, "two of the buildings had a sign painted on them, a four-leaf clover on fire."

Fire? Something twisted inside Michael at the word. Surely no one would be so stupid as to start a fire here, with wood to burn everywhere. Did Seattle even have a fire company yet? He'd heard no blowing of horns calling them to duty.

Beside him, Maddie shivered. "Is it a threat, then?"

"That's the way my partners took it." Clay put his free hand to her arm. "Look out for yourself, Maddie. If you have any more trouble, let me know immediately."

"Clay's already brought the matter to the sheriff," Allegra explained. "Surely something can be done."

Michael wanted to share her certainty, but too many people charged with upholding the law had looked the other way when it came to gang violence in New York. After a firefighter had been drafted despite assurances such volunteers were exempt, the men of the number thirty-three fire company had led a mob of mostly Irish men and women into the draft office three years ago, destroying property, threatening lives.

And even when the law officers had stood strong, they had been beaten down by the mob. Fire and destruction were the calling cards of the Dead Rabbits. Yet why target Irish concerns when it was the Irish they claimed to protect?

Though the sun remained high, the day seemed

darker as he walked Maddie and the children home. He'd been feeling as if his life was finally his own again. How could he relax, knowing that Maddie, Ciara and Aiden might be in danger?

As the children stopped to gaze at the display of brightly striped candy in a shop window, he drew Maddie aside.

"I'll have enough pay by this time next week to discharge my debt to Mr. Kellogg," he told her, fighting the urge to take her in his arms. "After that I could move out while I pay you over time for my passage. But with everything going on, I don't like leaving the three of you alone."

She hesitated. Would her pride keep him out even now?

"We'll be fine," she assured him as they started forward once more. "You heard Allegra—the law is keeping an eye out for trouble."

So was Aiden, it seemed, for he pointed to the side of the bakery as it came into view. "What's that?"

Michael caught his breath even as Maddie's steps faltered.

Painted in green on the side of the bakery, the color still dripping like the icing on one of Maddie's rolls, was a four-leaf clover, flames rising from the wilting leaves.

Just the sight of the clover sent Maddie's stomach plummeting. She'd told herself these attacks had to be Mr. Terry's retaliation against her bakery's success. But she could not convince herself the dapper businessman would paint a fiery shamrock on her wall or even hire someone to do it.

Michael put his arm about her shoulders as if to shelter her and nodded to Aiden. "The sheriff's office is on the corner by Kelloggs'," he said. "See if you can fetch him back for us."

Her brother ran.

"I'll check the rest of the bakery," Maddie said, almost afraid of what she might find.

"I'll make sure Amelia Batterby is safe," Ciara said, hurrying after her.

Maddie thought Michael might accompany her. His sturdy presence would have been welcome as she checked for her money canister and supplies, finding them all safe. Instead, he went prowling around the outside and met her back in the shop as Ciara carried a resigned Amelia Batterby down the stairs.

"No wagon tracks in the alley," he reported. "Whoever painted that sign came on foot."

"Carrying a bucket of paint and a brush," Maddie mused with narrowed eye.

Michael nodded. "At the very least we should be able to find out who bought green paint recently."

"And someone may have seen him crossing town," Maddie realized, spirits lifting.

As if determined to prick any bubble of hope, Ciara shook her head. "He didn't have to follow the boardwalk to get here. There's a trail along the ridge. Patrick told me about it. He said it's the fastest way to the university."

Though the Irishman was right, Maddie's concerns about her sister rose as well. "And just when were you speaking with Mr. Flannery that I wasn't around?" she challenged.

Ciara colored but lifted her chin. "He stops by from time to time. Apparently you're just too busy to notice."

Maddie stiffened, but Michael put a hand on her arm. "He's probably looking for me," he told Maddie. "I'll let him know he can meet me at the smithy if he has need."

As always, he found a peaceful, logical way to resolve her frustrations.

"Just see that you inform me when next Mr. Flannery comes to call," Maddie told her sister.

Ciara pouted, but Maddie directed her upstairs with the cat. Amelia Batterby's golden eyes were accusatory. It seemed Maddie wasn't the only one to find her sister's company lacking.

A short while later, Aiden led in a powerfully built man with a long narrow face half-covered by a thick brown beard. He brought the smell of tobacco and smoke with him. Maddie had heard that Sheriff Wyckoff had been Seattle's first blacksmith before hanging up his hammer to become sheriff. She thought his broad shoulders still spoke of days over the anvil. Small wonder Michael had taken to the work.

Deputy McCormick stepped around his boss and motioned to Maddie and Michael. "This is Miss O'Rourke and Mr. Haggerty. She came with Mercer's Maidens, and he arrived by ship from New York earlier this month, escorting young Aiden and his sister."

Aiden took the introduction as encouragement to talk. "Sheriff Wyckoff has a horse, Maddie! He let me ride on it with him. I wish we had a horse." He gazed up at her wistfully.

"Where would we be putting it and what would we be feeding it?" Maddie countered, then held up her hand as Aiden opened his mouth to respond. "No need to answer. Be off with you now. Mr. Haggerty and I must speak with the sheriff and his deputy."

Aiden nodded, then glanced at the sheriff. "Thank you for letting me ride your horse. He's a goer."

Sheriff Wyckoff smiled. "Blaze liked your company too, Master Aiden. Come by and say hello anytime."

Aiden beamed. "I will."

As Aiden clambered up the stairs, Maddie squared her shoulders. "Did you see that sign on my wall, Sheriff?"

Wyckoff nodded, widening his stance on the floor as if preparing to defend the bakery from all comers. "Indeed I did. And there were complaints of another one this morning as well."

Michael stepped closer to Maddie as if to protect her. "Where?"

"On the other side of town," the sheriff told him. "There were more earlier this week."

"And did you check to see who'd bought green paint?" Maddie challenged.

"First thing," McCormick assured her. His eyes narrowed. "Mr. Terry had some brought up from San Francisco, but he says it was stolen from his shop."

Maddie bristled, but Sheriff Wyckoff held up a hand to forestall her. "By the fact that the paint in both locations today is still wet, we may be looking for two miscreants."

"Or a gang," Deputy McCormick drawled, gaze on Michael.

Maddie reached for Michael's hand, not only for strength but to let him know that she didn't believe he was part of this trouble. His fingers felt cold in hers.

"Mr. Haggerty and I have been concerned that there may be a member of the Dead Rabbits in town," she told the sheriff.

Wyckoff frowned. "The Dead Rabbits?"

"An Irish gang, powerful in New York," Michael explained.

"Known for criminal conduct," McCormick added. "Mr. Haggerty has had dealings with them."

He made it sound as if Michael endorsed such things. Anger at the injustice lifted Maddie's head and her voice as well.

"Mr. Haggerty refused to support their dirty dealings, you mean," she informed the deputy. "At great personal expense for refusing, I might add."

"Maddie," Michael said, giving her hand a squeeze, "I can speak for myself."

Well, of course he could. What was she thinking to jump into the fray like that? As Michael went on to explain the reason he'd come west, she clamped her lips shut. He was a clever, well-spoken man, with a much easier way of talking than she'd ever cultivated. She had no call to step between him and the sheriff, defend him to her dying breath.

But for a moment there, all she'd wanted to do was fight to protect him.

Was that how he felt? Is that why he stepped between her and trouble, smoothing her way with Ciara and Aiden? Did he see her as a friend worthy of defense?

"That's why I doubt it's a gang," Michael finished. "I think we're looking for one, maybe two people who are intent on stirring things up."

"Two people newly off the ship," McCormick insisted with a look to his superior. "This trouble only started recently."

Sheriff Wyckoff cocked his head as if considering the matter.

"This trouble could have been brewing for years," Michael argued. "Old prejudices die hard. Old fears seldom quiet for long. But if you truly think the Irish in Seattle are mobilizing to form a gang, talk to them yourself. They'll be meeting in the alley behind the bakery in less than an hour."

"What?" Maddie cried, and all eyes veered to her. "Why are they coming here?"

"Because I asked them," Michael said, putting a hand to her elbow. "They're afraid, Maddie. They've had the same trouble you have. I thought if we all talked, maybe we'd see a pattern other than us being Irish. At the very least, we might be able to band together for safety."

"So you are starting a gang," Sheriff Wyckoff challenged.

Michael flinched. "No. Never that. But you can't blame us for wanting to protect our families."

"Sounds like a pack of vigilantes to me," McCormick said. "That still puts you up against the law." He widened his stance as well, hand hovering by the hilt of the gun on his hip.

Did he think to bully them? Maddie could hardly believe it. He'd been nothing but kindness to her and the Wallins, looking out for them, riding out to check on things. Why was he being so obstinate now?

She shook a finger at him. "For shame, Hart McCormick! Have you no understanding of protecting the ones you love?"

His jaw worked, as if he struggled with his response. "Apparently not," he gritted out. "I'll just go about my duty, then. Good day, ma'am." His spurs clanked his displeasure as he strode out the door.

Wyckoff sighed, but he relaxed his stance on the floorboards. "He understands, Miss O'Rourke. The woman he loved died trying to protect him from his own gang of outlaws. They didn't take kindly to him changing his stripes, you see."

A wave of remorse swamped her. "Oh, the poor man.

I'll be begging his pardon the next time I see him, you can be sure."

"But Mr. McCormick's past doesn't change our present," Michael said, voice firm with his convictions. "We have families to protect, along with businesses and livelihoods. You can't ask us to stand by and do nothing."

"I can ask you to trust me and my deputy to get to the bottom of this," Wyckoff said, voice equally firm. "And I'll go further. One of us will be at that meeting of yours to explain our stance on the role of Seattle's law-abiding citizens in keeping things safe." He tipped his hat to Maddie. "Ma'am."

Maddie nodded, and he turned and left.

Michael shook his head. "The others won't like it, but maybe Wyckoff can talk some sense into them."

"Sure-n but he won't be the only one talking," Maddie said, chin rising. "I intend to have a few words with my fellow Irishmen myself. And then we'll be seeing what's what."

Oh, but she was in a temper. Red splashed her cheeks, and fire hotter than her brick oven burned in her eyes. How could he not rush to put out the flames?

"Now isn't a good time for scolds, Maddie," he said, keeping his tone level, calm. "These fellows are agitated enough as it is."

"Agitated by a prime agitator, I'm thinking," she countered, heading for the kitchen. "Someone's after trouble. Until I find out who it is, I'll be trusting no one."

Michael stopped in the doorway, watching as she pulled out the last of the sugar cookies she'd baked the previous day.

"Not even me?" he asked, trying for a smile.

She glanced up as she set a bowl on the worktable.

"Of course I trust you. I know you're not involved in any gang."

"Deputy McCormick didn't seem so sure," he reminded her. He'd had to force his hands to relax from fisting at the lawman's implications.

"Mr. McCormick was speaking nonsense," she said with a lift of her nose in disdain. "You've proven you want nothing to do with violence."

Something inside him uncoiled, and he felt himself standing taller. "Thank you."

"No need to thank me for saying the obvious." She crossed to the water bucket and drew out a cup. "You've been nothing but kindness to me and mine. But I'll not be letting you walk this road alone, Michael. I'd be no true friend otherwise."

Friends. That's what they should be. Two people with a common background, common goals to succeed in this new world. Two people with shared values—family, faith. Being friends with Maddie would give him ample reason to help and protect her, and to remain close to Ciara and Aiden.

Why, then, did part of him protest that he wanted more?

She went to the larder to retrieve a cone of sugar and began to pound it with her pestle, shoulders bunching, mouth tight.

Michael chuckled. "I know why you smash your ingredients. It's easier than taking your frustrations out on me."

"Legal too," she said with a grin.

Her smile pulled him closer, and he found himself walking into the kitchen. "What are you making now?"

"Powdered sugar," she said. "To make icing for the

cookies. Sure-n it's the best I can do with less than an hour until company arrives."

She was asking for trouble. He tried again to dissuade her. "Maddie, they won't like having you there. You're what they want to protect."

She eyed him but kept pounding. "Then they should have met farther away from my bakery. I've been affected by trouble too you know. It's my right to attend."

Michael couldn't argue with her there. But he thought the others might have different ideas.

They started arriving a half hour later, a man alone or with a friend, until the alley was crowded with what had to be every fellow of Irish descent in the city of Seattle and its environs. Narrow-brimmed hats and tweed caps tilted as broad shoulders bumped wiry ones in the afternoon sunlight. The scent of leather and an honest day's sweat drifted on the breeze. Rough voices grew louder as more joined in. Michael could see concern on every face, determination in most gazes. He expected Maddie to come marching out to join them, but the time to start the meeting came and went with no sign of her.

"Well?" demanded a short, scrawny fellow with hair nearly as red as hers. "Why are we all here? Who's organizing this?"

Michael stepped to the front. "I am. I'm Michael Haggerty, newly come to your shores, but I can see trouble brewing."

Shouts of "Aye!" and "Too true" rose around him, like some of Maddie's fiery cinnamon thrown into the air.

"Some of you have been robbed," Michael continued. "Others have had property destroyed or defaced. I asked you here today so we can begin to understand why."

"There's nothing to understand," someone yelled. "It's all because we're Irish!"

Voices growled in angry agreement. As Michael raised his hands and called for quiet, he saw Deputy McCormick stroll up to the back of the crowd. The men standing there took one look at him and gave him wide berth.

"Right now, all we know is that Irish businesses have been affected," Michael told them. "Many of us have faced hostility in other places. But that doesn't mean we're facing it here."

"Are you mad, man?" A broad-chested fellow in plaid trousers pushed himself forward. "My store's been robbed twice. There's a giant shamrock on my door!"

Patrick wound his way through the crowd to join Michael at the front, nodding his support before turning to face the crowd. "Shamrocks aren't a sign of anger. They're a sign of Ireland."

"Well, this one's on fire," someone else called out, pointing to the sign on Maddie's bakery. "That's a threat."

Once more voices exploded in debate. From what Michael could hear, some argued that it had been a mistake, only to be shouted down as fools. Others called for vengeance. Deputy McCormick's steely eyes narrowed.

"This could turn ugly," Patrick murmured to Michael. "We have to take the lead, Michael, help them see the path."

Just then, the gate from the yard creaked open, and Maddie strolled into their midst, platter of cookies held in her hands. She still wore her church dress, and the russet color brought out the copper of her hair. Voices quieted, men stood taller, pulled off hats, adjusted ties or coats. Maddie's smile embraced them all.

"Well?" she challenged as she came to stand beside

Michael and Patrick. "Did you come here to argue or did you come here to find a solution to our problem? I've cookies for those who want to help and nothing but contempt for the rest."

Pride raised Michael's head. He'd said she was what they all fought for—home and family and a prosperous future. Every one of them was gazing at her, and for once he didn't think it was because of her smile or the icing dripping off her cookies.

But would Maddie's influence be enough to turn this fearful crowd into a force for good?

Chapter Eighteen

As Maddie gazed out at the sea of faces, some red with anger, others white in concern, she found she cared to know only one person's opinion of her challenge. Turning, she looked to Michael. He stood still, solemn, but the light shining in his blue eyes said he had never been more proud. Her smile spread.

Around her, deep voices and burly arms raised in support, accepting her call.

"To Ireland and the Irish!" someone shouted, and the cry was taken up by a dozen men.

Maddie felt as if a balloon had inflated inside her, lifting her heart and her head at the same time. She motioned to Ciara and Aiden, who were peering out of the gate wide-eyed, waiting for her as she'd asked. Her brother and sister brought out the rest of the cookies, and the three of them passed among the crowd, offering the goodies to their guests. Soon arms were coming down, smiles were forming and voices were quieting.

"Nicely done, Miss O'Rourke," Deputy McCormick said as she held out the platter to him. His chiseled features were as tight as usual, so she could not tell how deeply she might have hurt him earlier.

"Better than my previous speech," she acknowledged. "And I'll be begging your pardon for my presumptions."

He nodded and bit into the cookie, mouth turning up at one corner as he chewed, and she knew she was forgiven.

As Ciara and Aiden returned to their spots by the gate, Maddie went to the front to offer Michael the last cookie.

Hand on her shoulder, he bent to put his mouth next to her ear. His breath was like a caress. "Keep it for yourself. You earned it."

Patrick went so far as to tip his hat to her as she took the cookie and joined Ciara and Aiden at the gate.

"Now that we're all in agreement, or at least well fed," Michael said with a smile, "let's see what we can learn. Sheriff Wyckoff and his deputy have been looking into our troubles. Deputy McCormick, give us a report."

The deputy made his way to the front. His broad-brimmed black hat shaded his eyes as he turned to look at the other men, as if he thought he needed to protect his face from them. Maddie was just thankful he did not reach for his gun.

"In the last week," he said, "there have been a total of six robberies in Seattle. Four of those were from Irish businesses."

The murmurs started again. Maddie glared them into silence, then caught Michael smiling at her and blushed.

"So we are a target," Patrick said, watching the lawman.

"Businesses are a target," Deputy McCormick warned him. "Anytime you have more, someone with less is bound to notice."

She'd certainly seen that lived out in New York. The

other men must have realized it too for they shifted, muttering.

"More, he says," someone scoffed. "Do you call it having more when you can barely put food on your table?"

"Or when you're in debt?" another demanded.

Michael held up his hand. "We all came to Seattle in hopes of building better lives. No one said we wouldn't have to struggle first."

"No one said we wouldn't face persecution either," Patrick put in around the deputy to Michael. Then he focused on McCormick. "Can you promise you'll protect these good people from further harm?"

Deputy McCormick hooked his thumbs in his gun belt. "That's my sworn duty."

One Maddie was fairly sure he took seriously. Yet despite all his hard work, people had been robbed, had their property damaged.

Patrick waved one hand to the shamrock on the wall. "But you're not protecting us, are you?" he challenged the deputy. "You come in after the damage is done to catch the criminal. We need help now, to stop the criminals before they act."

Voices rose again, loud in consensus. Aiden leaned closer to Maddie, brow puckering in concern. Ciara was white, but her gaze was fixed on Patrick.

Michael lifted both hands this time, then took a step forward before everyone quieted.

"I heard of a protective force," Patrick volunteered, looking at Michael. "The ship owners on the Thames were losing thousands of pounds to theft. When the government would do nothing, they chartered their own police force. We could do that. I'd be proud to lead you."

Maddie could see Michael frowning, but murmurs ran through the group.

Deputy McCormick stepped toward the crowd. "There's one law in Seattle, and that's the county sheriff."

Maddie thought the men would argue him off his feet the way they rushed toward him, shouting, threatening.

"Enough!" Michael's voice roared over the din. Once more, he was the warrior prince, head high, shoulders back, determination glowing in his gaze. Around him, men stepped back, closed their mouths, cocked their heads to listen.

"With all due respect, Deputy," he told the lawman, "there's no reason we can't watch our homes and businesses to protect them. We don't have to hire our own police force," he added as a few called their support for the idea, "but we can organize a watch. If we see a problem, we can send for you."

Heads began nodding like daisies in the breeze, the murmur of voices positive, encouraging. Leave it to Michael to find a logical, peaceable solution. Only Patrick, Maddie noticed, looked less than pleased with his idea.

Even Deputy McCormick snapped a nod. "Just see to it that you call," he warned. "If you take matters into your own hands, I'll arrest you too."

Oh, why did he have to confront people, and just when Michael had quieted them! Visages darkened, fists came up once more. She would not watch Michael's good work come undone.

She broke away from Ciara and Aiden and marched to the front. "Have a cookie, Deputy," she said with her best smile, holding the last one out to the lawman. "Sure-n but you need something to sweeten your disposition."

Chuckles and laughter greeted her comment, and even Deputy McCormick, bless him, managed a smile as he accepted her offering.

Michael raised his voice again. "That settles it, then. If you've a mind to help or want your property included on the list for protection, come see me. Otherwise, be watchful and contact the sheriff's office at first sign of trouble."

The crowd began to disperse. A few men left. More surged forward to talk to Michael and Patrick. Maddie sent Ciara into the bakery for paper and pencil to write down the names of the volunteers and draw up a map of the properties.

"Your cookies are good enough to soothe the savage beast, Miss O'Rourke," Patrick said as she held the paper to the fence and wrote what Michael repeated to her.

"Sure-n but it's hard to be angry with someone when you're breaking bread together," Maddie said. "Or, in this case, cookies."

Patrick chuckled, then left them to their work. He stopped to have a word with Ciara. Though his face remained polite, like that of an uncle or an old family friend, her little sister blushed at his attention. Maddie wasn't sure whether to remind the girl of the age difference between the two or hope that Ciara would find other things to interest her here in Seattle. Perhaps she should discuss the matter with Michael. He always seemed to know how to handle her sister.

It was nearly dinnertime before the last of their compatriots returned home and Maddie finished making a copy of the list for Deputy McCormick and the sheriff so they knew whom they might meet on their rounds as well as the businesses that were being protected.

Because more than a dozen men, including Michael, had signed up to help patrol, the gentlemen had set up two-person teams, rotating members so that every man served no more than once a week. Given the villain's tendency to strike at night or on a Sunday, the watchmen would concentrate their efforts at those times.

"We'll be keeping an eye on things," Deputy McCormick told Michael as the lawman folded the sheets Maddie had given him. "I'll hold you to your promise to notify us of any trouble."

"None of us wants to escalate this," Michael assured him.

Maddie hoped he was right. She could not shake the feeling that someone was determined to start trouble in Seattle. All she could pray was that the precautions Michael had put in place would offer protection while the lawmen worked to catch the culprits.

Standing at the gate, she offered him a smile as the deputy departed. "Sure-n but you did a good thing here today, Michael Haggerty."

"Sure-n but it might not have turned out so well if it wasn't for your baking, Maddie O'Rourke," he countered, returning her smile. Opening the gate for her, he motioned her through. "But I'll sleep better tonight knowing we have help, and the others will too."

Maddie linked her arm with his, feeling the strength of him. "I'll be needing your help before you sleep, sir. With all this talk, I've had no time to start dinner much less the mixings for tomorrow morning's bread."

He pressed his hand over hers, smile warming. "Anything you want. But who knows? Maybe Ciara started something."

As they stepped into the kitchen, however, it was evident Maddie's sister had done nothing about dinner.

Instead, Ciara stood on the floor of the kitchen, wringing her hands, face white.

"I can't find Amelia Batterby," she said, voice catching in a sob. "I think someone let her out, and now the wolves will get her."

Michael felt Maddie tense beside him. He very much doubted that someone had purposely let out the cat. With so many people arriving, it would have been easy for Amelia Batterby to slip through the door and out the gate. Still, he didn't want either of his ladies to worry.

He took Maddie's hand and gave it a squeeze as he looked to Ciara. "We'll find her."

Maddie called for Aiden, and together they scoured the bakery. No little gray cat with a concerned face looked back at them.

Maddie raised her voice. "Miss Amelia Batterby! Here, kitty, kitty, kitty."

Ciara scowled at her. "As if she'd ever come to anything so silly." She put her hands to her mouth. "Miss Amelia, dear Miss Amelia, come out, come out wherever you are."

Michael thought a more practical approach might be needed. He reached into the larder and pulled off a bit of ham. "She may not come when she's called," he said, bending to wave the salty meat close to the floor, "but she'll come when she's hungry."

"But that could be days!" Ciara protested. "I tell you, she's outside, in the rain and cold."

Maddie frowned at her. "Did you open the door while Michael and I were out at the gate?"

Ciara pulled away, head coming up. "Why would I do that? I'm supposed to watch Aiden, remember?"

"Then why are you so sure she's outside?" Michael asked, straightening.

Ciara threw up her hands. "Because I can't find her *inside*! For all I know, you let her out when you came back in, the two of you were so lovey-dovey."

For someone who had encouraged Michael and Maddie to make a match, she seemed rather annoyed with the idea now. Was it only the loss of the cat that concerned the girl?

Aiden, who had been looking under the worktable, made a face as he straightened. "She's probably hiding. Ciara wouldn't let her eat."

"Because you tried to feed her a piece of cake!" Ciara accused him. "I told you she wouldn't like icing."

"Never mind that now," Michael said. "The important thing is to find her. We'll check outside."

Keeping his smile pleasant and his tone encouraging, he led them out to the rear yard. Again, they searched, calling her name, promising treats. Aiden even leaned under the chicken coop, coming out speckled with grime and dotted with feathers.

Maddie grew more quiet and tight with each step. "I should have kept an eye out for her," she murmured to Michael. "I was so busy handing out cookies I didn't watch my feet."

Ciara must have heard her, for she shook a finger at Maddie. "You had to show off for those men!"

Maddie drew in a breath as if to keep from shouting back, but Michael had had enough. "Pipe down, Ciara. Your sister was doing her best to stop a riot in your own backyard."

Instead of deflating as she usually did when challenged, Ciara put her hands on her hips and glared at Michael. "Well, there wouldn't have been a riot in our backyard if you hadn't invited all those men to begin with."

"That's enough," Maddie said before Michael could answer. "There are bigger things happening here than you understand, Ciara, and I'll thank you to stop complaining about it."

"I understand," Ciara insisted, eyes narrowing. "People hate us because we're Irish. We need someone to protect us. We could have had our own policemen, and you and Michael refused. You're the one who doesn't understand!"

Aiden, who had been poking behind the washtubs, came to join them, face pinched. "Could you please stop fighting so we can find Amelia Batterby? She's probably scared."

Michael thought the cat wasn't the only one scared. Aiden's look and Ciara's outburst proved they knew enough about their circumstances to fear. Their earlier heartbreak must have made them wonder whether the adults around them could protect them from further harm. They loved the little gray cat and were genuinely worried about her, but they needed to find her alive for their own peace of mind as well.

"Right you are, Aiden," Michael said, laying a hand on the boy's head, the feathers lodged there tickling his palm. "Amelia Batterby is a part of this family. We won't abandon her."

"Never," Maddie agreed. She cast Ciara a glance out of the corners of her eyes. "We stick together, through thick and through thin."

Ciara did not answer.

Michael glanced around at them. "But you know something? Though we think of Amelia Batterby as family, the truth is that she's a cat."

"Shh! Don't be telling her that," Maddie murmured, a whisper of a smile returning to her lips.

Michael smiled back. "My point was that we need to think like a cat if we're to find her. Picture it—suddenly, you're free, with all of Seattle to explore. Where would you go?"

"To Kelloggs' for candy," Aiden said, eyes lighting.

"That's what you'd do, silly," Ciara told him. "She'd follow her nose. Down to the shore for fish."

Maddie nodded. "She might at that."

Aiden darted toward the gate. "What are we waiting for? Let's go!"

Michael opened the gate for the boy, and Ciara and Aiden hurried ahead. Maddie came more slowly. Michael could almost see the concerns weighing her down.

"She'll never get over being left behind, will she?" she murmured as she fell into step beside Michael.

He knew she wasn't talking about the cat. "Ciara and Aiden have had cause for concern, just like all the children who came to Sylvie and me. Most of them had lost parents. Some curled inward, had to be coaxed to smile again. Others lashed out the way Ciara is."

She sighed. "And my temper isn't helping. I don't know what to say to her."

"She'll come around," Michael promised. "She's smart. The more stable we make their lives now, the easier it will be to learn to love it here."

"Stable, he says." Maddie snorted as she lifted her skirt free of the mud. "The ups and downs of a new business, a new home and school, a whole new world all around them! There's nothing stable here, even if we didn't have these threats."

"The threats will be over soon," he reminded her. "We just need to hold firm." He called to Aiden to slow down as the boy darted across Occidental Avenue, Ciara not far behind.

Maddie eyed him as they started along the next stretch of boardwalk. "There's a time to hold firm and a time to give up, and it's hard to be knowing which is which." She glanced at the building they were passing, and he felt her shiver. Glancing up, he read the sign over the doorway: Eureka Bakery. So this was Maddie's competition.

The square building was painted a crisp white, with a high false front that proudly proclaimed the name of the shop and its proprietor. Every pane of the wide front window sparkled, and he could smell the now-familiar scent of baking bread.

He took Maddie's hand and squeezed it. "No need to give up, on Amelia Batterby or your bakery. We'll succeed. We're too determined not to."

"So you say," she replied, but without any of her usual spark of courage. "But I left New York when trouble came, and so did you."

The sadness in her tone broke a hole in his heart. And it suddenly struck him that Ciara and Aiden weren't the only ones needing stability. Maddie had lost a father and two mothers. She'd traveled halfway around the world, first from Ireland to New York and then around two continents. She'd risked everything to start a new business, one that now faced challenges on every side. Small wonder she didn't believe his promises.

Ahead of them, Ciara and Aiden ran down to the pier and wiggled over the edge. Aiden's cry hastened Michael's steps, and he outpaced Maddie to the rocky shore. The tide was out, leaving masses of kelp lying on the damp rocks like streamers of green and brown. Brine made the air sharper.

Amelia Batterby sat near the high tide line by the carcass of a salmon, its silver skin flayed wide, pink meat open to the sky. She was calmly licking fish oil off her dainty paws while seagulls protested overhead. She glanced up at Michael as if accusing him of dawdling.

Ciara snatched her up and held her close. "Oh, Miss Amelia, you had us so worried!"

"Don't you ever scare us like that again!" Aiden scolded her, hand rubbing down her fur.

Michael's gaze met Maddie's over the children's heads. He didn't think he was imagining what was going on behind those deep brown eyes.

Though relieved to find Amelia Batterby safe, Maddie was wondering about him. He'd said he'd stay until everyone was safe. But she'd faced adversity before, and alone. Now she wasn't so sure of him. Would he really hold firm for her when trouble came, or would he give up and flee the scene as he'd done in New York?

Chapter Nineteen

Maddie stayed close to Ciara and Aiden as they all returned to the bakery with a smug Amelia Batterby. Dark clouds were crowding the mountains. She felt as if they gathered inside her as well, pushing at her to run, to hide.

Why? Amelia Batterby was safe; Maddie's countrymen were prepared to protect each other; she had the supplies and recipes ready for the wedding that would make her fortune. She should be celebrating. Instead, she felt weighted down, as if more than mud clung to her skirts.

She couldn't help glancing at Michael, who walked on the other side of Ciara and Aiden. Catching her gaze on him, he smiled, and she hastened to look away. He'd doubted her abilities at first—questioning how she wanted to raise her brother and sister, the debt she'd taken on. Now he seemed certain of her success. Why did she suddenly doubt?

For we know that all things work together for good to them that love God, to them who are the called according to His purpose.

The remembered verse nearly stopped her in the

mud. Could all these troubles and turmoil turn into something good?

Would You be talking to me now, Lord? Are You truly interested in the simple folk like me?

Once more, her gaze was drawn to Michael. She'd been so certain he was a problem to be solved—taking the money meant for her helper, interfering in the way she was trying to raise Ciara and Aiden. Yet he had helped her so much—in running the bakery and learning to understand her brother and sister. Now a smile kept playing about his mouth as he glanced down at the cat held so firmly in Ciara's grip.

Maddie could not imagine any other man of her acquaintance being so willing to spend his afternoon searching for a beloved feline. Her father, bless his heart, would likely have told Maddie good riddance and one less mouth to feed!

She wanted to believe Michael would stay by her side. That what they felt for each other would only grow deeper. But what if she was wrong? How could she break not only her own heart but Ciara's and Aiden's as well if his love turned cold?

Heart and mind full of questions, it was all she could do to lead everyone home. She even enlisted Ciara's help in getting dinner on the table. As Ciara began peeling potatoes, Michael drew Maddie aside.

"I think we should explain this situation to Ciara and Aiden," he murmured, gaze on Maddie's. "They understand enough to worry. We can put those fears to bed."

That he would ask her permission before going straight to the children told her he was trying to honor her position in the house. How could she not admire him for that?

"Agreed," Maddie murmured back. "We'll tell them at dinner."

"It's not nice to keep secrets," Ciara said from her place at the sideboard.

"Why?" Aiden asked, chasing Amelia before him into the room, body bent and arms wide as if to prevent her from escaping again. "You do."

Maddie went to fill a pot with water and set it on the stove to boil. "And what secrets would your sister be keeping?"

"Nothing," Ciara said with a look to Aiden as if daring him to contradict her.

Aiden humphed, ducking to reach under the table and retrieve the cat. Amelia Batterby sighed for him.

As close as they all lived, Maddie was fairly certain she'd have stumbled across any major secrets before now. Still, she could not help glancing at her sister. Ciara's hands moved surely with the knife, slicing off the dark skins, coring away the black spots, all her focus on the work. When had she put up her hair? The thick braid wound around her head, pinned properly in place.

Just like Maddie's hair.

Maddie's lips trembled. So, despite all Ciara's bravado, she still looked up to Maddie. Maddie wanted to hug her sister as close as Ciara had hugged Amelia Batterby, tell the girl that she understood and would never leave her again. She settled for complimenting her on her good work. Ciara's cheeks turned pink.

She and Ciara finished the potatoes and set them in the water to boil, then Maddie carved some pieces off the venison and fried them, making gravy with drippings. She was thankful to see Michael corner Aiden and clean the boy up after his foray under the chicken coop.

At last they said grace and began eating. Maddie caught Michael's gaze on hers and drew in a breath.

"You were both a big help today with our visitors," she told Ciara and Aiden, setting down her fork. "I know all this must be confusing to you."

Aiden nodded, but Ciara rolled her eyes.

"It isn't confusing in the slightest," she informed Maddie. "Bad people are doing bad things to us, like always. And we're starting a gang like the Dead Rabbits to stop them."

That brought Michael's head up. "We are not starting a gang, Ciara," he said. "The Dead Rabbits aren't heroes. They're a vicious mob intent on having their own way, in everything. Would you want someone telling you how to live, who to love?"

Ciara frowned. "It's not like that."

"It's exactly like that," Maddie told her. "I know it seemed as if the Dead Rabbits were fighting for Irish interests, but they robbed businesses and killed people who didn't agree with their way of thinking."

Ciara paled and looked to Michael. "Is that true?"

Michael nodded. "I was given a choice to help them and I refused. Because of that, they threatened to hurt Sylvie and her children, even you and Aiden. That's why we left New York."

Aiden stabbed his fork into the ham. "I hate them!"

"No one needs to be hating anyone," Maddie said. "That's how it all starts. We should be caring about each other, not hating and hurting."

Ciara scrunched up her face. "So we should care about the Dead Rabbits even if they're as awful as you say?"

Michael chuckled. "No one said it would be easy, my girl. But even though we turn the other cheek, that doesn't mean we can't protect ourselves. That's why we organized the watch. Every night and during services on Sunday, Irishmen of good intent will be watching over the city."

"Like you," Aiden said, raising his head.

"And Patrick," Ciara added with a smile.

Maddie decided not to correct her sister's use of the fellow's first name this time.

"That's right," Michael agreed. "They'll notify the sheriff of any problems before those problems get too big for us to handle."

Aiden went back to his dinner. "Good. When I'm old enough, I'll join them."

Maddie smiled at him. "And an excellent watchman you'll make, I know. When you aren't being a sailor."

"I don't want to be a sailor," Aiden said. "I want to be a sheriff and ride a big black horse."

"Maybe I'll be a sheriff too," Ciara said. "That way I can protect everyone."

Maddie laid a hand on her sister's. "That will be a grand day. For now, please believe that Michael and I can protect you. I would never have left you behind in New York if I thought I had any other choice."

Ciara attacked her venison. "I could have given you lots of choices if you asked. You could have married the grocer. That way he wouldn't have asked you to pay off Da and Mum's bill. Or you could have married Michael."

Maddie's face was heating, but her gaze was drawn to Michael's once more. He winked at her.

"But if Maddie and I had married in New York," he told Ciara, "we'd never have come to this wild country where you and Aiden can be sheriffs if you want."

Ciara chewed on her venison, frowning in obvious thought.

"Then you can just get married now," Aiden put in brightly. "Maddie's already figured out how to bake the cakes."

"As if that's all there is to marrying!" Maddie protested.

Aiden glanced between her and Michael. "Is there more than cakes?"

"Of course," Ciara scolded him. "There's the wedding gown and a minister, and all your friends and family around you. But we can take care of all that. Miss Underhill already said she'd make the gown."

Maddie felt as if this ship was about to sail without her. "I don't need a wedding gown, because I'm not marrying anyone."

"I don't see why not," Aiden said, flattening his potatoes with his fork so that gravy ran out across the plate. "You and Michael are together all the time anyway."

Maddie looked to Michael for assistance. He didn't seem nearly as concerned as he should be, grin forming on his handsome face.

"I believe he's planning on moving out soon," she said. "Aren't you, Mr. Haggerty?"

That wiped the smile from his face. Ciara and Aiden reacted nearly as badly. Her sister stopped eating in midbite, and Aiden's face puckered.

"You're leaving now, Michael?" he asked, voice plaintive.

Oh, what had she done? Trying to protect herself from marriage, she'd taken their stability and thrown it out the window like dirty water.

"Not right away," Michael assured Aiden. "I promised your sister I'd stay until all the trouble is over."

Maddie nodded, watching as her brother and sister relaxed.

"Good," Aiden said, returning to herding his gravy back toward the potatoes. "There's always trouble, so you'll never leave."

Maddie stared at him, but Michael laughed and reached for more of the venison.

She managed to keep the conversation away from weddings for the rest of the meal, then settled her brother and sister into bed and heard their prayers. Michael was waiting for her near the stove when she came out of Ciara's room.

"I'm going to work at Kelloggs' tonight," he said, taking her hand and cradling it in his own. His touch sent warmth flooding through her. "But I meant what I said earlier, Maddie. Even when I move out, I'll still want to be part of Ciara's and Aiden's lives. I'll still be your friend, ready to help when needed. All you have to do is ask."

And asking was the hardest part. Asking meant she had to have faith in the other person. It was easier on her heart to rely only on herself.

She pulled back her hand. "Thank you, Michael. I'd best get some sleep now. You know how early morning comes."

"Not early enough for me," he said with a smile. "But good night, Maddie. Sweet dreams."

She was fairly sure her dreams would be more troubled than sweet. To her surprise, though, she slept so well the sun was already up when she opened her eyes. She lay there a moment, smiling at the light.

The light? Her bread!

She leaped out of bed, threw on her clothes and scurried down the stairs.

Michael looked up as she careened into the kitchen.

"Easy," he said, catching her shoulders. "Aiden and I have it in hand."

Her brother waved from the worktable, where he stood on a stool, slathering icing on sugar cookies. By the stains on his shirt, more was going on him than on the cookies.

"When you didn't get up, Aiden and I checked on you," Michael said, turning for the oven. "You looked so peaceful we didn't have the heart to wake you."

"But the bread," Maddie protested, brain feeling fuzzy as she followed him.

"Is done," he replied. Taking the peel from the wall, he opened the oven. Dozens of loaves, golden and plump, shimmered in the heat.

"Michael said we shouldn't try cinnamon rolls," Aiden supplied, knife flashing as he spread the icing. "But we managed bread and cookies."

They had indeed. Maddie helped Michael line the loaves on the display counter to cool, then rescued the cookies from Aiden's eager grasp and laid them out as well. Everything was ready by the time her first customers arrived.

While Aiden gathered eggs and took them upstairs, promising to wake his sister, Maddie and Michael served the loggers and mill workers. The mad scramble went even faster than usual. She said as much to Michael as he helped her clean up afterward.

"Maybe you're just getting used to it," he said with a smile.

Perhaps. But another thought struck her. In fact, the truth of it resonated through her body. No matter what happened, everything was easier with Michael beside her.

Oh, but she'd done it now. Despite all her efforts and firmly held beliefs, she was falling in love with him. Just what was she willing to do about it?

Michael glanced at Maddie as he finished sweeping the floor. He thought it had been a good morning. She'd been able to sleep in, and the bakery had still earned a pretty penny. Yet now her cinnamon brows were down, and her mouth worked as if she chewed on thoughts far weightier than her bread. He was almost afraid to ask.

She looked up then, and her frown deepened. Following her gaze, Michael saw a beaming bearded face peering in at them from the window.

"Now, what could he be wanting?" Maddie asked as Mr. Terry waved from the other side of the glass.

"Perhaps he's come to admit defeat," Michael suggested with a grin.

She shook her head as if she couldn't believe that, but she went to the door and let her competitor in.

Mr. Terry whipped off his narrow-brimmed hat and gave them a nod. "Miss O'Rourke, Mr. Haggerty," he greeted. "I was concerned you might have closed when I saw the place empty."

"We're open," Maddie assured him as if determined to put that rumor to bed. "Every day but Sunday."

"Maddie's customers bought her out again this morning," Michael added, unable to keep the pride from his voice.

"It's hard to keep up with demand," Mr. Terry agreed. "Which brings me to the reason for my visit. I understand you've had some trouble at the bakery, and I thought I could help."

Maddie's gaze narrowed. So she still harbored some

suspicions toward the other bakery owner. Though Michael was equally sure the man was innocent, he had to admit that Mr. Terry had reason to want to see Maddie fail.

"I'm doing well despite the troubles," she told him. "But I thank you for thinking of me all the same."

He refused to give up. "You're making do with your current clientele," he corrected her. "The Wallin wedding will be a different matter. From what I hear all over town, James Wallin intends to feed the entire city of Seattle. That's a big job, for any bakery."

"It is," she agreed, "but I have every intention of helping the family who's been so kind to my friends. I can manage."

He had to hear the steel in her voice, but still Terry persisted. "With having to care for your sister and brother too?" he asked, cocking his head. "And I hear you're involved with organizing this watch. I've had more than my share of irons in the fire, Miss O'Rourke. I know how difficult it can be to keep them all flourishing."

"Funny thing about irons," Michael put in. "The more you have in the fire, the more things you can make." He glanced at Maddie and nodded, trusting her to respond in her own way.

Terry didn't wait for her. He seemed to think her silence meant agreement. He rubbed his hands together briskly. "We're prepared to take the burden off your shoulders. We'll bake for the Wallin wedding. I'm sure that will be a relief." He smiled as if he'd done her a great favor and stood ready for her to fall on her knees and kiss his hand in gratitude.

Michael knew he would have a long wait coming.

"Sure-n what a noble offer," Maddie said, red flaring into her cheeks. "You'll take the wedding that would establish my bakery as the best in Seattle and leave me the crumbs, all in the name of kindness, of course. I can't imagine why I wouldn't jump at the chance."

A more experienced man would have escaped while he could. Terry just stood there, smile fading. "I don't think you understand the effort involved."

"Oh, I understand." Maddie swept to the door and held it open for him. "I understand you'll do anything to hinder my success, and I won't be helping you do it. Our business is done, Mr. Terry. Good day."

He clamped his mouth shut, clapped his hat on his head and strode from the shop. The moment Maddie closed the door behind him, Michael let out a laugh.

"Now, that was some fine talking, Miss Maddie O'Rourke," he said, crossing to her side. "You told him what's what."

For a moment, she shared his grin, then turned away.

"That's all well and good," she said. "But we'll have to keep an eye on him. I wouldn't put it past him to try to damage the bakery again."

"We'll be on guard," Michael promised her. "I won't fail you, Maddie."

He reached out and touched her check, marveling at the silk of her skin. She closed her eyes as if savoring his touch. Before he knew it, his lips had met hers, tender, sweet. This was what men fought and died for, what sent them across oceans and continents: the precious love of a fine woman.

He pulled back, stunned. Face turned up to his, cheeks as pink as her soft lips, she was the finest woman he'd ever met. And it was kiss her again and never let go, or leave while he still could.

He took a step toward the door. "I should go. I'll be on watch tonight, but I'll see you in the morning." He turned and hurried out the door before she could chase after him and demand an explanation he couldn't even give himself.

Chapter Twenty

A few hours later, a cough pierced Michael's attention.

"Did you leave your brain at home with your other shirt?" Smitty demanded. The smith took the mangled iron out of Michael's grip and threw it back into the forge, sending sizzling sparks flying up the chimney.

Michael grimaced. "Sorry. I'll do better next time."

His employer peered at him, craggy brows down over his short nose. "So are you deeper in debt than you thought or is it woman trouble?"

"Neither and both," Michael said with a rueful laugh. "But I'll try to focus for the rest of my shift."

Muttering about the vagaries of youth, Smitty went back to his anvil on the other side of the forge.

Michael shook his head. He knew why he was woolgathering. He couldn't get Maddie off his mind. All he wanted to do was hold her close, shelter her from all harm. Somewhere along the line, she'd become a part of him. That wasn't what she wanted, but he didn't know how to let go.

"It's not like anything I've ever felt before," he confided in Patrick as they made their rounds that night. With the exception of some whooping and hollering from one of the establishments near the mill, Seattle slept quietly under a cloudy sky.

"I don't know," Patrick said, raising his lantern to peer into a darker corner of the boardwalk. "You were crazy over Katie O'Doul too, and look where that led you."

"I've been thinking about that," Michael said as they came around the corner. A few lights were still on upstairs at De Lin's hotel, but the buildings around it were shut for the night, with no sign of any trespassers. "I think I wanted Katie because she was the prettiest girl in Irishtown."

Patrick cast him a glance. "It seems to me the same could be said of Maddie O'Rourke. I don't think there's a bachelor in town who isn't sweet on her. What makes you think she's any different from Katie?"

"I didn't at first," Michael admitted as they headed west. At the end of Washington Street, he could just make out the swirling mass of gray that was Puget Sound. "Katie flirted with everyone. I convinced myself I was different, better. That she truly loved me and I loved her. But I wonder now if it was all a game. She was the best, and I thought I deserved only the best back then. What did I really know about her?"

"Not enough, my lad, or you'd have seen her for what she was sooner." Patrick stopped at the top of the pier and nodded in obvious satisfaction at the empty planks. Michael could hear the waves lapping at the supports below them, the tart scent of sea spray hanging heavy in the air.

Michael turned toward the shops. "That's just it, Pat. I feel like I know Maddie, for all we've been here less than three weeks. I'm with her so often. I see how hard she works. I hear her praying with Ciara and Aiden at night." He chuckled. "I can tell you she doesn't fuss over her hair in the morning, and she isn't coherent before that first few sips of tea. But is that love?"

Patrick clapped him on the shoulder. "Love or indigestion, me lad. And given how well Maddie O'Rourke cooks, I'm guessing it's not indigestion."

Michael laughed at that. They ventured past the mill toward the boardinghouses along First Street. "I envy you," Patrick told him. "You have a family, a job. Me? I'm more afraid of these troubles. Shouldn't we be doing more, I wonder."

Michael eyed him as they passed the last boardinghouse. "Such as?"

Patrick shrugged. "Start a police force, as I said. Charter a city government. Run for mayor."

Michael laughed again. "Sounds like you have your future all planned."

Patrick's teeth flashed as he grinned. "Indeed I do. What about you? Will you be pursuing Maddie O'Rourke?"

How was he to answer? He'd always believed the tales of love at first sight. Certainly that's what he'd felt for Katie. What he felt for Maddie was softer, warmer. With Katie, he'd always been thinking of how good she looked on his arm, how her connections could help his career.

He wasn't that man anymore, and though he'd once lamented that fact, he felt now as if only good had come from leaving New York. He'd found a profession where he could make things instead of just carrying other people's things. He'd found friendship, encouragement, purpose in helping others here.

Had he found love as well?

He felt the answer inside him. Love was patient and

kind; it did not envy or puff itself up. It rejoiced in the truth. That's what he felt for Maddie.

"Yes, I will, Pat," he said as they headed back toward the bakery. "I'll ask her to marry me."

Patrick gave a low whistle. "I'm thinking she won't be easy to convince."

"She won't," Michael agreed. "I'll have to find the right time and place to even have the discussion."

"The Occidental Hotel," Patrick suggested. "Tomorrow night, before you lose your nerve. It's the finest setting Seattle can provide for a proposal, me lad."

Patrick was right. Just his one peek inside the hotel when he'd been looking for work had told Michael the place was the best Seattle had to offer. He couldn't imagine anything finer than a quiet dinner there with Maddie, Ciara and Aiden.

Though with her siblings along, dinner might not be all that quiet.

Still, perhaps there in the hotel, he could give her another taste of what it could be like if they were really a family. But, given her feelings on love and marriage, would she ever say yes to his proposal?

Maddie was certain the easiest way to escape her feelings for Michael was to avoid him. Accordingly, she rose, dressed and slipped down the stairs early the next morning without waking him.

That didn't stop him from bringing her tea a little later. She was scooping dried currants and apples from where she'd soaked them in tea overnight and preparing to mix them with the *barmbrack* dough when a movement caught her eye. Michael was standing in the doorway of the shop, cup in each hand, watching her work.

The smile on his face warmed her more than the heat seeping out of her baking oven.

"Lots to do this morning?" he asked, crossing to the worktable and holding out a cup.

She nodded to him to set it on the table, glad for the excuse of her work to prevent her fingers from brushing his. "I'll be starting to bake for the wedding today," she told him.

"I have a few minutes before I have to go to the smithy," he said, leaning against the worktable. "How can I help?"

By staying away from her. "No need," she assured him, dropping the fragrant fruit into the dough. "Ciara will get herself and Aiden ready for school. I'll check on them before they go. You can be on your way with no concerns."

He nodded, straightening, and she let out a breath, thinking he was leaving. But he paused a moment. "Have I done something to offend you, Maddie?"

"Not in the slightest," she assured him, whipping the mixture together with her wooden spoon. "You know me. I'd be telling you otherwise."

"I do know you," he said ducking his head to see up under her gaze. "You take your feelings out on your cooking. By the look of things, that dough doesn't stand a chance. Who's ruffled your feathers now?"

"No one," she insisted, dumping the dough onto her floured worktable. "As I told you, I have a lot to do. Just leave me to it."

He held up his hands as if in surrender. "All right. But don't start dinner today. I'll be back after work to take you and Ciara and Aiden to eat at the Occidental."

The Occidental? She'd never been inside a fancy hotel eatery in New York, but she would have loved a look inside this one. Yet a dinner in public with Michael made a statement somehow. Her stomach dipped. "Perhaps that's not a good idea."

His look darkened. That expressive face showed his least emotions, and she knew she'd hurt him.

"Why?" he asked, tone polite. "I've heard the food is very good. Probably not as good as your cooking, but good enough."

Maddie plunged her hands into the dough, working the soft mixture, gaze on the speckled mass. "You'll be wanting a house soon, your own things about you. Sure-n but you shouldn't be wasting money on me."

She looked up to find him right next to her.

"Spending time with you is never a waste," he said, gaze holding hers. "If you don't want to go out to dinner with me, just say so."

She could feel her jaw working, but no words came out. What was wrong with her? She'd never had the least trouble giving her opinion on any matter. Her friends and family had occasionally had cause to rue her frankness.

But this time she simply didn't know what to say. She couldn't admit her feelings when she had no intentions of acting on them. That wasn't fair to him. And she couldn't explain why she was keeping her distance without confessing her feelings!

She brushed past him. "I told you, I have a lot of work that needs doing. If I can spare the time, I'll join you, but I'll be making no promises."

He caught her hand. "I'll wait for you in the dining room. If you aren't there by six, I'll know you're not coming."

The tension in his face, the grip of his hand, told her

there was more at stake here than a dinner. For some reason, he needed her beside him tonight.

That only made her all the more determined to stay away.

"Go about your business now, Mr. Haggerty," she said.

Looking pensive, he left her alone at last.

Maddie sighed. She didn't want to hurt him. He'd been kind, thoughtful, helpful since the day he'd arrived. He held her trust as gently as he held Ciara's and Aiden's. How could she not fall in love with a man like that?

But how could she believe he'd stand by her when the hard times came? For richer, for poorer, in sickness and in health, the wedding vows said. Yet no one she'd known had been able to live by those vows and keep their love alive. Her friends from the expedition were newly married, with the glow of a honeymoon still in their eyes. She doubted they'd be objective. They thought everyone would be as happy in marriage as they were at the moment. They hadn't seen the struggles her father and stepmother had gone through.

A small voice inside her urged her to believe that what she and Michael felt was different, stronger. She wanted to believe it! But something held her back.

So, she thrust herself into her work. When the first customers arrived, she had loaves of bread, crusts crisp and insides still steaming; savory barmbrack with the fruit plump and juicy; iced lemon cookies; and tart gingersnaps laid out on the counter. All were gone within the hour.

She checked Ciara and Aiden, and sent them off to school with lunches, started the dough to rising for the afternoon sales, paid the man who came to replace the broken pane in the front window, tidied the upstairs, began soaking Aiden's dirtied clothing in the washtub, inventoried her supplies and gave Amelia Batterby a good brushing.

The cat eyed Maddie over her shoulder as she stalked away, smiling as if she were more pleased with her role of comforter than mouse catcher.

But no matter how hard Maddie worked, she couldn't erase Michael from her mind. She caught herself saving some sugar cookies for him from the afternoon batch and made herself put them out for sale instead. A pair of his socks made their way into Aiden's laundry, and she dropped them like hot coals the moment she realized what they were. Even inventorying her supplies reminded her of the sacrifice he'd made to purchase them.

She obviously needed to work harder.

That afternoon, she did three tubs of laundry, thankful for the nice day to hang most of the clothes to dry in the yard. A few she strung on a line near the oven. She could not get the ropes as high as Michael did, of course, but she upended one of the tubs so she could stand taller. And wouldn't he be pleased with her ingenuity.

Oh!

She launched herself into the baking for the wedding. Knowing the likely number of attendees, she'd calculated that she'd need hundreds of rolls and at least eighteen wedding cakes. The Wallins and Howards were providing the meat and vegetables. But anything baked was up to her.

Her rolls would keep well covered for a week, the cakes for only a few days. With the wedding four days away, she began with the rolls, mixing an extra batch in her trough. She was kneading the dough when Ciara and Aiden returned from school.

"Miss Reynolds says Seattle has only been here fifteen years," Aiden declared, tossing his lunch pail up on the worktable with a clang.

"She's obviously mistaken," Ciara said, setting her pail down more carefully. "You can't build a whole city that fast."

"Cities can spring up in a few months, given the will and money," Maddie told her. "Ask any miner about the boomtowns he's seen."

"Boomtown," Aiden said, smacking his lips as if he liked the taste of the word. "I changed my mind. I want to be a miner and live in a boomtown. Boom! Boom! Boom!" He punctuated his statement with a jump on the kitchen floor that set Maddie's bowl to rocking. Amelia Batterby dashed out from under the worktable and ran for the stairs.

Ciara rolled her eyes at her brother. "I'm not moving to a boomtown," she said. "I'm going back to New York first chance I get. There's nothing to do here."

Maddie barked a laugh, thinking about her day. "Oh, there's plenty to do here, me girl, if you look." She eyed her sister, who was toying with a loose thread on the only dress Nora hadn't fixed. Ciara had consistently complained about not having enough to do. Perhaps Maddie had been wrong not to oblige.

"Miss Underhill offered to teach you to sew," Maddie said. "Would you like that?"

Ciara straightened, eyes brightening. "Oh, Maddie! That would be wonderful! Then I can sew pretty dresses."

"If you help around the bakery like Aiden," Maddie said, emboldened by her sister's response, "I can pay you a bit so you can buy cloth."

Her sister threw her arms about Maddie and hugged her tight. "Oh, yes! Thank you! You're the best sister!"

Tears pressed against Maddie's eyes, and she smiled at her sister as Ciara pulled away. "And you're a dear girl for saying so. It's a perfect time to be helping, you know. I'll have much to do before this wedding."

Ciara's look turned dreamy, and she leaned against the worktable. "Oh, I love weddings. Pretty clothes, vowing undying devotion, dancing. It's so romantic."

Aiden made a face. "More kissing! I can't wait for the food. I'm going to take a bite out of every cake."

"Mr. and Mrs. Wallin might have something to say about that, me lad," Maddie told him. "Now go on upstairs and clean yourself up for dinner."

Aiden glanced around the kitchen. "What are we having?"

"Stew," Maddie supplied, turning her dough.

"But I thought Michael was taking us to the Occidental," Ciara protested.

How did her sister know? Had Michael confided in her? She hated to disagree just when she and Ciara were getting along, but she couldn't sit like a family with Michael over a public dinner when she couldn't bring herself to join her life to his. "Sure-n but we shouldn't be wasting his money when he has debts to pay and a new life to be starting."

Ciara's mouth was set, her eyes narrowed. "You just don't want us to have any fun."

"It has nothing to do with fun," Maddie informed her, temper rising with her dough. "I'm merely being practical."

Ciara humphed. "But we have to go. You'll ruin the surprise."

Maddie frowned at her. "What surprise?"

Aiden was eyeing his sister as well, as if he wasn't sure of the matter either.

Ciara took a step back. "If I told you, it wouldn't be a surprise," she scolded. "Now, come along. We have to go to dinner. I promised."

Maddie wasn't sure what her sister and Michael had dreamed up. This surprise must have been why he'd been so intent on Maddie coming to dinner when they'd talked this morning. She simply could not trust her feelings.

"Promise or no," she told Ciara, "we are eating dinner here and that's that. I'll give Mr. Haggerty our regrets later."

"Give him your own," Ciara retorted, backing for the door. "I'm going to dinner. If you want to stop me, you'll have to catch me." She turned and ran out the door.

Aiden glanced at Maddie, eyes wide. "Should I go after her?"

That was clearly what her sister wanted. Maddie wasn't about to gratify Ciara's bad behavior.

"No," she said, raising her head. "Ciara will come to no harm between here and the hotel, and Michael will send her back once he realizes we aren't coming. I'll have words with her then."

And she'd talk with Michael when he returned as well, tell him her concerns, confide her feelings. The very thought set her hands to shaking. But it had to be done, even if she ended up breaking his heart, and her own.

Chapter Twenty-One

Michael sat at the table in the dining room of the Occidental Hotel, shifting on the curved-back wooden chair. Beeswax candles in brass candlesticks, fine crystal glasses and silverware graced the table, but it was the white cloth draping it that gave him pause. Thanks to Maddie, he now knew just how hard someone was working to keep it white. He was afraid to so much as touch the thing lest he leave a mark.

Around him, Seattle's finest sat together, murmuring pleasantries. The scent of good food vied with flowery perfume to color the air. The stage was set to propose. The very thought had him reaching for the glass of lemonade the waiter had brought him.

Ciara flounced into the room and looked around. Michael rose, and she hurried to his side. Her blue gown looked a bit rumpled from her day sitting in class, but the fire in her eyes reminded him of her sister in a taking.

"Good afternoon, Ciara," he said as she sat opposite him. That chair probably should have gone to Maddie, but Michael couldn't mind. If Ciara was across from him, Maddie had to be next to him at his right or left at the four-person table. And that meant it would be easier to take her hand.

He glanced to the door, spirits lifting as he waited for Maddie to make an appearance, Aiden at her side. Maybe she'd wear her russet dress. He could imagine the room's light reflecting in her hair.

The doorway remained empty.

"They aren't coming," Ciara announced, scooting her chair forward with a squeak on the hardwood floor. "Maddie says it's a waste of money."

If Maddie thought dining out was so costly, she probably wouldn't like the gold band that was burning a hole in his pocket. Mr. Kellogg had assured Michael he had kept engagement rings in stock ever since Mercer's Belles had arrived. This one might be too big for her capable fingers, but he knew Smitty could size it to fit her.

"A shame," Michael said, disappointment warring with relief that he wouldn't have to test the degree of affection Maddie held for him. "Then perhaps we should go home as well."

In the act of placing the linen napkin on her lap, Ciara frowned at him. "Why can't we eat here?"

He wasn't about to confess that he'd been hoping to eat with her sister instead. Ciara would likely tell Maddie, and he wasn't sure how her older sister would take it.

"A young lady like yourself must be careful of her reputation," Michael reminded her, rising. "What would folks think if they saw us out alone together and me not a member of your family?"

Ciara shook her head. "Oh, Michael, you're already part of the family. Everyone knows you're going to marry Maddie. Everyone but Maddie, that is."

He sat down, hard. "So your sister has something against me."

She wrinkled her nose. "Maddie doesn't like boys."

That wrung a chuckle out of him. "Well, the boys certainly like her by the way they buy her bread."

"That's not the same," Ciara said. "They aren't suitors that I can see. She wouldn't allow it. Oh, she has no understanding of romance."

More than her eleven-year-old sister, Michael thought. "And why is that, do you suppose?"

Ciara shrugged. "I don't know. All her friends back home got married and they had lovely weddings."

"There's a bit more to marriage than a wedding," Michael told her as she began glancing around as if admiring the clothing of the other diners. "And we aren't staying for dinner, Ciara. We're going home to Aiden and Maddie."

Gaze returning to his, she crossed her arms over her chest. "Why? She's trying to be nice, but she doesn't want me any more than she wants you. We're just a burden to her."

"She never said that," Michael protested, but Ciara sat taller, arms coming down.

"No, you said it. I heard you in New York, talking with Sylvie. You said Maddie would sail away and never give us another thought. Sylvie said Maddie would do her duty. That's what we are, a duty. She doesn't love us."

He'd put Ciara's airs down to the loss of her parents and being left behind for a time in New York. Now he saw that her attitude was at least in part his fault. He'd blamed Maddie for being like Katie before he'd ever seen the size of her heart. Guilt wrapped around him.

"She loves you, Ciara," he promised the girl. "It

wasn't duty that had her working so hard to pay your way out here. It wasn't duty that put her in debt for the bakery and all the fine things in it. She wanted a better future for you and Aiden."

Ciara's face was tight, as if she struggled to believe him. "If she has so much love in her, why doesn't she marry you and give us a father?"

His heart hurt for the girl. "Just because she loves you doesn't mean she loves me," Michael explained.

Ciara gazed at him. "Do you love her?"

The answer came easily. "Yes. Yes, I do. In fact, I was hoping to ask her to marry me tonight." He pulled out the ring, which gleamed in the candlelight, just like his hopes.

Ciara's eyes widened. "Oh, Michael. It's beautiful!"

He smiled as he tucked it away again. "Not nearly as beautiful as your sister."

The waiter came up just then, smile both apologetic for the interruption and eager to serve. "We have fried chicken, salmon and beefsteak on the menu tonight. What can I get for you?"

Michael looked to Ciara, who raised her chin.

"Nothing," she said. "We have to go home for dinner. Our family is waiting."

Michael rose, handed the waiter a coin for his trouble, then escorted Ciara to the door. Outside, the sun was setting behind the Olympics, turning the Sound to rippling sheets of gold.

"She'll say yes," Ciara said as they headed back toward the bakery.

Michael chuckled at her confidence. He could only hope she was right. Maybe the distance he'd felt between him and Maddie this morning was only his nerves. Maybe she truly had been too busy today for dinner. Maybe all he had to do to ensure a future with Maddie was to ask.

He glanced up the block toward the bakery, where the windows glowed red. It took him a moment to realize it wasn't a reflection of the setting sun.

And then he ran.

After all Maddie's efforts to forget about Michael, she knew she hadn't succeeded because she burned the stew. One minute it was simmering nicely on the stove, and she'd paused in her stirring to think about what she could say to him. Unless she missed her guess, he had feelings for her and deeper ones than the calf-love sent her way by some of her customers. Them she could turn aside with a smile or a promise of a cookie later. Michael deserved more.

Yet what could she say? "I don't believe in love" sounded jaded and not entirely the truth. She believed in love. She just didn't trust it to stay.

"That doesn't smell very good," Aiden said from where he was setting the table for her.

Maddie yanked the pot off the stove, shoving her thoughts away as well. The rancid odor filled the flat as she managed to scrape up enough bits for her and Aiden to eat on bread. She wasn't sure what she'd do when Michael and Ciara returned, but perhaps she'd been wrong and the two would eat dinner at the Occidental after all.

She could hope for a little more time to gather her thoughts.

Aiden poked at his soggy bread. "Couldn't we go find Ciara and Michael?"

Maddie forced herself to fork up the charred mass. "And miss my most original dish? I thought you were an adventuresome lad." She wiggled her eyebrows at Aiden over the top of the food, and he giggled.

Amelia Batterby stalked out of Ciara's room and went to stand by the stairs. Fur rising on her back, she looked at Aiden and Maddie, tail tense.

"And what has offended you, Miss Amelia?" Maddie couldn't help asking.

"Maybe she wants some stew too," Aiden said, grabbing his plate as if fully prepared to sacrifice his dinner.

"What do you think, Miss Amelia?" Maddie asked. "Would you like to try my masterpiece?"

Amelia Batterby glanced between the two of them, opened her mouth and screeched. The sound reverberated in the little room. Aiden fell back in his chair even as Maddie stared at the cat.

"She talked!" Aiden cried.

In answer, the cat screeched again, a long, drawn-out cry that raised gooseflesh all along Maddie's arms.

She rose. "Something's wrong."

Aiden dropped out of his chair and darted toward the cat. Amelia Batterby wasn't about to be caught this time. She veered around Aiden, scooted under the table and popped out on the other side. But no matter how Aiden chased her, she refused to take the obvious exit down the stairs.

Was there a thief even now stealing Maddie's supplies again? She snatched up the broom from behind the door and started down. Oh, but the fellow had made a mistake this time. She was in no mood to be trifled with. She'd just reached the shop when she saw the glow.

Her kitchen was on fire. She could see the clothes on the line, flapping in the rising heat, like live things trying to escape. Even as fear washed over her, the flames licked through the doorway into the shop. From the kitchen came the pop and whine of her other extracts breaking. Tongues leaped along the icing that had dropped from her afternoon rolls, lapped up the mud her customers had tracked in. The floor lit, blocking her way to the door, and the blaze reached greedy fingers for her skirts. She ran upstairs and shut the door.

Aiden's face was white. "What's wrong?"

"There's a fire," Maddie said, hurrying for her room. Now that she realized what was happening below, she felt as if the heat was pulsing through the floor at her. All she knew was that she had to get her brother to safety. She would not let him die the way his father and mother had died.

She yanked the covers off her bed and threw them to Aiden, who had followed her into her room.

"Tie those together in a rope," she ordered. "Use the good strong knots the sailors taught you."

Trembling, Aiden bent his head to do as she asked.

Maddie heaved the tick off the bed. It wasn't much, but it might break their fall if the rope didn't hold. Dragging the bag across the room, she shoved open the window overlooking the street.

People were gathering below, pointing, exclaiming.

"Bring buckets!" Maddie shouted to them, and men went running. Others shouted up, urging her to flee. If only it were that easy.

"Watch out below!" Maddie cried, then she stuffed the tick through the open window until it slid from her grip and tumbled to the ground.

"Here," Aiden said, puffing as he brought her his makeshift rope. She saw he had taken the time to tuck his *feadóg* in his waistband.

Maddie tugged on his knots. "Well done, me lad. Now, I need you to be brave enough to climb down this."

"What about Amelia Batterby?" Aiden asked, eyes fearful.

"I'll be right behind, with her in my apron," Maddie promised. She took the rope and wound it around the base of the stove, tying it off tight. The rest she slung out the window. It ended five feet from the ground.

"Go on, now," Maddie told Aiden. "Someone will help you."

"Maddie!"

Michael's voice pierced the fear that was enfolding her in fiery arms. Looking out, she saw him and Ciara below, faces turned up in anguish.

"We're all right!" she called. "Aiden is coming down. Help him!"

She didn't wait for an answer, pausing only to kiss her brother's silky hair.

"I'm scared," Aiden whispered. "I'm not brave like you, Maddie."

"I'm not so brave, me love," she told him. "Da always said true courage meant being afraid and doing the right thing anyway. You can do that now, can't you?"

He nodded and inched out the window onto the rope. Maddie clung to the material, holding it taut. *Please, Lord, help him!*

It seemed forever before a cheer from below told her that Aiden had reached the ground. She peered out and could barely catch sight of his dark head among the well-wishers. From down the street, church bells began tolling a warning.

"Come on, Maddie!" Michael called from below, hand up as if to help her.

"Coming!" she promised.

She tugged on the rope again to make sure of it and heard the unmistakable sound of tearing cloth. Strings jutted up around the base of the stove where the metal of the legs had cut into the material. The rope would never hold her weight now.

She sat down hard on the floor, and Amelia Batterby ran and cowered in her lap. Maddie held her, crooning comfort, as she tried to think of any other way to escape. Facing the bedchambers as she was, she could see smoke streaming from between the floorboards, filling the space. Just the sight of it made her cough.

"Sure-n but we're in a pickle now, me girl," she murmured, hands on the soft fur of the cat's back. Tears stung her eyes. She'd told Aiden that courage meant acting through fear, and her little brother had believed her. He thought she was brave. After all, she'd sailed around the world, started her own business, made them a family again.

Maddie knew the truth. She was a coward. She'd left New York because she'd been afraid she couldn't handle raising her sister and brother under those circumstances. Worse, she'd let fear stop her from loving Michael. She'd seen so many marriages ruined by privation that she hadn't been willing to try. That was wrong. And now there was no way to make it right.

Forgive me, Lord. I see how You've been working. I needed help, and You sent me Michael. You gave me love, and I refused to accept it. Help Michael and Ciara and Aiden, for I'm thinking I won't be here to help them meself.

A crash from below sent a shudder through the floor. How long before the boards gave and sent her tumbling into the flames?

Footsteps thudded on the stair, and the door burst open. Michael threw off the smoldering sheet that had covered him. Maddie clambered to her feet and met him halfway across the room.

"You're a fine man, Michael Haggerty," she said, giving him a hug. "But you're a fool for coming after me, for now you've doomed us both!"

Chapter Twenty-Two

Michael's heart was beating so hard he couldn't make out Maddie's words. All he knew was that she was alive.

And he intended to keep it that way.

"Is there water in the bucket?" he asked, balling up the sheet.

"Aye," Maddie answered, disengaging from him. "But not enough to make a difference on those flames."

"I don't need it to douse the fire," he said, crossing and dunking the material into the water. "I just need it to douse us."

He'd seen firefighters in New York use the trick to enter burning buildings, but he'd never thought to have to use it to save someone he loved. Now he knew if he focused on Maddie, his fears would swallow them both. So as she came to join him, cat still clutched in her arms, he watched as the material soaked up most of the water, then yanked out the sodden mass. Lifting the bucket with the remaining water, he upended it over Maddie's head.

"What are you doing?" she sputtered.

"Saving your life," he said.

He grabbed the wiggling Amelia Batterby and tucked

her under one arm, then threw the soaked sheet over the three of them.

"They're working a bucket line," Michael told Maddie, leading her toward the door. "From what I can tell, the fire is mostly contained in the kitchen now, but it hit the larder hard and the stairs could give any moment. Stay close to me."

"For the rest of my life," Maddie murmured. "Which may not be too long."

"Courage," Michael said. "We'll talk about the rest of our lives when we're outside." He opened the door, and heat rushed upward, nearly stealing his breath even through the sheet. "Ready?"

Maddie's look narrowed in determination. "Ready."

Together, they started down the stairs. Michael moved as fast as he could, mindful of her shorter stride and full skirts. Amelia Batterby dug her claws into his chest as if fearing he'd release her. He wasn't about to lose either of his ladies.

A man stood in the shop, throwing buckets of water at the fire, handed to him from a line of helpers that stretched out the door, into the street and to the pump. Maddie and Michael passed him to be met by willing hands outside.

Sucking in a breath of the cool air, Michael pulled the sheet off their heads.

"Maddie!" Aiden cried, running over to hug her, and Ciara squeezed in as well, sobbing. Michael handed the girl the cat to wrap his arms about them all.

Thank you, Lord, for saving Maddie, for saving our family.

A crash inside told them the stairs had fallen. The man who had been inside ran out the door as the flames brightened the windows.

Maddie pulled back. "We have to stop it. If it reaches the other buildings, we could lose the whole town!"

Michael felt cold despite the heat pulsing from the building. "Where's the engine company?"

Maddie shook her head. "There isn't one. There's no steam engine, no hand pump. Seattle hasn't even organized the volunteers yet."

Michael stared at her, then at the building, where the glass on the window was starting to buckle with the heat. With the roof and walls still whole, they might have a chance of beating back the flames, if they only had more men.

And then, from down the street, came the sound of singing. Michael turned with Maddie to behold the men of the Irish watch, marching up the street toward them, armed with buckets and axes. Men ventured out of homes and shops to join them, swelling their ranks. Like a tide, they surged toward the bakery.

"The newly organized Irish volunteers, at your service, Mr. Haggerty," Patrick said with a salute. Voices rose in chorus behind him as the men brandished their tools.

Something hotter and fiercer than the fire rose inside Michael. He lifted his fist in tribute to them all.

"Quick now, lads," he called. "You and you, use your axes to break out the window so we can go in three deep. The rest of you, form three lines and fill those buckets from the pump by the livery stable."

The men sprang into action, and Michael moved to join them.

Maddie caught his arm.

"No you don't, Michael Haggerty," she said, face still pale from her fears. "I thought I was lost to you. Don't you be going and leaving me now."

Michael enfolded her in his arms. "I'll never leave you, my darling girl. But this is your dream going up in smoke. I'll not let you lose it without a fight."

Maddie pulled back. "Then we'll all help, you and me and Ciara and Aiden. Let's show Seattle what it means to be Irish."

A few hours later, Maddie stared at the bakery from the other side of the street. Darkness had fallen, and the charred remains of the building stood like an ancient ruin, silver under the rising moon. The last of the Irish volunteers were making their way home after she and Michael had thanked them for their bravery and generosity. Once again, she had no home to call her own.

But she still had her family. She gathered Ciara and Aiden close as Michael crossed the street to join them.

"You'll stay with us," Allegra said next to Maddie. The Howards had seen the trouble from their house on the hill and had come to help. They'd already rescued the chickens and sent them to safety in the Howard coop.

"We'll rebuild," Clay promised as he stood next to his wife. "Whatever you need."

Maddie smiled her thanks. It was all she could do at the moment. She didn't want to think about what it would cost to rebuild the bakery. She leaned against Michael, and he put an arm about her and rested his head against hers.

Aiden hugged the cat. "At least Amelia Batterby is safe."

"We have a lot to be thankful for," Michael said.

She felt the same way. She and Aiden and Amelia Batterby might have died in the inferno. As it was, though she wouldn't be able to go into the remains of the bakery until tomorrow at the earliest, she was fairly certain she'd lost her clothes, her equipment and her supplies. Ciara and Aiden now wore the only clothes they owned as well.

Yet they were all alive, all safe. They would face the future together.

No more running, Father, from fears, from love, from You. Today You gave me back my life. I won't be squandering the gift.

Deputy McCormick, who had been part of the bucket brigade earlier, came to join them now as well.

"I know you have a lot of work ahead of you, Miss O'Rourke," he said, pausing to wipe soot from his cheek. "But when you have a moment, come down to the sheriff's office and make your statement."

Maddie glanced up at Michael, who straightened as if he understood the deputy's meaning. She didn't. "My statement?" she asked, looking back at the lawman.

"About the fire," he explained. "How it started. Who might have wished you harm."

Michael's arm fell away from her shoulder, leaving her cold. "You think someone started it intentionally?" he asked.

"I thought it must have been the oven overheating and catching fire to the laundry," Maddie protested, glancing between the two men. "I saw the shirts burning. I thought it was my fault."

Beside her, Ciara wrapped her arms about herself as if she was ready to believe it of her. But for once she didn't scold Maddie.

"With all the other incidents around town," Deputy McCormick said, "I wouldn't be so sure the fire was an accident. This could have been arson."

Maddie's throat was tight. "So you're thinking this is more of the trouble we've been facing?" she murmured.

McCormick nodded.

Allegra pressed a hand to her chest. "Oh, Maddie! How horrid!"

"We'll find out who did this," Clay vowed.

"The sheriff and I will find the culprit," Deputy McCormick told him, head coming up to meet Clay's gaze. "That's our job. You can rest assured the fellow will be brought to justice. The last thing we need is a bunch of vigilantes going around hanging people without due process."

"Hanging people?" Ciara clutched Maddie's skirt, face pale in the moonlight. "They don't really hang people here, do they, Maddie?"

She found it hard to believe herself. There hadn't been a hanging in New York for years, and then only for murder. "Deputy?" she asked.

McCormick tipped his hat to her sister. "Yes, we do, Miss Ciara, but only when they've been tried and found guilty by a jury of their peers." He turned his gaze on Michael and Clay. "Not when they look or act differently from us, or we think we need to take matters into our own hands."

"You've made your point, Deputy," Michael said, voice hard. "If we have any suspicions, we'll talk to you first."

Clay nodded as well.

"Good," Deputy McCormick said. "I take it you all have somewhere to stay until you rebuild."

"The O'Rourkes and Mr. Haggerty will be staying with us," Allegra told him. The chilliness in her voice said she didn't like the way he'd spoken to her husband and friends. "You can bring any news about your investigation to them there."

"And thank you, Mr. McCormick," Maddie added. "For everything."

The harsh planes of his face softened, and he tipped his hat to her. "Always at your service, Miss O'Rourke. Good night." He strode off down the street.

"Let's get you settled," Allegra said.

Maddie took Amelia Batterby from Aiden and followed her friends up the hill, moonlight bathing their path. Michael walked beside her with Ciara and Aiden in front behind Clay and Allegra. Maddie hadn't realized she'd sighed aloud until Michael put an arm about her shoulders again.

"It will all come out right, Maddie," he murmured. "I promise."

"Sure-n I believe that, Michael," she said, gaze on the uneven ground. "But I'm not sure what to do in the meantime. I don't see how I can bake for James Wallin's wedding. That was to pay off most of my bills and bring customers to my door. I suppose I'll have to offer the work to Mr. Terry after all."

"There will be other weddings," Michael said. "Perhaps not as grand but good enough to make a name for yourself among the ladies."

"Or maybe I could just invite them over for tea," Maddie said with a chuckle, "like the grand society hostess I am."

Michael gave her shoulder a squeeze. "Maybe you should. There has to be more than one way to make their acquaintance and impress them. We'll think of something."

How easy it would have been for him to walk away, leave the future to her. Yet there he was, taking her burdens onto his own broad shoulders once again. How could she fail to love a man like that?

As they reached the top of the hill, the Terry house gleamed like a pearl in the moonlight. She wanted to hold it close. The dream was farther away than it had been this morning, but not out of reach. Not yet.

"Clay spoke of rebuilding," she told Michael. "It will put in me deeper debt to him, but I can't give up."

"I know a way," he said, and the hesitancy in his voice told her he doubted she'd like it. "I'll take the loan to rebuild. You work to pay off the first loan. I'll work to pay off the second."

"But your future," Maddie protested. "You won't be able to have your own place for years."

He pressed a kiss against her hair. "You are my future, Maddie. I'm only investing in us."

Tears pressed against her eyes, clogging her throat. "'Tis a fine, fine man you are, Michael Haggerty," she murmured, content to walk in the shelter of his arm.

Gillian and Mrs. Adams were waiting for them when they reached the Howards' home. The housekeeper exclaimed over Maddie and the children, but Gillian only had eyes for Amelia Batterby.

"Oh, what a pretty kitty!" she cried, her blue eyes meeting the cat's golden ones. She put out a hand, then drew back.

Amelia Batterby inclined her head as if finally meeting someone worthy of her glory.

"You can pet her," Aiden told Gillian. "Her name is Amelia Batterby."

Gillian curtsied. "A pleasure to meet you, Miss Batterby."

Amelia Batterby began to purr.

Allegra, however, could not be satisfied until everyone was settled. She and the housekeeper heated water, and Maddie and Michael took turns in the brass bathing tub to clean off the soot and smoke. The scent of the lavender soap somehow made Maddie's tense muscles relax a little.

Afterward, Clay offered Michael clean clothes. The shirt fit, but the waist of the trousers bagged a bit against the suspenders that hugged Michael's chest. Allegra brought in a lovely purple gown for Maddie to wear, but they had to pin up the hem for Maddie's shorter height and put an extra chemise under it because the tapered bodice wouldn't close properly over her curves. Maddie was glad Ciara's and Aiden's clothes needed only a brushing to serve another day.

They had finished a dinner for which no one had much appetite except Gillian and Aiden, and Maddie and Allegra were seated in the parlor discussing sleeping arrangements when Ciara approached Maddie.

The girl had been quiet since they'd arrived. Maddie had put her hesitation down to shock over the events of the day, and the grandness of Allegra's home, but she could not help noticing her sister's continued pallor now.

Maddie scooted closer to Allegra on the sofa and patted the space beside her. "Come sit with us, Ciara."

Ciara shook her head. "I can't. I don't deserve to sit. I don't deserve any of this." She waved a trembling hand that took in the whole house. "It's my fault the bakery burned down. I didn't know what he was going to do, but I could have stopped him. Can you ever forgive me?"

Chapter Twenty-Three

Michael had taken Clay aside after dinner. Knowing Maddie agreed with his plan to help rebuild the bakery, he couldn't wait to put their proposal to the entrepreneur.

"How much will it cost to rebuild the bakery?" Michael asked him.

Clay rubbed his chin. "A little less than it cost to build it in the first place, assuming we can salvage the bricks for that oven. But I wonder whether Maddie will agree to rebuild. She doesn't like going into debt, even when it's a friend offering. I had to convince her to take as much as she needed the first time."

That sounded like Maddie. And here Michael had thought her too interested in money. How wrong he'd been.

"She and I have a plan," Michael said. "I want the debt under my name, if you're willing. I've found work at the smithy, and I can see about taking a second job in the evenings if needed. She has a dream, and I won't see her lose it because of all this."

Clay nodded. "I have every faith her bakery will succeed. I'll make you a partner investor. Consider the money yours." He stuck out his hand, and Michael shook it. He'd just put himself under a burden, yet he felt lighter than he had in months.

A movement caught his eye. Ciara was waving her hand as she stood before Maddie and Allegra. Her voice pierced the air.

"It's my fault the bakery burned down. I didn't know what he was going to do, but I could have stopped him. Can you ever forgive me?"

Michael was moving toward her even as Maddie blanched. Aiden and Gillian, who had been taking turns dangling a ribbon for Amelia Batterby, looked up from near the hearth as well.

"What are you talking about?" Maddie demanded.

Ciara was worrying her hands in front of her blue dress. "I'm sorry I didn't tell you, but I didn't think you'd understand." She flashed a glance at Michael as he came to a stop beside her. "We wouldn't have had to sneak around if you had any idea about romance."

Michael frowned at her. "Who are you talking about? If some boy at school wanted to play with fire..."

"Not a boy," Maddie said, voice tight. "Oh, Ciara, what have you done?"

The girl's usual defiance flared, and her head came up. "He said I was the only one who believed in him since we left New York. He said he was going to make the Irish great in Seattle."

A sick feeling crept over Michael. "You're not talking about Patrick Flannery."

Ciara threw up her hands. "Of course I'm talking about Patrick! He'll marry me one day, I know he will. When I'm old enough. He understands how I feel."

"If he's laid one hand on you," Maddie started.

"It's not like that!" Ciara protested. "He won't even

kiss my fingers, that's how highly he holds me in his esteem. And don't you tell me otherwise. I just wish I'd known why he wanted in the bakery yesterday. He said he had a surprise for us. All I had to do was make sure everyone went to dinner and leave the door open for him. I thought you'd follow me." She stomped her foot. "You were supposed to follow me! Now everything's ruined!"

"Nothing's ruined," Maddie said, rising. "We will rebuild the bakery. What I don't understand is why Patrick Flannery would want to harm it."

"Neither do I," Michael said, his voice coming out as grim as hers. "But I intend to find out."

His frustrations must have been written on his face, for Ciara grabbed his arm. "Don't hurt him!"

Allegra rose as well. "Surely Mr. Flannery didn't intend to burn down the bakery. It must have been an accident."

"Don't be defending him," Maddie scolded her. "He used a schoolgirl's infatuation to further his own cause. He'll get no sympathy from me." She looked to Michael in challenge.

"Or from me," he assured her. "But I won't believe it of him until I hear it from his own lips."

Clay started for the door. "I'll find him and bring him to the house."

Michael followed. "I'm coming with you."

Ciara ran after them. "No, you mustn't! Leave him alone!"

"Ciara." Maddie's call stopped them all in their tracks. She swept across the room and stopped beside her sister. Michael had never seen her so sure of herself.

"You did not cause the fire, Ciara," she said, voice kind yet firm. "But whether you like it or not, you are an eleven-year-old girl and under my guardianship. Michael and I will deal with Patrick Flannery. I need you to sit with your brother and help Mrs. Howard. And there will be no more outbursts, or I will know that you aren't ready to learn from Nora."

Michael wasn't sure what Maddie meant by that, and he thought the girl might fight, but Ciara nodded as if she believed her sister. She went to sit near Aiden and Gillian, who were watching wide-eyed. Gillian handed her the ribbon as if in consolation.

Maddie turned her gaze on Michael next, and he stood taller, ready to face her temper. If Patrick was the cause of their troubles, he'd been the one to bring the man to her door. She had every reason to order him out of her sight.

She reached up for his face and pulled him down, lips brushing his, filling him with hope.

"You daft man," she said as she released him. "I love you. If you want to find Patrick Flannery and have it out, I'm coming with you."

Still reeling from her kiss, he couldn't muster an argument to stop her.

"I'll watch the children," Allegra said. "Go."

They went.

An owl called from the forest behind them as they made their way down the hill by the light of Clay's lantern. Maddie marched along, hands fisted in her skirts. Michael thought her grip had as much to do with her emotions as with the need to keep her borrowed finery out of the mud. Her determination was like a hearth beside him, keeping him warm.

But warmer still was the memory of her words. She loved him. She was willing to stand beside him. He felt as if they'd turned a corner and found a whole new world waiting for them. They were going to be all right.

He wasn't sure where to start looking for Patrick, but as they reached Main Street, a light near the pier caught his eye. Shadowy figures clustered around the last building on the row.

The smithy.

Michael put a hand to Maddie's shoulder. "Go to the sheriff's office. Find McCormick. Tell him there's trouble."

She must have seen the crowd as well, for she patted Michael's hand before taking the lantern from Clay and running down the boardwalk, shoes clattering on the wood, skirts flaring behind her.

Clay drew a pistol from inside his coat. "Let's join this party."

Together, they approached the smithy. Michael could see more torches inside, the light glowing off the faces of the surrounding men. He recognized Hennessy immediately, along with Clay's partners Aherne and Disney. Voices murmured in concern. But one voice rose above the others.

"Now do you see what we face?" Patrick was demanding. "It's one thing when they come for us, but when they harass a sweet, innocent woman like Maddie O'Rourke, we cannot stand by."

Agreement was immediate and enthusiastic. Michael entered the group, and men made way for him. He saw Clay slipping into the back.

"What crime had she committed?" Patrick asked, face impassioned in the flickering light as his gaze speared the group. "What wrong had she done that she deserved to have her livelihood burned to the ground, every last thing she owned destroyed?"

"Nothing!" someone yelled, and the others roared agreement.

Patrick pointed at them. "Nothing but being born in Ireland!"

Michael pushed his way closer, meeting nods of recognition and smiles of approval that he'd joined them.

"Organizing to protect our homes isn't enough," Patrick continued. "We need to know our families are safe. If there's punishment needed, we need to be the ones bringing it!"

"Aye!" they chorused.

"For Maddie O'Rourke!" Patrick cried, raising his fist over his head.

Around Michael, voices took up the chant, until the words set the rafters above them to trembling. Light shone in every eye. This wasn't the type of fire he could fight. How would he convince these men that the very fellow stirring them up had been the one to cause the trouble to begin with?

As the sound died down, a clear female voice spoke from the doorway.

"You'll pardon me for saying so," Maddie said, stepping out of the shadows, "but I'm not liking the way you're using me name."

Every voice quieted as she made her way to the front. Her red hair burned as bright as the torches, but brighter still was the look in her eyes. She came to Michael's side and held his hand. The squeeze told him that Deputy McCormick was somewhere in the crowd. Michael knew the lawman must be fully ready to arrest the lot of them. It was up to Michael and Maddie to see that the right person was brought to justice.

"Happy I am to see you, Miss O'Rourke," Patrick

said fervently. "I only wish we'd been able to save your bakery."

Murmurs ran through the crowd, regretful, angry at the injustice.

"Do you, now?" Maddie asked. She turned to address the other men. "I've thanked many of you for helping today, and I thank you again. Sure-n but I might have lost my life without your help. Who would be so brazen as to put the torch to my bakery, in broad daylight, while my brother and I were still inside?"

Patrick took a step forward, blanching. "You were inside? But you were supposed to be at dinner with Michael."

So at least he hadn't meant to harm anyone. Yet even as the thought entered Michael's mind, he realized the rest of Ciara's story must be true. Anger licked up him faster than flames.

"And why would that matter to you?" he demanded of Patrick. "Unless you had to be certain no one was inside when you started the fire."

So it was true. Maddie could barely stand to look at Patrick's handsome face, knowing how he'd betrayed both Michael and her sister. The others took the news nearly as hard. Gasps echoed around them, and voices turned dark as gazes fixed on Patrick once more.

"Careful, Haggerty," Hennessy said. "You're accusing one of our own."

"There was plenty of trouble directed against the Irish before Miss O'Rourke's bakery was burned," someone else reasoned.

"And none of it before Mr. Flannery came to town," Maddie insisted. She could not let the man get away with this. He had to be stopped before someone else was hurt.

"I have it from my own sister's lips," she told them all. "Patrick Flannery cozened a little girl to gain access to my shop for the purpose of setting it on fire."

Again voices rose, some questioning, others scoffing.

Michael's voice thundered beside her. "Listen to her! Patrick Flannery is not the man he claims." He glanced at Patrick. "He's not the man I thought him."

She was sure Patrick would demur, claim innocence. Instead, his head came up, and his eyes narrowed.

"I'll not apologize," he said, anger darkening his voice as well as his look. "I was ever after the raising of the Irish." He glanced out at the men, who quieted again in the face of his rage. "I saw what gangs like the Dead Rabbits did in New York. Their ways were hard, but they got results. That's what we need here, a group of men who aren't afraid to protect their own."

"We didn't need protection until you came along," Maddie told him.

"Didn't you?" His face twisted with a sneer. "You think you're safe here? You think they won't come for you? You're wrong. You were sheep waiting for the butcher. I showed you the dangers! I showed you the future!"

Michael was pale. "We knew oppression in New York, Pat. How could you have brought it here?"

Patrick laughed, the sound sharp and brittle. "It was already here, me boy. I merely helped it along. Don't you see? They needed a leader. It could have been us. We could have been important for once."

"Sure-n but he's already important," Maddie scolded him. "A finer man I've never had cause to meet."

Hennessy shoved men out of his way until he was

standing directly in front of Patrick, his head down like a bull. "I'm not the smartest fellow, so let me understand this. All the thefts, the broken windows, the marks on people's homes and shops, those fancy pants Miss O'Rourke found in my laundry sack, the fire that ruined her bakery—that was you?"

Patrick met his look, defiant. "Aye. I thought the pants would be enough to wake up Michael to the need, but it seems I had to do more to get your attention so you'd understand the reason we had to organize. It was for your own good, Hennessy."

Hennessy drew himself up, towering over the others. "This isn't Ireland, Mr. Flannery. The British crown doesn't tell me what's to my own good. I do." His meaty hand reached out to grab Patrick.

The smithy erupted. Men shouted, fists flew. Maddie was jostled one way and another. The hem of Allegra's gown, so hastily pinned, caught on her feet, and she felt herself tumbling. Michael's hand seized her, and he sheltered her against him as anger rose on all sides.

Near the far wall, a shot rang out. Maddie flinched. Glancing back, she saw Deputy McCormick lowering his gun as all eyes turned to him.

"That's enough of that, now," he drawled. "I'll be taking Mr. Flannery into custody for theft, vandalism and arson. If you have knowledge of his deeds, I want to hear from you. The rest of you, go home."

The men shuffled off. Several stopped to apologize to Maddie, promising they hadn't known of Patrick's plan. Others waited for Deputy McCormick, and she could only hope they were confessing what they knew. Beaten, Patrick stood beside the deputy, head bowed as if accepting his fate.

Maddie turned away from him, wrapped her arms

around Michael and held him tight, thanksgiving welling up inside her. "It's over," she murmured. "We're safe."

Michael rested his head against hers. "It's over. And it's just beginning. You have a business to rebuild and a wedding waiting for your cakes."

She shook her head, feeling his chin firm against her hair. "There's no time. James and Rina are to be married in four days."

"Then you have a lot of work to do," Michael insisted.

His determination was infectious. Could she really do it? She had no bakery, no equipment and no supplies, and she was already behind schedule with the loss of today's rolls.

They'd just stopped a madman from setting the entire city ablaze with his anger. What were a dozen cakes and a few hundred rolls? Together, she and Michael could do anything.

Maddie leaned back to eye him. "How much time do you have between now and the wedding?"

"Seeing as I must have earned my employer's everlasting gratitude for breaking up a riot in his business, probably quite a few hours," Michael assured her. "What do you need?"

"Help," Maddie said with a smile. "And I know just where to get it."

Chapter Twenty-Four

Four days later, every man, woman and child within a five-mile radius of Seattle was crowded in the yard of the Brown Church. Ribbons fluttered from the trees, and yellow bunting draped the tables, which groaned under rolls and cakes that were rapidly disappearing with cries of delight. James and Rina Wallin sat at the head table and smiled and thanked everyone who had come to wish them happiness.

Standing beside Michael near the church, Maddie heaved a satisfied sigh. One of her former travelling companions closer to her own size had loaned her a green gown with white cuffs and collar, another a paisley shawl. She fancied that, with her hair curled up at the nape of her neck, she looked rather festive.

Michael had also managed to cobble together clothing for the day—brown trousers, tan wool waistcoat and a tweed coat. The narrow brim of his hat allowed the sunlight to sparkle in his blue eyes. His smile now was all pride in what they had accomplished.

Mr. Terry strolled past with his lovely wife on his arm.

"Well done, Miss O'Rourke," he said. "You and your army waged quite a campaign."

"And how would we have won without your command post?" Maddie said with a smile. She and the rival businessman had come to an agreement. She would bake for the wedding in his ovens, and the Eureka Bakery would get some of the credit for catering the wedding. James had made sure to mention both businesses in his welcome speech to the guests.

Of course, if it hadn't been for James and his brothers, she might still have failed. The logging family had dropped everything at her call for help. Under Michael's direction, they'd carried in supplies, helped mix and knead the dough, and shuffled products from worktable to oven and back. She'd never forget the sight of massive Drew Wallin swathed in an apron, powdered sugar speckling his chin, as he broke a wooden spoon attempting to beat the icing.

All the Wallin men were beaming now at the marriage of their brother. Even Simon, the only one to match Drew in height if not brawn, looked happy for a change as he tucked his fiddle under his chin to play the bride and groom a song in celebration. The soft melody floated on the air, bringing a smile to every face.

Ciara and Aiden came running up just then, eyes bright over the finery Nora had sewn for them in time for the wedding. Now that Patrick had been taken into custody and the extent of his dark deeds revealed, Maddie's sister had shed much of her animosity. She and Maddie had finally come to an understanding, and there had been few outbursts.

Oh, Ciara still had her queenly ways. That was evident as she eyed a passing youth with her nose in the air. But Maddie felt as if she finally knew what her brother and sister needed, and she had hopes she and Ciara would have a much easier time of it in the future.

Michael cleared his throat. "I can think of no finer

time than a celebration of marriage to ask you an important question." He reached into the pocket of his wool waistcoat.

Maddie stared at him. The smile on his face, the hope shining in his eyes, told her what he was about to do. She caught his hand, closed his fingers over the ring that glittered in the sunlight. She wanted no doubts for either of them as to her answer.

"After all we've been through, Michael Haggerty, it is I who should be going down on my knees." She suited word to action, tears coming to her eyes as she gazed up at him. "I was afraid to love you, afraid to watch that love die in the trials and tribulations of life. But you never wavered. You made me see that love doesn't have to die in adversity. It can grow stronger."

"Maddie," he murmured, fingers caressing her cheek.

She put her free hand over his, holding the warmth close. "I hope someday to be a lady of means, but right now, I'm poor as a church mouse. So all I can offer you is a dream—of a life and a family held together by love. Will you marry me?"

Michael laughed, but she could see the answer in his eyes as he lifted her to her feet. "Always have to be the one in charge, don't you, my girl?" he teased. "Nothing would make me happier than to marry you and make us a family. I love you, Maddie, with all I am and all I will be. I know together we can make something beautiful of this world."

He bent his head and kissed her, and she was certain an entire orchestra had joined Simon in a song of celebration.

As Michael drew back with a smile, Aiden stared at them. "Does this mean we all get to live together forever?" he asked.

"Yes, silly," Ciara said. "It means we'll be a family for real now."

Michael put his arms around them all. "I like that. A forever family."

A forever family. The ingredients had been there all along, but it had taken mixing and kneading and even heating to bring them all together, Maddie realized.

And the love between her and Michael was the most important ingredient of all.

* * * * *

Dear Reader,

I hope you enjoyed Maddie and Michael's story. I knew it would take a very special man who understood the importance of family to make a match with the feisty redhead. I couldn't resist adding the part about chicken races. My great-great-grandmother and her siblings raced the family chickens, until their widowed father figured out why the hens had stopped laying!

You'll find more information about pioneer Seattle and my books on my website at reginascott.com, where you can also sign up for an alert to be notified when the next book is out.

Blessings!
Regina Scott

REQUEST YOUR FREE BOOKS!

2 FREE INSPIRATIONAL NOVELS
PLUS 2 *FREE* MYSTERY GIFTS

Love Inspired HISTORICAL

LIHI5

Turn your love of reading into rewards you'll love with
Harlequin My Rewards

**Join for FREE today at
www.HarlequinMyRewards.com**

Earn **FREE BOOKS** of your choice.

Experience **EXCLUSIVE OFFERS** and contests.

Enjoy **BOOK RECOMMENDATIONS**
selected just for you.

PLUS! Sign up now
and get **500** points
right away!

Earn
FREE
REWARDS
Join
Today!
HarlequinMyRewards.com

MYR16R